D0007389

Grace in Autumn

Heavenly Daze Book Two

By

Lori Copeland and Angela Hunt

WORD PUBLISHING
NASHVILLE
A Thomas Nelson Company

ISBN 0-7394-1873-4

Printed in the United States of America

And this same God who takes care of me will supply all your needs from his glorious riches, which have been given to us in Christ Jesus.

—Paul, writing to the Philippians

PROLOGUE

Sometimes, when the autumn wind sweeps in from the ocean and wraps icy tendrils around your neck, life on an island off the coast of Maine can be a far cry from comfortable. I suppose that's why humans don't always relish the thought of visiting our little town in the month of November. I also suppose that's why the folks who live on Heavenly Daze year round are not what you'd call soft. I've heard them describe each other as "tough as pitch knots"—and intend the phrase as a high compliment.

Maine folks are peculiar that way, and Maine island folks are the most peculiar of all. I've been watching the comings and goings of the humans on Heavenly Daze for over two hundred years, and they never cease to entertain, amuse, and inspire me.

Maybe *inspire* is the wrong word—I'm not quite as handy with the English language as some of my brothers. They live among the humans here, while I tend to remain in the background, acting as a messenger between the Lord and his servants. What I meant to say is that humans inspire me to wonder . . .

Long ago, when the Creator breathed life into dust and called forth a man, I wondered at his purposes. Generations later, when the Son stepped down from his throne to offer his life for the sons of Adam, I marveled at his love. And now, as I watch those who are called by Jesus' name struggle to do his will, I am amazed by his faithfulness and patience.

Over two hundred years ago, you see, a child of God called Jacques de Cuvier begged the Lord to guard the inhabitants of this tiny island. In answer to Jacques's sincere prayer, the Lord dispatched me and six others of the angelic host. Our mission is simple: We guard and serve those who live in the seven original buildings on the island of Heavenly Daze.

I am Gavriel, the captain of this little company, and I guard the church. Unlike the others, I rarely find it necessary to don mortal flesh, for most of my work is done in secret. But the others—ah! My brothers live in mortal flesh and age along with the humans they serve, retiring to heaven at the end of an ordinary human life span, then returning in renewed flesh to continue the work they have begun. The cycle of life continues unbroken, as does our careful watchcare. Through it all, the sons of men continue to go about their daily lives, unaware of their unique position.

And so we enter another November, a time of increasing chill and frostiness. The first snow is falling as I write this, snowflakes spiraling through bare branches and gently dusting the sloping roofs of our historic homes.

But no matter. All hearts are warm in Heavenly Daze.

CHAPTER ONE

Trailing a frosty breath vapor up Main Street, postmistress Beatrice Coughlin huddled into her jacket and pressed harder on the pedal of her golf cart. Cold wind mixed with rain and snow swept from a pewter-colored sky. Maine winters could be a right down fright—pure misery for mail carriers and meter readers.

Wheeling the cart around the corner, Bea groaned when she felt the vehicle's right back wheel hit a pothole.

Ruts.

Heavy fall rains had turned the entire island into one big rut. If recent precipitation was a reliable forecast of the coming winter, she was going to be a gormy cuss by January, for certain.

Springing from the cart, she bent into the wind, peeking at the trapped back wheel. Wind whipped her flannel scarf and stung the tip of her nose.

Delays, delays. She still had to deliver a handful of encouragement cards for Edmund de Cuvier and the usual bills for the Grahams before she could seek shelter and a warm fire.

She glanced up, blinking snow out of her eyes. She might be a senior citizen with legs that felt remarkably like two rusted rain gutters, but she could walk the rest of her mail route if need be. She couldn't, however, leave the cart sitting at this cockeyed angle. Floyd Lansdown was likely to take his cart out for a quick trip to the bakery, and if he'd been fool enough to forget his glasses (not unusual for Floyd), he was bound to smack straight into her vehicle.

Bea looked up to see Buddy Franklin rounding the corner in long, purposeful strides. "Oh, my," she murmured. "Look what the wind blew in."

The flaps of a fluorescent orange cap hugged Buddy's angular face and accented the wiry goatee sprouting from his youthful chin. Maxwell Franklin, known to the islanders as Buddy, was as friendly as a six-week-old pup and often as irritating. Buddy lived with his sister Dana Klackenbush at the Kennebunk Kid Kare Center. Unlike Buddy, Dana worked hard and took pride in her accomplishments while Buddy drifted from project to project with no real purpose. After coming to Heavenly Daze last year broke and down on his luck, he was managing the Lobster Pot during tourist season. Rumor was he was trying to buy the restaurant and turn it into a taco establishment. Bea shuddered at the thought. A taco hut in Heavenly Daze? Who'd ever heard the likes?

"Hey, Bea." Buddy approached in the whirling snow, hands buried in his heavy down jacket. On a coatless day, Buddy's arms revealed evidence of his stint in the navy. His multicolored tattoos (Mother, Kiss My Biscuits, and Don't Take Bilge from Nobody!) ran the length of his spindly arms. Buddy had apparently intended to make a career of the navy, but after one week at sea he was shipped home, green as a gourd. A doctor said the sea and Buddy would never get along. He was landlocked for the remainder of his duty and took an early out.

"Morning, Buddy." After giving the young man a curt nod, Bea shifted her gaze to the stuck wheel.

Dark chocolate brown eyes shaded by heavy brows followed her gaze. Buddy studied the wheel as if it were a novelty instead of a usual occurrence this time of year. Then: "Are you stuck?"

Bea narrowed her eyes at the boy, thinking about what her sister Birdie would say in response to such a silly question: *A mind is a terrible thing to waste.*

Bea shoved the cynical words to the back of her mind. "Ayuh. Stuck."

Buddy's eyes moved to the opposite side of the cart, as if the answer to her predicament lay along the axle between the airborne wheel and the one in the rut. Finally he said, "Want me to go get Abner?"

"Abner's baking pastry." She sighed, resigned to the inevitable. "How about you helping?"

Buddy looked up, blank faced. "Me?"

"You." Bea motioned to the back of the cart. "It's a little cart. A lift and a push will get me going."

Buddy shrugged, his face pale against the dark color of his jacket. "Whatever." He stepped around her, then slid behind the wheel.

Crossing her arms, Bea waited. Did he expect her to push and him to drive? Apparently.

He glanced up, one eyebrow shooting almost to his hairline.

Bea glared at him. "You push; I'll drive."

Shrugging, he meekly got out. "Whatever."

Bea settled behind the wheel, keeping an eye on Buddy as he sauntered to the back of the cart. Adjusting his gloves, he pulled the collar of his coat tighter, then bent to tie his boot.

Bea drummed her gloved fingers on the steering wheel. Spitting snow was pelting the golf cart, and her bones ached when she thought of home. Right now Birdie was probably brewing hot tea to go with the cherry Danish Abner was sliding out of the oven.

Straightening, Buddy fished in his back pocket for a handkerchief. Bea watched as he blew his nose, wiped his chin, then wadded the hankie into his back pocket.

"About ready," he said.

She nodded, huddling deeper into her coat, aware that *about* was the operative word. Closing her eyes, she mentally conjured up sunshine and balmy breezes, even though warm weather in Heavenly Daze meant she'd spend more time renting bicycles to tourists than dispensing stamps and postage. But she lived a comfortable life and had ever since returning to the island all those years ago.

Had Frank been dead fifteen years now? She opened one eye to do the math, then shut it again when the wind blew snow into her face.

After her husband's death, Birdie had insisted that Bea come home and work at the small post office and handle the bicycle and binocular rentals. Binoculars didn't do so well this past summer season, but Birdie kept insisting they were a sound investment. Abner thought portable beach cabanas might be more profitable, but what did a pastry chef know about tourists?

Bea's lips curved in a smile at the thought of Abner Smith. The man had proved to be a godsend to both her and Birdie. He'd come to the island—well, she didn't know exactly when he'd arrived, but he'd been there long enough that people no longer referred to him as an off-islander. The small man, whom tourists frequently mistook for Dustin Hoffman (albeit a Hoffman with a spare tire around his middle), worked tirelessly. Whether Birdie asked him to decorate a cake, cut out gingerbread, or bake dog biscuits, he never complained. In fact, Bea had never known him to say a bad word about anybody. For two women getting on in years, Abner Smith was a real blessing—though Birdie didn't admit to aging a-tall.

"Shake a leg, Buddy. My old bones can't take much of this weather," Bea called. "It's blowin' fit to make a rabbit cry."

The young man unwrapped a piece of gum, frowning when the wind snatched the paper and sent it spiraling toward the ferry. As he leaned forward to take off in hot pursuit, Bea stretched across the cart and snagged the hem of his coat.

Their eyes met. "The cart, Buddy. Push." She leaned forward. *"Now."*

He nodded.

After releasing him, Bea turned the key and heard the electric motor spring to life. Finally, Buddy was in position. He hunched forward, ready for action, his hands on the back bumper.

"When I give it the juice, you push!" Bea yelled over her shoulder.

Shoving his hands in his coat pocket, Buddy straightened and squinted at her. "What?"

"Get your hands back on the cart! When I give it the juice, you push!"

"Seems to me," he spoke slowly, as if carefully considering each word, "I ought to lift first. You're in a hole, Bea, and the only way to get something out of a hole is to pull it out."

"Fine. Then pull."

He screwed his face up into a human question mark. "Maybe we should make that a lift? I'd pull that tire out, but the cart's sitting on top of it and in the way—"

"Lift, push, pull, whatever! Just do something."

"You don't have to holler." Sulking, Buddy bent again, placing both hands on the rear fender.

Seizing the moment, Bea eased her foot down on the accelerator, then glanced over her shoulder to see the young man straining, eyes bulging, pushing for all he was worth. The cart rocked back and forth, spewing a wide arc of mud-colored snow pellets and splattering Buddy from head to foot.

Backwash rained down on the metal roof as the old cart endeavored to break loose. Surely it needed only a bit more power—

Slamming her foot down, Bea gave it all she had. The cart sprang forward, free at last, but Buddy Franklin must not have been expecting success. From her rearview mirror Bea saw him teeter off balance for an instant, arms wildly flailing, before falling face first in the mud.

The cart jumped the curb, took out one of the Grahams' shrubs, then returned to the pavement. After throwing a shouted thanks over her shoulder, Bea yelled, "Stop by the bakery and tell Abner I said to give you a hot Danish!"

Still sitting in the mud, Buddy Franklin straightened and stared after her with a dazed expression.

Shaking her head, Bea returned her gaze to the road. "Whatever," she said, grinning as she headed north on Ferry Road.

Plink.

Sitting at the worn desk in her kitchen, Babette Graham lifted her gaze and stared at the ceiling. Snow had been falling outside her window for half an hour, and that long awaited plink assured her that her containment system was working. The snow had melted upon her tin roof, dripped down the broken seams, seeped through the rotten wood, flowed along the attic rafters, traversed her bedroom from ceiling to floor, found the lowest spot in her worn pine planks, insinuated itself through the space between the upstairs and downstairs, then landed in her kitchen bucket. Mindless molecules of water were lining up to obey the law of gravity and follow the paths of least resistance.

She stood to check the pail's position. Another drop, hanging in the dead center of the brown spot on the kitchen ceiling, launched and landed squarely in the center of the bucket. Plink. She sighed heavily. With no other visual aid than her own house, she could teach a physical science class. Gravity, erosion, entropy, degeneration—in any given room she could illustrate a law of science at work.

Sinking back into her chair, she made a mental note to towel off her bedroom floor when the snow stopped. She used to keep a roasting pan upstairs, but quickly discovered that she had more ceiling drips than pots. Fortunately, the second-story floor had only two low spots, and as water tended to flow downhill, she could catch it with one pail on the first floor—two, if a storm arose or the spring sun decided to melt an entire winter's snow in one afternoon.

Plink.

She closed her eyes and steeled herself to the realization that things would get worse before they got better. This was only the first of November, and the big storms wouldn't hit the island until January or February. By then she'd either have the roof repaired . . . or she'd have to invest in an entire battalion of buckets.

Reluctantly, she opened her eyes and considered the two letters on her desk. Both were estimates from roofers in Ogunquit, and both bids had come in at over $10,000. "You can't slap just any kind of roof on these old houses, lady," one of the men had told her. "You gotta stay in character with the history of the house, and you gotta be artistic about it. 'Specially since this place is an art gallery."

"Trouble is," Babette murmured, setting the bids aside, "we're an art gallery only six months out of the year. And we barely make enough in those months to carry us through the winter, so how am I going to pay for an artistic new roof that doesn't leak?"

Her gaze shifted to a single business card propped against her pencil mug. Handyman Roofing, headquartered in Kennebunk, had not yet responded with a bid. The nice man who came out had measured and squinted and scribbled on a notepad, then touched the brim of his hat and said he'd get back to her.

She hadn't heard a thing from him, but at this point, maybe no news was good news. As long as he dawdled, she could hope for a miracle . . . an affordable estimate.

The teakettle on the stove began to rumble, so Babette stood and moved to the cabinet where she kept the mugs. She hated to think the worst of her fellowman, but she suspected the first roofer had come to Heavenly Daze, eyeballed her historic house, and spied the expensive paintings in the gallery showroom. Given her surroundings, he'd assumed she and her husband were rich, when nothing could be further from the truth. He estimated her new roof would cost $15,000.

When the second roofer arrived, she made a point of confessing that she didn't own the gallery paintings—she'd only taken them in on consignment. He figured she could replace her roof for $12,000.

When Babette met the third roofer, she managed to casually mention that she and her husband had inherited the house—and they were supporting an active five-year-old who would almost certainly need braces in a few years. As he left, she apologized for not offering him a cup of hot tea. She was out of sugar, she had said, and with sugar prices at the Mercantile being what they were . . .

She frowned at the fellow's business card. Maybe she had overplayed the sugar thing. Maybe he wouldn't get back to her at all. Maybe none of her conniving mattered. Even if the last guy came back with a bid of two thousand dollars, that would require two thousand dollars they didn't have.

Plink.

Click, click, click, zing!

She glanced toward the staircase, then bit her lip. The clicking sounds came from Charles's manual typewriter, so apparently he had finished priming his creative pump and was ready to continue his work on the Great American Masterpiece II. He had finished his first GAM last winter, and that ponderous tome was still making the rounds of New York publishing houses—or so Charles hoped. Last April he'd sent it out to a dozen publishers, a handful of agents, and his favorite novelist, Stellar Cross. At last count, replies from two publishers, an agent, and Mr. Cross were still pending.

Babette never asked what the rejection letters said. But from the expression on Charles's face, she knew the news wasn't good.

Plink, plunk!

Click, click, clickity, click.

At least the house was musical. Shaking her head, Babette poured hot water into a mug, dropped in a tea bag from the canister, then crossed her arms, letting the fragrant tea steep.

The house actually seemed quiet at times like these when Georgie was at kindergarten. He attended the Kennebunk Kid Kare Center, run by Dana Klackenbush, and was Dana's only student in the off-season. Because Dana's schedule was relaxed, Babette never quite knew when her son would burst through the door and noisily announce his return.

She moved to the desk with her tea, then picked up her pen and studied the bill at the top of the heap. Coastal Gas wanted $300 this month, and she'd only budgeted $275. That meant she'd have to siphon twenty-five dollars from another account, probably clothing, if they were to make it through the winter. Of course . . . her gaze fell upon the envelope stamped Heavenly Daze Community Church. Since the beginning of their marriage, she and Charles had made tithing a regular practice, giving the first 10 percent of their income to support their church. She could hold back the tithe check to avoid dipping into her clothing account . . .

Plunk, plink!

. . . but the church had to pay Coastal Gas, too. And wouldn't that be like doubting that God would provide? She'd heard too many sermons about God blessing those who obediently gave the first tenth of their income to hedge on tithing now. And in the entire ten years of their marriage, though they'd often been broke, they had never gone without food, clothing, or a roof over their heads. God had been faithful.

Click, clickity-click, click, click, zing.

Charles's typing picked up as Babette pulled out the checkbook. She wished he'd try to write something salable like articles or news features, but he seemed set on toppling Stellar Cross from the bestseller lists. She'd hinted that he should paint in the winter, for his popular seascapes always sold for a nice profit, but Charles insisted that summer was for painting and winter for writing. She'd muttered that he ought to invest as much energy into caring for the house and the business providing a roof over their heads, but he pointed out that organization was her gift, not his, and he produced enough during the tourist season to deserve a break during the winter months.

She found herself unhappily dissatisfied as she wrote out the gas check. She loved her husband, truly she did, but living with an artistic personality could drive a woman crazy. Charles didn't exactly howl at the moon, but his occasional fits of melancholy and his live-and-let-live philosophy often forced her to shoulder the burdens of budget and child rearing and . . . roofing.

Plink.

Riiiiiiiiiiiiiiiiip.

She grimaced at the sound of paper being torn from the typewriter. If she were to climb the stairs and enter the spare bedroom, she knew she'd find Charles surrounded by crumpled wads of typing paper, a few reference books, and at least six Stellar Cross novels, all standing upright with the glossy author photos facing Charles at his typewriter. "For inspiration," he had told her when she first noticed this odd arrangement. "Stellar and I are kindred spirits. With his help and support, I'm going to make it."

Babette had wisely refrained from pointing out that Stellar Cross had never written or spoken to Charles . . . and she had also bitten her tongue when Charles insisted on sending a copy of his first manuscript to the best-selling novelist.

"Five pounds of paper wasted," she muttered, ripping the Coastal Gas check from the checkbook. "Cross won't read it. He probably won't even open it."

Charles, of course, couldn't see the impudence in his action. He never minded taking chances in his art—he painted big paintings, he wrote big books, and he dreamed big dreams.

If only he didn't want to spend big bucks.

Just last night he'd been hinting that they could use a computer. "Just think of all we could do with it," he'd said, bringing a computer magazine to bed—not her idea of romantic bedtime reading. "You could advertise my paintings on-line. You could set up an auction page for the gallery. And Georgie could use the Internet for research—"

"Georgie is five years old!"

"Age doesn't matter." Charles propped his elbow on his pillow, then settled his head on his hand as he waved the magazine before her bored gaze. "You can find anything on the Web. Art supplies, books, recipes, information—"

"If I need the Internet, I can always go down to the Mercantile." Babette crossed her arms and glared at him. "Vernie said I could use her computer anytime, so we don't need one."

"I could write faster on a computer." Charles's voice took on a dreamy tone, and his heavily-lashed eyes went soft. "I could write better. I could sell my book more easily, maybe even e-publish it."

"I don't want to hear a list of coulds," Babette answered, her patience evaporating. "I need to hear wills. I will write faster; I will sell my book. We need to survive the winter, Charles, and we don't have money to waste on luxury electronics. So unless you can come up with a surefire moneymaker, you can forget the computer."

After that pronouncement she had turned over and closed her eyes, a little ashamed of how harshly she'd spoken to him. Charles was a wonderful husband and father—a little too preoccupied sometimes to be practical, but he'd never said a harsh word to her or Georgie.

She had apologized the next morning but couldn't resist following up her confession with a warning: "We only cleared enough to make it through the winter, Charles. We can't be spending money on extras. There is no financial safety cushion this year."

Plunk.

No cushion even for a new roof.

A sudden clattering at the front porch interrupted Babette's musings. She rose and hurried through the hallway, then caught a glimpse of Olympia de Cuvier's mounded hair through the window in the door. Olympia, owner and resident of the town's stateliest house, Frenchman's Fairest, stood on the porch, her hand firmly wrapped around Georgie's upper arm.

Was the child out of school already?

Bracing herself for the inevitable, Babette opened the door and forced a smile. "Olympia! I didn't expect to see you out in the snow—"

"I wouldn't be out in the weather if not for this young hooligan," Olympia interrupted, jabbing a finger into Georgie's puffy blue jacket. "Caught him about to throw a ball into Annie's garden. We can't have that, you know."

Olympia's bony, sharply-angled face wore the remnant of a flush. "Annie would be absolutely devastated if she came home to find her tomatoes injured. The good Lord knows we've had enough troubles with that tomato patch."

Babette reached out and pulled her son away from the older woman's stabbing finger. Everyone on the island knew that Olympia and her niece, Annie, had squabbled on account of Annie's experimental tomatoes, and the truce they'd declared was fragile at best. No one would have dared harm those spindly plants, for they were the reason Annie came home every weekend to visit Frenchman's Fairest.

"I'm sure Georgie didn't intend to hurt the tomatoes, Olympia." Babette's tone strengthened as she looked down at her son. "Did you, Georgie?"

"No, Mom." His face was a picture of innocence. "I was playing ball with Tallulah. I threw the ball; she brought it back. I threw it again, and she brought it back. I was about to throw it again—"

Babette clapped her hand over his mouth. "I get the picture." Shifting her gaze to her angry neighbor, she softened her tone. Olympia had been cut of stern and sturdy cloth, but it wasn't like her to fuss openly. The stress of caring for her terminally-ill husband, Edmund, must be getting to her.

"I can promise this won't happen again, Olympia," Babette said, trying her best to be compassionate. "Georgie will not be allowed out to play for the rest of today or tomorrow. And when he can play outside again, I will give him strict instructions never to play near your house."

"Mmmmmmmm!"

Babette smiled, glad her hand muffled Georgie's protest.

Some of the anger seemed to leave Olympia's face. "I don't know that I'd go that far, Babette," she said, tugging on the heavy knitted collar at her neck. "We like the boy. Tallulah adores him, and I don't have much time to play with her these days, with Edmund being so sick and all."

Her faint smile held a touch of sadness when she met Babette's gaze. "Just be sure he minds the tomato patch, okay? Those experimental tomatoes will have a hard enough time with the snow."

Babette reached out and squeezed her neighbor's wrist. "I understand, Olympia. And I'll take care of Georgie. You take care of yourself, okay?"

Olympia nodded, then turned and moved down the porch stairs with much less energy, Babette suspected, than she'd expended escorting Georgie from her house.

After drawing her son inside, Babette closed the door and knelt to take off his heavy jacket.

"I didn't mean to hurt the tomatoes, Mom," he said, his teeth chattering despite the warmth of the clanging radiator beneath the foyer window. "But Tallulah kept leading me that way. First she wanted crullers, and when I didn't have any, she went under the house and brought out her ball and asked me to throw it, so I did, then she brought it back but told me to go 'round to the front of the house, so I did, and then we went to visit Blaze in the barn, but Caleb said to stay back 'cause old horses might kick a kid, so Tallulah and I went back 'round to the front, where Dr. Marc saw me and said hi and then gave me a lollipop but said ask your mother, but I said my mom didn't care so I ate the lollipop and gave Tallulah a lick, but she said she liked crullers better."

Despite her irritation, Babette laughed when he paused to draw a breath. Though children poured onto Heavenly Daze in the summer tourist season, in the winter months her poor son was the only child on the island. No wonder his best playmates were the local dogs and horses.

"You." She tousled his brown hair. "You're the light of my life and the root of my gray hairs."

His face crinkled into a questioning expression. "Whaddya mean, Mom? Your hair's not gray."

"It's getting there," she said, standing. "Give it time." Placing her hands on his shoulders, she turned him toward the stairs. "Up to your room, young man, and no more playing outside today. I'll be up to talk to you later."

Birdie Wester shivered as the back door opened and a gust of chilly wind blew into the room.

"Mercy!" Bea said, coming in. "I'd swear the wind's kicking up a line storm if I didn't know better." She stomped snow off her feet, then slammed the door, eyeing the steaming teapot on the stove as she stripped off her gloves.

Smiling, Birdie looked up, knitting needles poised in midair. "It isn't fit for man or beast out there today. You must be frozen."

"Like a popsicle." Bea took off her coat, then moved into the kitchen.

"Get the mail delivered?"

"Ayuh." Bea lifted a cup from the cabinet, then poured a cup of tea. "Got stuck in that rut on the corner of Main and Ferry. Floyd needs to do something about that hazard before I blow another tire." After unwinding her scarf, she gravitated toward the fire with a cup of steaming liquid.

Birdie sighed, settling deeper into the comfy recliner. Thank goodness her job kept her indoors.

The sisters' living quarters adjoined the bakery, and their home was considered one of the coziest in Heavenly Daze. After Frank Coughlin's death, when Bea came to live with Birdie, the sisters had built an addition onto the back of the house, increasing the square footage to nine hundred square feet—more than enough for two little ladies and a small business.

A Kodiak wood stove kept the rear sitting room as warm as toast. The bedrooms in the center of the building got a little cool during January, but Birdie added another blanket to her bed and made out quite well. And in the early morning, when Abner fired up the big oven on the other side of her bedroom wall, Birdie would stretch out and breathe in the delicious scents of baking bread and pastry . . . what a glorious way to wake up!

The kitchen, a tiled space between the sitting room and the bedrooms, was tiny by most standards, but it held everything the sisters needed: a large white Tappan gas range, a wooden table with four chairs, and a dependable Whirlpool refrigerator. Bea brought her microwave when she came, but the sisters didn't use it for much other than warming leftovers and making popcorn. Birdie liked her coffee perked, her tea steeped, and her meat cooked with real heat. Bea had fussed at first, having developed an unusual dependency on the appliance, but she'd adapted nicely to doing things Birdie's way. It took just one question—"What if that radioactive stuff leaked out?"—and Bea had agreed to use the microwave sparingly. One could never be too careful.

A slant-roofed back porch separated the house from the wild emptiness of the northern end of the island. The sisters' washer and dryer sat on the covered back porch, along with a fifty pound sack of birdseed, salt for melting ice, and an assortment of muddy boots and galoshes.

"There's cream in the refrigerator," Birdie said. She bit off a piece of thread, then tied it.

Bea glanced at the empty plate in the center of the kitchen table. Ordinarily, it would have been filled with two of Abner's finest pastries.

"Abner running late this morning?" Bea asked.

"Ayuh." Birdie got out of the recliner and adjusted the lace draperies in the sitting area. This was her favorite room in the house. Flanked on three sides by six windows, the space featured two La-Z-Boy recliners, a polished cherry end table with a trailing philodendron, and a floor lamp positioned so Bea could read and Birdie could do handiwork. Her current project, knitted dishrags, spilled out of a basket by her chair.

Across from the chairs stood an entertainment center they'd ordered from Sears and put together themselves—now that was a day to remember. They'd spent the better part of an afternoon down on all fours, trying to figure what went where. All those bolts and screws and instructions—why, it'd take a Harvard graduate to understand them.

The best thing about their small abode, however, had to be the delicious scents that continually filled the living quarters. Now the aromas of cherry filling and flaky pastry wafted from the front of the building. Bea sniffed the air. "Smells like those cherry Danish are about ready."

Straightening a lacy tieback, Birdie turned from the window and proceeded toward the hallway that led to the bakery kitchen. Folks claimed Abner had a gift when it came to baking. Birdie liked to say that the good Lord gave Abner a golden rolling pin.

Bea trailed Birdie into the bakery, sniffing with appreciation. The cheerful baker was taking a large pan out of the oven, exchanging small talk over the counter with Vernie Bidderman. The tall, raw-boned owner of Mooseleuk Mercantile, swathed head to foot in a man's overcoat and green earflap cap, greeted Birdie and Bea with a nod and went on yakking.

"Did I tell you I got the new Web site up and running? Selling pure Maine maple syrup—got four more orders just this morning."

"Is that right?" Abner smiled, transferring Danish onto cooling racks with a steel spatula. "That's good to hear, Vernie. Selling many candles?"

"A few—expect sales to pick up any day now with the holidays coming on."

"Vernie Bidderman, you should be ashamed of yourself," Birdie scolded, tying an apron around her trim waist. "Everybody takes the easy way out these days. Internet this, Internet that. Why, if we keep working with computers our children will forget how to use a book. Can't people buy syrup and candles at the grocery store?"

"Not if they want pure Maine syrup and Bidderman candles—unless they live around these parts," Vernie answered, grinning.

Birdie bit her tongue. Criticism rolled off Vernie like water off a duck's back. Especially criticism about the Internet. Vernie loved the World Wide Web. Wasn't a finer sales vehicle around, she was quick to tell anyone who questioned her preoccupation with cyberspace.

All a waste of good time, Birdie contended. Didn't people use libraries anymore?

"I don't know anything about computers," Bea began, but her words trailed away when the front door opened and Salt Gribbon blew into the bakery.

Birdie felt her heart skip a beat when the curmudgeon stamped his feet in the sudden ringing silence. Snow lay in white skiffs on the sea captain's navy pea coat. Salt, a gaunt man not especially known for cordiality, scowled at Bea and Vernie as he shuffled to the counter. Lowering her gaze, Birdie put her hands to work lining a display tray with paper doilies.

Abner set the spatula aside. "Morning, Cap'n."

"Ayuh." Gribbon's eyes scanned the display counter. Salt Gribbon, retired swordfish boat captain of the Salvatore 2, had long since lost the desire to prove anything to anyone. In his late-sixties, Birdie supposed, he lived alone in the lighthouse and still cut a vibrant figure—vibrant enough to make her hands tremble.

Abner leaned across the counter. "What can I get you today? The Danish are nice and hot."

Gribbon's eyes lifted and focused squarely on Birdie. "A loaf of rye and two dozen molasses cookies."

Excusing herself, Birdie stepped to the end of the display case, out of Abner's way. Her heart did a silly flutter and she flushed. If a crusty old sea goat could do this to her, she needed to get out more.

"A loaf of rye and two dozen molasses cookies coming right up." Abner reached for a bag.

With his gaze fixed on Birdie—she could feel it across the room—Gribbon inclined his head in her direction. "She can get it."

Birdie's lips firmed when Bea shot her a narrow warning look. Lifting a brow to confirm she wasn't about to get Salt Gribbon's rye, she nodded curtly.

Never mind that her cheeks were burning.

"No trouble for me to grab the order." Smiling, Abner sacked twenty-four saucer-size molasses cookies, adding three extra for good measure.

The old sea captain's eyes followed Birdie's movements as she struggled to separate the paper doilies. Heat suffused her neck, and she toyed with the idea of cracking the window to cool things off a bit.

"I want her to get the bread."

Apparently sensing an approaching clash, Vernie crowded closer to the counter. "I'll take a dozen of those cherry Danish, Abner. And a half-dozen bear claws—they're fresh, aren't they?"

Abner smiled. "All our pastry is fresh, Vernie."

Gribbon's steely voice cut though the conversation. "I want Birdie Wester to get my bread."

Every eye swiveled back to the sea captain, who appeared to brace himself for an oncoming gale.

Gribbon captured Birdie's irritated gaze.

"One loaf of rye," he repeated.

Silence hung over the room. Though she didn't dare lower her eyes, Birdie knew Bea and Vernie were exchanging glances and probably wondering if it'd be wise to move toward the nearest exit.

Gribbon stared at Birdie as if he were determined to win the contest of wills. She could stand here and stare all day, or she could give up and let him move on—

"Oh, for heaven's sake," she said, dropping the doilies on the tray. "One loaf of rye." *For one stubborn old goat.*

Moving toward the bread case, she removed a brown loaf and wrapped it in plastic, avoiding Bea's aggravated look. "Anything else, Cap'n?"

Vernie eyed the old captain with a stringent glance. "There've been some complaints about rock throwing from tourists visiting the lighthouse. You know anything about that?"

Ignoring the question, Gribbon continued to stare at Birdie.

"You're going to have to stop throwing rocks, Cap'n." Vernie picked up her order and dropped her money on the counter. "People will think there's a bunch of heathens living around here."

A muscle moved at Gribbon's jaw. "People need to stay away from my place."

"It's not your place—it's a historical monument owned by the city. Your job is to take care of it, not to scare people off."

Without so much as a ripple of concern, Gribbon calmly opened his coat buttons and pulled out a book. Melted snow dripped from his white beard as he handed it to Birdie.

Birdie perused the title. *"Curious George?"*

Gribbon nodded. "Bought it at Graham's yard sale last month. Is it fittin' reading?"

"Ayuh. It's a classic, excellent for children and adults, too." Birdie thumbed through the pages, refreshing her memory. Curious George was an adorable little monkey, adopted by a man from the city and treated to all sorts of adventures . . .

Nodding, Gribbon took the book from her hands and wedged it between his blue flannel shirt and pea coat. "Thought you might know, seeing how you're a librarian."

Birdie felt her cheeks burn in a blush. "That was years ago, Cap'n, before I retired and bought the bakery. I have nothing to do with books anymore other than to enjoy hours of reading."

Apparently satisfied with the information, Gribbon picked up his bag of cookies and bread. Before leaving, he looked up, his eyes locking with Birdie's. "You bake good bread."

Birdie clasped her hands to her cheeks in an effort to hide what had to be a pronounced flush. "You go on now, get along."

Surprisingly, he obeyed. Buttoning his coat, he turned and nodded. The front door closed behind him a moment later.

Birdie stepped quickly aside when Bea butted between her and the counter, wielding a spray bottle and paper towels. Bea said nothing but made reproachful clucking sounds as she set about cleaning the counter. Bea had never had a kind word to say about the old skipper and frequently accused him of being a salty craw that gave the town a bad name. But Birdie found him fascinating. There had to be a book in that man's life, a very interesting book.

Vernie hustled to the door, opened it, and leaned out to shout, "No more rock throwing! I mean it! We can replace you."

"No, we can't," Birdie corrected under her breath. "No one wants to live at that Godforsaken point and stare at the sea all day." Raising her voice, she called, "Shut the door, Vernie, you're lettin' all the heat out."

Vernie took her leave of the sisters, too, muttering something about selling rye bread on the Internet, and for a moment silence reigned in the bakery.

But not for long. "I declare, Birdie." Bea moved to the window and craned her neck. "That man's got a crush on you."

Warmth flooded Birdie's neck and pooled at the base of her throat.

"Bea, you're getting addled. Go on, now. Get away from the window."

Tight-lipped, Bea squirted cleaner on a windowpane, mumbling under her breath. Birdie could have sworn Bea was jealous, but she had no cause to be. Birdie had no designs on that man, none whatsoever. Their relationship, if she could be so bold as to call it that, was based on mutual respect and a sort of grudging admiration.

"Why do you suppose he had that children's book?" Bea asked, swiping at the glass. "A man his age, buying *Curious George*? Who ever heard of such a thing?" She scrubbed a resistant fingerprint, squeak, squeak against the glass.

Birdie shrugged. "Maybe he wants to read it."

"Read? Ha!" Squeak. "I bet he can't read."

"He can, too!"

"Can not."

"By the way, Bea," Abner called from the baking area, "there's another piece of mail waiting for you."

Bea rolled her eyes. "I have to go out again?"

"It's general delivery."

Straightening, Bea absently touched her hair as she moved away from the window. "I declare, there's no rest for the weary."

Abner came forward, wiping his hands on his apron. "Captain Stroble overlooked a piece that must've fallen out of a mail tray. He dropped it off when he stopped in for coffee and doughnuts. Said he thought you might want to see to it right away."

Birdie had been about to arrange the freshly baked Danish on the display tray, but she glanced up at this news. "Could be important, Bea."

"Probably Publishers Clearing House wanting to know where to deliver my million dollars. Thank you, Abner."

Setting her cleaning bottle aside, Bea pulled her shawl from the front hook and hurried next door to the post office.

Grateful for a moment in which to compose her thoughts about Salt Gribbon, Birdie went back to her work.

A few minutes before noon, Bea wandered back into the bakery and held up a letter. "Would you look at this?"

Setting aside a large pot she'd just washed, Birdie wiped her hands on her apron. "Who's the letter for?"

A frown hovered between Bea's brows. "An angel."

Birdie laughed. "Around here?"

From where he was working in the pantry, Abner coughed.

Bea held up a creased sheet of notebook paper. "Listen to this:

Dear Angel,

My name is Lewis, and I visited your island with my mommy and daddy this summer. I liked your houses and the pretty trees and plants that grow there. I like the saltwater taffy, too. It tastes good but pulled my front tooth out, but that's OK. Mom said I was gonna lose it anyway.

I can't write very good yet, Angel, so Mom is writing this letter for me. I am very sick. I have something called leukemia and I have to take medicine that makes me very tired and makes all my hair fall out. I hope I will get better, but Mama says that is up to the Lord. Mama says the Lord is your boss. Could you please ask him to make me well?

I would like to have a new bicycle for Christmas and if I don't get well I won't feel like riding it much. Mama says God can do all things. Is this true? If this is right, please ask God to make me well. I don't like being tired and sick all the time. And while you're talking to God, will you tell him I want a red bicycle, not a blue one? I have a blue truck and a blue tractor and a blue ball. I don't want a blue bicycle.

Thank you very much, Angel.
Lewis Anthony Morris, five years old

"Ah, the poor tyke," Birdie murmured, her throat aching with regret. "Wonder what makes him think angels are living here?"

"Heavenly Daze," Abner supplied. Birdie turned in surprise. He must have come out of the pantry while Bea read the letter. Now his eyes were dark with concern. "The child associates the island with the Father."

"That, and the fact that the tour guides get a little carried away when they take people through Frenchman's Folly—er, Fairest." Birdie shook her head. "I've heard that they're telling people that Jacques de Cuvier called down continual angelic protection for the town."

Bea blanched in astonishment. "Olympia lets them say that?"

"Olympia," Birdie lowered her voice, "will let them say anything as long as it makes Jacques de Cuvier look like a saint. Besides, the story adds a touch of color, and that's what brings the tourists back again and again. You can't knock local color."

Shaking her head, Bea folded the letter and slipped it back into its envelope. "Well, I'd like to answer this letter, but I can't allow the boy to think an angel is writing to him. What would you do, Birdie?"

Birdie waved her hand in confusion. "Why, I don't know. I suppose I'd thank him for writing and tell him that our prayers are with him and his family . . . but that seems like so little." She paused and looked at Abner. "I wonder how the post office handles letters sent to Santa Claus?" Birdie slanted a brow in Abner's direction. "Have any ideas?"

Abner shook his head and moved toward the counter where he'd been mixing up a batch of sugar cookies. "Considering the island's name, I'm surprised there haven't been more letters of the same nature. It doesn't help that the tourist brochures call this a little bit of heaven on earth."

"If they stayed here a week, they'd know that isn't true," Bea said. She paused thoughtfully. "I suppose I could write and say I'm an angel assistant . . ." Frowning, she looked at Birdie, then Abner. "Would that be a lie?"

Abner smiled as he poured sugar into his mixing bowl. "You are an angel's assistant, Bea. Haven't you heard?"

"Right, and I'm Miss America, too." Dismissing his lighthearted banter with a smile, Bea turned to Birdie. "I certainly can't promise the child a red bicycle or good health, but I can promise to speak to the Lord about his problem."

Birdie nodded. "That would be nice, Bea. And assure the mother that lots of angel assistants on Heavenly Daze will be praying for her son."

Birdie felt a sense of rightness as she turned away and wiped the counter over the display case. In a way, all God's children were assistants, so Bea's answer to little Lewis's letter seemed appropriate.

Besides, autumn days were long and often uneventful, so praying for five-year-old Lewis Anthony Morris would give Bea something to do.

What harm could come from it?

CHAPTER TWO

Confined to his quarters for the rest of the afternoon, Georgie sat on his bed and bounced the mattress, enjoying the rhythm of the squeaking springs. Everything in their house made noise, especially when the wind blew strong off the ocean. The painted radiators beneath the windows hissed and sometimes clanged when the nights grew cold, and something in the walls moaned like an old man whenever Mom ran the water for his bath. He knew about old men and the sounds they made because he'd heard Mr. Edmund moan several times when he visited Frenchman's Fairest with Tallulah. His mom didn't moan, exactly, but she groaned a lot, especially when she sat at the kitchen table paying bills. His dad didn't moan or groan but tended to grunt almost constantly when he typed on his book.

Georgie didn't know how grownups could sit still for as long as they did. He had a terrible hard time sitting still in church, and only a stern glance from his mom or dad could make him keep quiet until Pastor Wickam finished his long sermons.

Bored with the mattress, he scanned his room for something else to do. His easel sat in the corner, near the window, and a half-finished painting of a puffin hung from the clip. He liked painting puffins. He had seen several of the funny little birds on the far side of the island when he went for a walk with his dad. They were sort of like penguins, but more colorful. Puffins were especially colorful in his paintings.

The island puffins had black backs and white bellies, orange feet, and white faces. Their beaks were red, yellow, and blue-gray. Best of all, their beaks were flat—not side-to-side flat like a duck's, but up-and-down flat, like a puffin's. His dad said the bright colors of the beaks went away after the birds laid their eggs, so Georgie painted his birds with extra bright beaks so the color would never wear off.

His mom didn't care much for puffins. She said they were as silly as penguins, and some people were spending too much money trying to save silly birds when their neighbors were facing hard times. But Dad understood the puffins and told Georgie all about them. They weren't penguins at all, he said, but from the auk family, whatever an auk was. Puffins could swim like a fish and fly like a bird, and they were the only birds who could actually fly underwater and catch fish.

Best of all, Dad said, puffins had learned the value of community. They traveled together, lived together, and made their nests together, because a single puffin alone could never survive against the sea. But puffin colonies were strong because they had learned how to work as a team.

Georgie slid off the bed and walked to his easel, then considered his color tray, a mismatched collection of watercolors and leftover oil paints from his father's box. He could finish the picture . . . but Mom, who never threw anything away, already had a couple of his puffin paintings in a drawer. She even had one in the gallery.

He had given it to her one night during the summer, hoping she could sell it and stop groaning about the bills. But she smiled when he suggested that someone might buy it. "Why, Georgie, I wouldn't want to sell this puffin. It's special."

Georgie looked away, a little baffled by his mother's answer. "I can make more, Mom. I'm an artist."

"Like your father." He heard a smile in her voice, though her lips had straightened.

"Yeah." He slipped his hands into his pockets and stepped back, feeling pleased with himself. "So sell it, and you'll have money for the bills. Okay?"

The picture now stood under a plastic sheet with a group of other framed paintings in the gallery. Georgie didn't worry about it selling because he knew some pictures took time. After all, one of his father's paintings had hung in the gallery ever since Georgie was a baby. Some paintings, his dad said, waited for years until just the right person stopped by to buy them.

But his puffin painting would sell soon, he knew it. After saying his prayers every night with his mom or dad, Georgie whispered a private prayer in the darkness—that God would soon sell his painting so Mom could stop groaning and looking worried.

A clanging noise rose up from outside, breaking the snow-stillness of the afternoon. Georgie ran to the window and saw Zuriel by the garbage cans beside the house, wiping his hands on his apron.

Zuriel wouldn't mind if Georgie paid him a visit. Aside from Georgie's parents, Zuriel was the best person on the island.

Carefully creeping down the stairs, Georgie clung to the banister, remembering to avoid the last creaky step. His mom hadn't actually said he was forbidden to leave his room, but she hadn't exactly said he could go out to see Zuriel, either.

Better to not bother her with asking.

He peeked down the foyer hallway to be certain his mother wasn't standing at the back door, then heard the slam of the desk drawer. She was still in the kitchen.

Pulling his jacket from the peg rack by the front door, Georgie slipped his arms into the coat and made a face when his shirt sleeves bunched up at his elbows. He hated bunchy sleeves, but there was no time to start over. Quick as a cat, he escaped out the front door, remembering not to let it slam, then rounded the corner of the house, skirted his mother's withered flower garden, and sprinted down the path to Zuriel's place.

The potter didn't live in a house, exactly—the building had originally been designed for a horse and carriage. But since only the de Cuviers actually owned a horse and carriage (and they made Blaze live in the barn), most of the little houses behind the town's big houses were used for apartments. Dr. Marc lived in the carriage house behind

Frenchman's Fairest, and a man called Elezar lived behind the Mercantile. Though Georgie liked Elezar a lot, he liked Zuriel especially. The potter never fussed, never got in a hurry, and never, ever told Georgie to be quiet.

He knocked three times because his mother told him he had to, then pushed the door open a crack. "Z?"

"Come in, George."

Georgie felt a warm flush steal over him as he closed the door and walked into the open space that served as Zuriel's kitchen, workroom, and living room. Z sat at his potter's wheel, his hands shiny and gray with water and mud. A large mound of wet clay sat on the spinning circular wheel, but Zuriel had not yet begun to pull it. His hands moved slowly over the mound, smoothing and patting.

Georgie tucked his hands into his pockets, trying to keep them still and out of sight. There were lots of breakable things in Zuriel's workshop. Bowls and vases and teapots crowded together on the shelves along the walls, and he knew the pieces of pottery would eventually be sold in his parents' gallery. Georgie didn't know much about pottery, but he knew enough about numbers to understand that Zuriel's pieces helped his mom and dad make a living.

Georgie stared at the clay lump. "Gonna make something today?"

"Maybe." Zuriel's hands never stopped moving over the clay. "I have to see if this clay is ready to be pulled. I need to discover what kind of mood it's in."

Georgie grunted as he sat on a stool near the wheel. "My mom's in a mood—a bad one. Miss Olympia got mad at me and Tallulah for playing ball near the tomato patch. And then Mom got mad. But I think she's really mad at the bills. She keeps groaning and mumbling in the kitchen."

Zuriel made a soft sound of understanding, then picked up his sponge with one hand and dipped it into a bucket of clean water. As he squeezed it and dribbled water over the spinning clay, he asked, "Do you think she's worried?"

Georgie shrugged. "I don't know. But I know she doesn't need to be. I gave her a painting of puffins, the bestest painting I ever did painted. When it sells, she'll have money. And then she can stop making faces at the bills."

Zuriel looked up, and for an instant his hands stopped moving. "You painted something for her?"

"Yeah."

"Why, George." A slow, shining smile blossomed out of Zuriel's shaggy brown beard. "I think that's quite gallant. Some nice gesture. I'm proud of you."

The warm rush returned, and Georgie shifted awkwardly under the weight of praise. "It hasn't sold, though," he said, looking down at the floor. "Nobody comes to the shop in the winter. So I don't know how God is going to answer my prayer."

"You asked the Lord for help with this?"

Georgie looked up. "I asked God to sell my painting."

Zuriel cocked a brow. "Prayers uttered in simple faith are always answered, George. But sometimes the heavenly Father takes time to work his will. You must be patient."

"I'll try." Georgie tightened his hands into fists and resisted the urge to put his own palms on the wet clay. Zuriel made the work look easy, but his mother said Z had a special gift and they should thank God he had agreed to exchange pottery for his room and board.

"Georgie!" His mother's voice echoed from the house. "Get back in here!"

Georgie looked up at Zuriel. "Uh-oh."

The potter smiled. "Busted?"

"I gotta go." Georgie slid from the stool and moved toward the door, then took a moment to run his finger over the shiny smooth surface of a teapot on a shelf. The piece was new, he thought—at least he'd never seen another like it. It looked like a little blowfish, with a spouty nose and a handle where the tail fins should be. It would sell. The people who visited his parents' shop loved to buy things that looked like puffins and fish and lobsters.

"Cool," he said, safely returning his hand to his side.

"Thanks," Zuriel called just before Georgie closed the door.

After the boy had gone, Zuriel sat in silence, his hands applying even, consistent pressure to the clay as his thoughts centered around Babette and Charles Graham.

When the Grahams moved to the island years ago, he had been delighted to discover that his latest charges planned to open an art gallery. Along with the qualities of emotion, intelligence, knowledge, and will belonging to all angels, Zuriel possessed a particular passion for the beauty of the creative arts. He had rejoiced to discover that God would allow him to use his gifts to aid humans with a similar mind-set.

Charles possessed a sensitive soul and a discerning eye, and while Babette had not been gifted with artistic ability, she had been given organizational skills and a sharp intellect. She ran the business and took care of Georgie while Charles carted his paints and easel all over the island in summer. In the winter, Charles typed.

Zuriel sighed as the leathery clay began to soften under his fingertips. Charles's gift did not extend to the written word, but the man had not yet discovered that painful truth. Zuriel bit his lip. His task was to do whatever God commanded, but he sincerely hoped the Lord's plan did not include a situation where he would have to burst Charles Graham's bubble.

Young Georgie, on the other hand, never failed to delight. Living in youthful innocence and sweet faith, the boy was still as tender as he had been on the day he entered the world. But he was five years old, and nearly capable of understanding that his home, this island, and this world were but a part of creation. He was almost mature enough to choose or reject the One who had created him.

Flipping the switch at the side of the table, Zuriel stopped the spinning wheel and pressed a fingertip into the clay. This lump finally felt right—ready for working. Unlike most professional potters, Zuriel did not use prepared de-aired clay. He took clay from the ground where God had placed it, mixing gummy clays with tough clays as necessary in order to get the best clay body for throwing on his wheel. This clay, dark with the impurities that would give it strength and color, would soon become a solid piece of stoneware.

He flipped the power switch again and leaned forward, his hands pushing firmly against the clay, centering the lump as it took on the shape of the space between his fingers. As he centered the piece, he moved his hands slowly and smoothly, remoistened them in the bucket, then lowered his hands onto the clay again. As always, he was surprised by how much pressure the clay required in order to center itself—just as God often had to use pressure to keep his people in the center of his will.

Zuriel closed his eyes, blocking out the sights and sounds of the ticking cuckoo clock, the humming refrigerator against the side wall, the sweet strains of Sinatra on the radio. He felt nothing but the clay, centering it and himself in one motion, moving his hands gradually up and down, feeling himself perfectly in the center of the will of God.

When the clay was perfectly centered, he lifted his hands entirely and looked down at the clay. The dark lump spun easily in the midpoint of the wheel, without wobbling, a perfect beehive ready to be shaped.

If only his humans were as malleable.

After firmly returning Georgie to his room with a sandwich and a juice box, Babette returned to the kitchen and wearily regarded the bucket of melted snow behind her chair. Too bad she couldn't bottle it and sell it on the Internet—maybe a few folks in Florida could be persuaded to buy genuine melted Maine snow . . . or maybe not. That moneymaking idea seemed about as reasonable as all the others she'd dredged up in the past hour.

She heard a creak from her front porch—the wind lifting the rusty lid of the mailbox. She hadn't yet checked the mail.

In no hurry for bad news, Babette trudged through the foyer, then stepped out into the cold. The aged mailbox (which she kept because now it was considered shabby chic) contained a letter from Handyman Roofing, three solicitations for new and improved credit cards (which she'd have to hide from Charles), and one Victoria's Secret catalog (which she'd have to hide from Georgie).

She grimaced as she tucked the Victoria's Secret catalog under her arm. Though she tried her best to keep her son safe and sheltered, the child was all boy. Last year they'd taken him to the Fogg Art Museum in Boston, and Georgie had all but gaped at the paintings of nudes. She'd breathed a sigh of relief when they sat in an open courtyard to have lunch, but Georgie wandered over to the fountain, where she found him studying an anatomically correct statue of Venus, goddess of love.

The art world was rife with child-rearing hazards.

She tore open the letter as soon as she reentered the house. This bid, bless Handyman's heart, was lower than all the others. For only $9,900.00, Handyman would give them a new roof and a five-year guarantee.

Sinking onto the deacon's bench beside the door, she considered the letter in the harsh light of reality. She finally had a low bid—but she still had an empty savings account. She felt empty, too. Worry, budgets, and penny-pinching had left her feeling drained. She couldn't go on without help.

Click, click, clickity-clack.

She lifted her gaze toward the stairs. Why was she carrying this burden alone? Wasn't the husband supposed to be the leader and supporter of the family? Stuffing the letter from Handyman back into the torn envelope, she straightened her shoulders and stood. The time had come for Charles to lift the burden from her back.

With her chin held high, she climbed the stairs. Charles sat before the typewriter in the spare bedroom, scowling at the printed page. As the floor creaked at her approach, he bent lower, as if to shield his precious paper from prying eyes.

"Charles," she began, not caring about his penchant for privacy, "we need to talk about the roof."

He pecked out another string of letters. "What roof?"

"The roof on this house. The one that leaks."

Charles hesitated, his fingers frozen over the keys, then swiveled his head to look at her. "You got bids, didn't you?"

"Ayuh."

His mouth pursed up in a small rosette, then unpuckered enough to ask, "And?"

"Fifteen thousand, twelve thousand, and ninety-nine hundred."

He closed his eyes, squeezing them tight in what appeared to be a colossal effort, then lifted his lids. "So what's the problem? Take the lowest bid."

Babette threw him a black look, but Charles had already turned back to his manuscript and placed his fingers on the keys.

"The problem," she said, taking pains to keep her voice low, "is that we don't have ninety-nine hundred dollars. We don't have one hundred extra dollars. With the high cost of gas this year, we'll be lucky if we can make it through the winter without maxxing out the credit card."

Charles's fingers kept hovering over the keys, but his head turned toward her again. "I'm not worried, honey. My book's still out there, and it's going to sell any day now."

She forced the words out. "And if it doesn't?"

Charles's shoulder lifted in a half-shrug. "You'll think of something. You always do."

Click, clack, clickity clack. His fingers moved over the keyboard. Already he had shut her out.

Babette swallowed hard and wrapped her arms about herself, feeling suddenly chilly. She had no answers, not this time. With winter approaching and the ferry running only three times a day, very few off-islanders even visited Heavenly Daze. The few who came might want to enjoy the bed and breakfast or sample saltwater taffy from the Mercantile, but with Christmas approaching, nobody would have money to spend on big-ticket art items from the Graham Gallery. They might sell a few pieces of Z's pottery, but those would barely cover the expense of heating the large showroom.

Gripping the Handyman Roofing envelope in her fist, Babette turned and left Charles alone, then walked slowly down the stairs. She wondered if anyone on the island knew about their money problems—after all, the Graham Gallery did not sell knickknacks or tourist trinkets. Their living-room-turned-showroom was well-stocked with paintings worth thousands. Even some of Zuriel's pottery pieces sold for over one hundred dollars. But most people didn't know that everything but Z's pottery and Charles's paintings were being sold on a consignment basis. When and if they were purchased, 60 percent of the money went directly to the artist. The remaining 40 percent went into the Graham Gallery business account to pay Babette's meager salary and provide a roof over their heads.

A roof that leaked.

Sighing, she dropped the letter from Handyman atop the stack of bills on her kitchen desk. Apart from taking out a loan—which she doubted they could get, much less pay off—she could do nothing but wait for spring and the few tourists who'd return and spend their discretionary income on a piece of art that would remind them of the idyllic weekend they'd spent on a Maine island.

She sank into her chair and stared out the window. The snow had stopped, and the steady plinking sound of the water had slowed. But she dared not move the bucket. If temperatures warmed, it could rain in an instant. Weather on the island could be fickle.

Crossing her arms, she leaned her head against the back of her tall chair and groaned. They could, of course, move to Portland or Boston. In an urban location they could turn the gallery into a twelve-month business and make money year round . . . but Georgie would have to live in the city. And the quality she appreciated most about Heavenly

Daze was the small town sense of community. Here, Georgie was growing up among people who prized and petted him. As far as she knew there were no guns on Heavenly Daze, no violence, and no crime apart from the occasional trouble that came over with the tourists. This island was as near as she'd come to finding to heaven on earth, and she didn't want to take Georgie away.

It'd be easier to buy more buckets.

Charles stopped typing nonsense and waited for the familiar sound of Babette groaning at her desk, then breathed a sigh of relief. Babette was a good woman and a great wife, but when she got in a mood . . .

He shook his head and stared at the confused page before him. He'd been in the middle of a scene when she interrupted, and now he couldn't think of anything but the leaky roof. What did she expect him to do about it? He knew nothing about roofing and would probably break his neck if he climbed up on the eaves and started ripping off shingles. His father had never been much of a handyman, and on the few occasions Charles had picked up a hammer, he'd routinely hit his thumb or injured some other part of his body.

Babette knew he wasn't handy, and she knew he didn't care a thing about accounting. Early on they'd agreed that she'd keep the books, and in the ten years of their marriage, she'd done a marvelous job of keeping their family and business solvent.

So why was she coming to him about their finances now? Sometimes he felt as though she wanted him to suddenly become the family executive, lawyer, and banker all rolled into one, but when she married him she knew he was none of those things. He was an artist, a dreamer, and a painter . . . and at the moment a very frustrated wordsmith.

He reread the first paragraph on the page:

> *"Devon," she whispered softly, her heart thudding like the bass drum that used to hurt her ears in high school band class, "I wanted to see you."*

Devon stared at her, his mouth going dry and his palms in need of a good swipe of antiperspirant. Wowsers, she was beautiful. She was passion and flowers and music and moonlight and magic and magnolias all rolled into a great big sticky gumball of loveliness. He needed her. He wanted her. But she must never know it.

"So see me," he answered dryly, his voice grating like nails over a chalkboard. "I'm here. I've always been here."

Akgyueiotywieotiutlgkshg

Charles blew out his cheeks, then ripped the page out of the typewriter, wadded it, and tossed it over his shoulder. Even with the gobbledygook he'd typed when Babette came in, he knew it wasn't working.

"Not compelling," he muttered. "Plodding. Tired and full of purple prose." Those words had become a jingle that echoed in his brain, a singsong chorus he couldn't wipe from his consciousness. The rejection slips he had received from his first book all contained some variation of those lyrics.

From a New York agent: "Not compelling. Keep your day job."

From Harbor House, home of best-selling author Stellar Cross: "Plodding and ill-paced. Needs revision."

From The Writer's Ink, a manuscript evaluation service: "Tired and redundant, but shows signs of promise. For $999, we'll make suggestions for improvement."

From Oprah's Book Club: no response.

But he had not given up hope, hadn't given in to the temptation to quit, hadn't moped or moaned or pouted. He'd merely outlined his second novel and begun to write again, holding out hope that those who still had his first manuscript would recognize fledgling genius when they saw it. Until they did, he would remain hard at work, polishing and perfecting and persevering at his task.

Let the roof leak. Someday, when he had made the *New York Times* best-seller list, he'd tell the story of how he suffered in his writing room . . . and laugh.

Later that afternoon, Birdie looked up from her accounting and saw that Abner was preparing to close the bakery. The devoted employee finished his baking by late morning, and early afternoon business usually slowed to a trickle—nothing Birdie couldn't handle if anyone happened to stop by for a cookie or an after-dinner dessert.

"If there's nothing else, Birdie, I'll be going." Abner appeared in the doorway, bundled up for the brief walk to the carriage house at the back of Birdie's lot. Though it would have been far simpler—and warmer—for him to walk through the house, he insisted that Bea and Birdie deserved their privacy. Also, he once confessed, the exercise did him good. (The poor man had developed a noticeable paunch—the result of sampling too many of his own delicious concoctions.)

Birdie often wondered what he did with his free time. She knew the carriage house was warm and comfortable. She'd furnished it herself with a soft bed, a small black-and-white television, a table, chair, and lamp. During summer months, when everyone on the island raised their windows to catch the sea breeze, she often heard him laughing at reruns of *Happy Days* and *Little House on the Prairie.* Six days a week his lights were out by 9 P.M., and he was back in the bakery by 4 A.M., baking again. By six o'clock, the first of the hot doughnuts, thick with shiny glaze, lay on cooling racks. Elezar and Zuriel would arrive, their noses red from the brisk, early morning walk, and the three men would sit around a table to enjoy cups of steaming coffee and fresh, just-baked doughnuts.

About a half-dozen sugary treats each.

Smiling, Birdie reached for a roll of adding machine tape. "I can't think of anything else I need, Abner. Have a nice afternoon."

"You, too, Birdie. May God smile especially on you today."

She grinned impishly. "He already has. I'm alive and apparently still foxy-looking enough to catch a certain skipper's eye."

"Ayuh, that you are." Wrapping his scarf around his neck, Abner winked, then left the shop.

After working another hour on her accounts, Birdie turned the CLOSED sign into place and pulled the shade on the front door. Sighing, she turned and walked through the kitchen and into the keeping room, careful not to disturb Bea, who was hunched over the small writing desk and apparently lost in thought.

Settling into her recliner, she picked up her knitting and began her work, her thoughts drifting back to young Lewis's letter.

Heavenly Daze had no angels, of course, but there was no reason she and Bea couldn't act as compassionate surrogates. They were two aging women with time on their hands, so what was to prevent them from helping out? They couldn't heal or dictate the color of bicycles, but they could lend a word of encouragement to a grieving parent and offer a word of comfort to a confused child. Perhaps they could write several letters over the winter, keeping tabs on Lewis's progress . . .

The thought of children brought Salt Gribbon to mind. Twice a week he came into the bakery for cookies and bread, and though Birdie didn't want to admit it (especially to Bea), she looked forward to his brief visits. He wasn't a conversationalist, but he always made a point of speaking to her, personally singling her out. Vernie like to tease her about the cap'n, but that didn't bother Birdie. Vernie could tease all she liked; Birdie rather enjoyed the man's attention, though she was powerless to understand why. Romance was certainly not in her future. Never married, she'd nonetheless made a comfortable life for herself on the island. She'd served as head librarian at the Ogunquit Memorial Library for twenty years before taking out a loan to purchase the bakery. When Frank died and Bea came back to Heavenly Daze, Birdie's life became even fuller. Sister took over the post office so Birdie could devote more time to the bakery and church work. Why, Edith Wickam literally glowed when Birdie offered to chair the annual quilt bazaar.

No, Birdie had no intention of changing anything, but a little male attention never hurt any woman's esteem.

But . . . what use could Cap'n Gribbon possibly have for *Curious George*?

Could Bea have been right when she said he couldn't read? He seemed intelligent enough. Was it possible he was using children's books to teach himself?

The image of such a flinty old character huddling over a children's book and stammering to pronounce the simplest words . . . that picture was all wrong.

Still, she could contact the Ogunquit library about buying some old books . . . and take them out to the lighthouse . . .

Her knitting needles clicked rhythmically. Knit three, yarn over, knit to the end of the row.

Even better—she could have Vernie order one of those lovely first edition copies of *Blueberries for Sal* from the Internet. She giggled, imagining the look on Captain Gribbon's face when she handed him the gift—assuming Bea was wrong and he could read, that is.

Sobering, she shook off the thought. There'd be no book ordering off the Internet. She would walk into an Ogunquit bookstore and place her order, thank you.

If she decided to order.

And buying Salt Gribbon a book wasn't a given.

Knit three, yarn over, knit to end of the row.

Not a-tall.

"Bea?" she called. "Remind me to take a loaf of fresh bread to Olympia. I'm thinking the oatmeal loaf would be nice."

Head bent over her work, Bea nodded.

"And it's high time we took Olympia up on her offer. What must she be thinking? She baked those lovely muffins and sent them to us with a note to join her for tea. Nearly a month's gone by, and we've yet to pay her a visit."

"We tried," Bea murmured absently.

"You mean the morning we received the muffins? We went too early, Beatrice. From what I heard, Olympia must have been up half the night baking. Sent every woman on the island a basket of those friendship muffins—why, no wonder she was still asleep when we got there! No, we need to go back, tomorrow morning."

When Bea didn't answer, Birdie lifted her gaze to look at her sister. Bea kept writing, her pen skimming back and forth over the paper in rapid succession. She had to be answering that boy's letter.

That boy—Birdie's thoughts returned to Salt Gribbon.

Books.

That'd set Vernie's tongue to wagging.

Dropping the knitting into her basket, she got up to wrap Olympia's bread.

CHAPTER THREE

As a watery sun tried to penetrate the island's midmorning chill, Birdie joined Bea in the golf cart for the short ride to Olympia's house. She'd dressed for the occasion, more for Olympia's sense of propriety than her own, and hoped that the hour would be put to good use—

Bea veered sharply, barely missing Tallulah as the de Cuvier's terrier trotted across the road.

"Beatrice, you're going to kill us!" Birdie shouted, her heart in her throat. "You're worse than Vernie and that infernal motor scooter." She held tight to her hat as the cart collided with the curb, then ricocheted back to the street.

"Olympia needs to keep that dog inside—she lets her run all over the island."

Gunning the cart, Bea rounded the corner as Birdie turned to make certain Tallulah hadn't suffered. Apparently not. The little mutt was prancing toward the Graham Gallery as if she hadn't a care in the world.

Wheeling into the drive at Frenchman's Fairest, Bea hit the brake, pitching Birdie forward and banging her knee on the glove compartment.

She drew a breath between clenched teeth. "As I live and breathe, Bea, the Japanese could have used you during the war. You'd have made a dandy kamikaze pilot." Easing out of the cart, Birdie hitched up her pantyhose, then frowned when she spotted a long run down her calf. "Look at this—another pair of hose ruined. That's two pairs this week. I'm going to start walking; it's cheaper."

"Gripe, gripe, gripe," Bea complained, taking Birdie by the arm and helping her up the row of concrete steps.

"Don't start that business with me, Bea Coughlin. Do you know the price of hose these days? Six pair cost me over twenty dollars. Break that down and it comes to three dollars and twenty cents a pair—that's six fifty in hose this week alone."

Bea lifted the brass knocker and rapped sharply.

"Six dollars and fifty cents. On hose alone—"

"I don't know where you learned math, Sister," Bea's voice was as sweet as honey, "but twenty divided by six comes to a little over three dollars and thirty-three cents, not three and twenty-five."

Birdie gasped. "Three dollars and thirty-three cents? Why, that's highway robbery!"

The door opened. Caleb Smith, the de Cuvier's butler, greeted them warmly.

The sisters broke into synchronized grins.

"Good morning, Caleb," Birdie chirped. "Is Olympia in?"

"Yes, in?" Bea echoed, straightening her parrot green felt hat.

"We thought perhaps she'd like to share a cup of tea."

"Yes, tea," Bea said.

The old butler's face lit with a smile. "Come in, ladies. It's blustery out."

"Oh, it is."

"Some blustery."

The sisters breezed through the doorway, unbuttoning their wraps. Caleb hung their coats in the hall foyer, then ushered them into the large front parlor where a rosy fire blazed in the hearth. "I'll tell Missy you're here." He left a moment later, closing the double doors behind him.

Sighing, Bea clasped her hands behind her back and meandered through the room, admiring various vases and knickknacks, murmuring an occasional, "Will you look at that" and, "Mercy, that must have cost an arm and a leg." Birdie, on the other hand, found herself drawn to the massive oak bookcases lining the longest wall of the room. Edmund's vast collection of books, ranging from beloved classics to volumes on the law and philosophy, never ceased to fascinate her. On the rare occasions she had been invited into the home, she'd spent most of her time perusing the titles and drinking in the scents of old leather and yellowed parchment.

As her gaze fell upon the children's section, she thought about Captain Gribbon and wondered what books he might like. What wonderful stories would capture his heart the way they had captured hers? Reading opened a whole new world, swept a body to far-off places. Why, in a book you could sail the open seas, fly to the moon, or visit a lazy stream on a hot summer afternoon. Ah, the delights reading brought—a pity so few people took the time to enjoy it these days.

The women turned when the door opened and Olympia appeared, a confused look on her face. Her eyes skimmed the two sisters, taking in every detail of their dress. "Good morning, ladies. Caleb said you wanted something?"

Crossing the room, Birdie smiled. "I told Bea yesterday, 'Beatrice, we're long overdue for tea with Olympia.' We were hoping you'd have time to share a cup this morning—though of course we've eaten the muffins long ago. And they were delicious."

"Delicious," Bea corresponded.

Olympia's eyes shifted to the mantel clock. "You want to have tea at 10:15?"

Birdie looked back at Olympia. "Is the hour a problem?"

One never knew about Olympia. Some days she seemed friendly, but other days she was about as personable as a public monument. Now she seemed uncomfortable with the idea of tea, yet last month *she'd* sent the invitation and muffins, not Birdie.

Olympia's right hand flew to the faded lace at her collar. "I'm not dressed for company, and look at you. All fixed up—"

"Oh, fiddle, don't worry about etiquette." Birdie took Olympia by the arm and ushered her toward the sofa. "Goodness, it's just me and Bea—and I have a runner in my hose." To prove it, she hiked up her dress and pointed to the run.

"Well . . ." Olympia glanced toward the door, where Caleb had reappeared. He carried a large silver tea service, laden with cups, cream and sugar, and a plate of what looked like lemon tea wafers.

He sent a smile winging across the room. "Would you ladies like to have your tea by the window?"

"Oh, that would be delightful, Caleb. Thank you." Birdie sighed with contentment. "What a perfectly glorious way to spend a gloomy, overcast morning."

"Yes, delightful," Bea agreed. "Perfectly lovely."

After casting Caleb a look—whether mystified or irritated, Birdie couldn't tell—Olympia proceeded to the small table in a south window and took her seat.

Birdie and Bea followed, smiling pleasantly as Caleb shook out linen napkins and placed them in the women's laps.

"Will you have lemon with your tea, Birdie?"

"Cream and sugar, please. Thank you, Caleb." Birdie preened under the pampering. Caleb was such a gentleman, mannerly to a fault. If only more Heavenly Daze men exhibited Caleb's fine breeding.

"Did I mention I nearly blew out a tire on the golf cart yesterday?" Bea asked, her eyes going wide. "Big rut on the corner of Main and Ferry. Floyd needs to do something about these roads—maybe he should spend more time on street maintenance and less time hoping for a fire."

Olympia nodded, some of her former stiffness slipping away. "Floyd is fond of crises, isn't he?"

Birdie offered a gentle rebuke. "We shouldn't be speaking ill of Floyd. He's a good man."

"Oh yes, a good man." Bea stared thoughtfully out the window. "He kept us in cucumbers all summer."

The conversation fell into a lull.

Reaching for the cream pitcher, Birdie stretched for a new topic. "Olympia, Bea and I haven't told you how much we appreciated the muffins you sent last month. They were simply delicious. You must share the recipe—Abner would love it."

"Muffins?" Olympia glanced at Caleb as he freshened her tea.

"Oh, they were wonderful," Bea echoed. "Friendship muffins, what a nice thought."

Olympia frowned at her butler, who promptly changed the subject. "Did you ladies happen to see Tallulah out and about this morning?"

"Bea nearly ran her over at the corner," Birdie said.

"Quite nearly," Bea agreed.

"Perhaps if you'd watch the road instead of yakking to your sister." Olympia lifted her head to stare out the window. "After all, Tallulah's always had the run of the island."

"That explains why she thinks she owns the place," Bea said, the corners of her mouth lifting. "She's a de Cuvier."

Birdie flinched, but Olympia seemed to take no offense. She looked exhausted, as if she'd spent another sleepless night with Edmund—which she probably had.

Leaning over, she covered Olympia's hand. "How is Edmund today?"

Moisture filled Olympia's eyes, then she looked away. "Growing very weak now."

"I'm so sorry."

"So sorry," Bea echoed. "Is there anything we can do to help?"

"Nothing." Straightening, Olympia cleared her throat. "Is this visit in regard to the quilt show? Because if it is, I've already given a donation, and I don't have the time to—"

Birdie stopped her. "No, dear. Bea and I are here to have tea, nothing more."

"Well"—Olympia leaned back, her tea sitting untouched before her—"I don't have a quilt to offer this year."

"Of course not," Birdie said. "Edmund's needs come before any old quilt." Taking a sip of tea, she searched for a more agreeable topic. "I suppose Annie will be home for the holiday. Thanksgiving's, what, three weeks away? How can that be possible? The months come and go so quickly—"

"Annie comes home every weekend, Birdie. You know that. Remember the tomatoes?"

Birdie blushed. "Ayuh, I knew that."

"She knew that," Bea offered in an apologetic tone. She lifted the plate to Olympia. "Won't you have a cookie? They're simply delicious."

"No, thank you." Olympia glanced at the clock. "I've just had breakfast."

Birdie sighed and picked up her teacup. "Oh."

"Oh," Bea echoed.

The two sisters swapped uncertain looks.

"Well," Birdie drew a deep breath, "Vernie says Dr. Marc's son is coming home for Thanksgiving. Wouldn't it be delightful if he and Annie hit it off? Your niece is such a sweet girl and so bright! Imagine, tomatoes growing in the winter, why—"

"Annie hasn't the least interest in men."

"Oh?" Birdie arched a brow and looked at Bea over the rim of her teacup.

Olympia didn't notice. "Her job keeps her sufficiently busy; she has no need for a man in her life."

Bea met Birdie's gaze and spoke in a disappointed tone. "Oh."

From where he stood, Caleb cleared his throat. "Olympia, perhaps Birdie and Bea would enjoy seeing your violets. They're so beautiful right now."

Olympia smiled in what looked like relief. "Lovely idea, Caleb."

The women obediently got up and trailed Olympia onto the sun porch. Bending over the delicate plants, Birdie and Bea breathed in unison, "Oh, they are lovely." Birdie had never had a green thumb; she killed nearly every green thing she encountered. But Bea was a bit more knowledgeable about gardening.

"My word," Bea whispered, "do my eyes deceive me? Is that a Swandley White?"

"Marie Louise." Olympia glanced at her watch.

Bea touched a velvety green leaf. "A sweet plant derived from Viola odorata."

"V. alba," Olympia corrected stiffly.

Bea smiled. "Well, it's gorgeous."

"Simply exquisite," Birdie concurred.

Consulting her watch for a second time, Olympia frowned. "My, my, look at the time. I don't want to keep you from . . . whatever you do every morning."

It's time to go, her eyes clearly stated.

Birdie straightened. "It is late, isn't it? I'd better get back to the bakery."

Bea took her cue. "And the mail's waiting. As the feller says, the mail never stops."

Birdie moved toward the door. "I didn't know it was so late, did you, Bea?"

"No idea."

The women strolled back to the parlor and obediently gathered their personal belongings. Olympia saw them to the front door, and her parting smile was the most relaxed expression she'd worn all morning.

"Do stop by the bakery some afternoon," Birdie called over her shoulder as Olympia briskly ushered the two women through the open doorway.

"Anytime," Bea lamely reiterated.

"Ladies, careful of the walk," Caleb called. "There's still a bit of ice in the low places."

The door closed, and the two sisters suddenly found themselves out in the cold.

They exchanged a series of peeved looks.

"Well," Birdie said, her irritation cresting in a wave of indignation, "how rude could she be?"

"Pretty rude, I'd say." Bea adjusted the brim of her hat. "Let's go, Sister."

Jerking on her gloves, Birdie followed Bea to the golf cart, giving her pantihose an irritable yank at the knee before she climbed aboard. Three dollars and thirty-three cents wasted on Olympia de Cuvier.

It would be a cold day in Heavenly Daze before she visited

Frenchman's Fairest again. Next time she felt the urge to do a good deed, she'd pick a more deserving recipient.

Olympia lifted the parlor curtain, snorting under her breath as the two sisters' cart whipped around the corner.

"Will there be anything else, Missy?" Caleb asked, cleaning up the remains of that pitiful tea party.

"A good head doctor."

"Pardon?"

She let the curtain drop back into place. "This town needs a good psychologist—that's the fourth time in as many weeks someone has dropped by babbling about friendship muffins and invitations. First it was Edith Wickam, then Vernie Bidderman. Last week Dana Klackenbush popped over, and now Birdie and Bea." She turned to face the old butler. "Must be something in the water, and I'm the only one not drinkin' it."

Ducking sheepishly, Caleb murmured, "I'll just carry these dirty dishes to the kitchen. If you need anything—"

"I know. I'll call you."

A few minutes before noon, Zuriel hunched into his coat as he walked to the ferry landing, bracing himself against the cold breath of the wind. The new day had dawned cold and gray, but now the overhead sun sent brilliant fingers of light through the cloud cover. The strident sound of gulls echoed over Ferry Road, but the only other sound in the stillness was the crunch of gravel as Bea and Birdie Wester wheeled their cart into the alley beside the bakery.

Zuriel paused at the intersection of Ferry and Main out of habit, watching for Tallulah and Butch, but nothing moved on Main Street. Smoke rose from the chimney of the Baskahegan Bed and Breakfast, where Cleta and Floyd were probably enjoying a lunch of chowder and shrimp salad sandwiches. The sweet scent of wood smoke filled Zuriel's nostrils and made him glad for the approach of winter. The other angels professed to favor summertime, but he liked the solitude of the quiet months.

A tiny whitewashed shed served as the ferry office. As Zuriel drew near he could see that the building stood closed and empty, but within the hour Captain Stroble would be holed up inside, warming his hands around a thermos of hot coffee. The ferry from Ogunquit ran only three times in the off-season: at 7 A.M., noon, and 6 P.M., returning to the mainland an hour after each arrival.

Zuriel checked his watch, then scanned the sea for a sign of the approaching boat. Nothing marred the horizon, so Captain Stroble must have been held up at Perkins Cove. Knowing he wasn't likely to encounter a crowd on a cold day like this, Zuriel moved toward the green bench next to the ferry office. He could wait.

Sinking to the bench, Zuriel smiled as he flicked away a peeling paint chip from one of the planks—the bench had been brown before—and considered his divine appointment. The man who would soon step onto the Heavenly Daze dock had no idea he was expected. Zuriel had only learned of his arrival this morning, when Gavriel materialized in his workroom and relayed instructions from the Lord. The Lord had spoken, Gavriel said, and Georgie's prayer was about to be answered. Zuriel was to facilitate the operation.

The wind caressed the angel's face as he turned to study the shafts of sunlight reflecting off the deep blue water. Ah—there she was. The squat ship was coming on with an impressive show of speed, a white foamy mustache at her bow.

Zuriel stood and walked down to the docks, smiling as a school of fish in the shallows darted away from his shadow. The ferry drew closer, slowing as it neared its berth, and two anchors fell from its nostrils. A deck hand threw out the towropes, then leapt to the dock to secure the heavy hemp spirals.

Zuriel stepped out onto the dock and rocked on his heels, his hands in his pockets as he regarded the boat. No tourists lined the deck as they might have in warmer months—the combination of cold wind and sea spray would not appeal to a landlubber. Not even the sturdy folk of Heavenly Daze would stand out here without a terrifically good reason.

The captain stepped out of the cabin first, the reddish-brown color of his face advertising his occupation.

"Hello, Z," he called, settling his cap upon his head. "If you were supposed to meet someone, I'm afraid they missed the boat. I got no one aboard but one little fella from Boston."

Zuriel met the captain's greeting with a smile. "I'll take whoever you've got, Captain. What's the off-islander's business here?"

Stroble crossed his arms, folding his ungloved hands into his armpits. "He says he's going out to photograph the lighthouse."

Zuriel stepped closer to the edge of the dock, breathing in a whiff of sea salt emanating from the captain. "I could take him out that way."

The captain's smile sent a single dimple winking in his left cheek. "Trying to earn some extra change, are you?"

"No." Zuriel felt a blush burn his face. "Just trying to be helpful."

At that moment Stroble's passenger emerged from the cabin. The "little fella" wore a down jacket, jeans, and a hat from which a fringe of brown hair sprouted at the back. A battered leather camera bag dangled from his shoulder, the mark of a tourist out for a pleasant excursion, but the expression on the man's face did not seem particularly pleasant.

The captain touched the brim of his cap. "Good afternoon to you, then," he called as the man negotiated the gangplank. "We'll be departing at one and again at seven, if you should need that long."

"I should hope not." The man clung heavily to the guide rope as he traversed the short walkway. Stroble winked at Zuriel, then leaned upon the deck railing.

"This fella here is Zuriel Smith," he called, pointing toward Zuriel. "He's a good sort, and he might be willing to show you the way out to the lighthouse. Might save you some time."

The man turned, his dark brown eyes taking in Zuriel's form in one swift glance. "I don't need a guided tour."

"It's not a tour, only a friendly point in the right direction," Zuriel answered, shrugging inside his coat. "I have to walk back that way no matter what you decide."

The man hesitated, lifting one gloved finger to stroke the end of his clipped mustache. "All right, then," he finally said, nodding at the captain. "I'll try to make it back in an hour. I only need a few shots."

Zuriel smiled to himself as the bantam-weight photographer led the way off the dock. He knew almost nothing about this man—only that he would somehow provide an answer to Georgie's prayer.

Lengthening his stride, Zuriel caught up to the man as they passed the ferry office. "First time to Heavenly Daze?" he asked.

The man nodded, his eyes set and serious beneath dark brows. "First and last, I hope," he said, glancing up and down Main Street. "What is this place, a ghost town? Not a soul around."

"I wouldn't say that," Zuriel countered. "I'm here. Everyone else, I expect, is busy with their duties. We've just come through a busy tourist season, and most folks are settling down for winter and the holidays." He nodded at Frenchman's Fairest as they walked past. "That household is keeping a vigil. The owner, Edmund de Cuvier, is near death."

The man made a face. "That's terrible. This place is bleak enough during the winter, but with death hanging over your heads—"

Zuriel cast the man a reproving glance. "On the contrary, there's nothing bleak about this island. You should come back when you have more time to look around."

"One look is all I need. The magazine I freelance for wanted a shot of this lighthouse for its spring edition. Though how I'm going to make it look like spring is beyond me."

Zuriel laughed softly. "The northern part of the island looks pretty much the same year round, except when there's snow on the ground. It's rocky up there, so we don't get much vegetation, even in summer. The landscape shouldn't be a problem, but getting close enough for a good shot might be. The lighthouse caretaker is a mite zealous in his responsibility. He doesn't like people getting too close."

"I've got a zoom lens," the man answered.

"You'll need it."

They passed through the intersection of Ferry Road and Main Street in silence. "Man," the visitor said as they passed the Mercantile, "I feel like I've stepped back in time."

Zuriel shivered as a gust of wind rocked the hanging sign outside the B&B. "Folks around here do like to keep things pretty much the same. That's what brings the summer tourists. Everyone likes to take a walk down memory lane." His voice softened as he thought about the two hundred years he'd passed on the island. "Even me."

He inclined his head toward the Graham Gallery as they approached. "Here's where I live. Could I interest you in a cup of cocoa before you head on up to the lighthouse?"

He stopped outside the tidy picket fence surrounding the property and noticed that his new acquaintance cast a longing eye toward the sheltering porch.

"Something hot sounds good," the man admitted. "The boat ride about froze me solid."

"Then come in for a cup." Zuriel opened the gate and gestured toward the cobblestone path. "Babette always keeps a pot of hot water on the stove, and there's instant coffee or cocoa or whatever you like."

"Your wife?" the man asked, passing through the gate.

"My landlady"—Zuriel flashed a smile—"and co-owner of the Graham Gallery, home of the finest art and most humble pottery in these parts. You can look around while you drink your cocoa, and I'd advise you to drink until you're pretty well defrosted. The lighthouse is still a good walk from here."

The bells above the door jangled as they entered, and a moment later Babette emerged from the kitchen, her face flushed and her hands wet. She hesitated, a question in her eyes, when she saw the stranger in her foyer.

"Babette," Zuriel stepped forward, "I was wondering if you had some hot water on the stove. My friend here is determined to walk out to the lighthouse, but I think we ought to fortify him for the journey by putting something warm in his belly."

"Why, certainly." Babette dried her hands on her apron, then came forward and smiled at the stranger. "I'm Babette Graham. It's nice to meet you."

"Pierce Bedell." After removing his hat, the man shook her hand and bowed his head in an almost-courtly gesture. "This is a lovely establishment. Quite charming."

"Oh." Babette blushed prettily and waved her hand toward the showroom. "It's a mess right now, with all that plastic over everything. Our sales season ended last month, and we generally keep everything put away until spring."

"An unexpected pleasure, to meet another art aficionado." Mr. Bedell patted the leather bag at his side. "I'm here as a freelance photographer, but I'm really an art dealer. I have clients in Boston, Portland, even as far west as Chicago."

"Really?" Babette's eyes widened.

Recognizing an opportunity to be of service, Zuriel took a step toward the kitchen, then turned. "Coffee, cocoa, or tea, Mr. Bedell?"

"Um, coffee. I take it black." The man moved toward the double French doors that led into the gallery showroom. "May I look around?"

"Please." Babette made a nervous gesture toward the doors, then pulled her hand back. "Help yourself."

Moving into the kitchen, Zuriel heard the creak of the doors that led into the gallery. An inch of dark brown liquid remained in the bottom of Charles's coffeepot, so he sloshed coffee into a stoneware mug, then set it on a tray and hurried into the gallery.

"This is an adorable piece." Zuriel entered the showroom in time to see Bedell point toward one of his salt-glazed teapots. "And so reasonable! Is the artist local?"

"As local as can be," Babette answered, her voice dry. "The artist is Zuriel—the fellow who's offering you coffee right now."

Bedell froze in surprise, then threw back his head and let out a great peal of laughter, the first glimpse of joy Zuriel had seen in the man.

"Wonderful!" he said, taking the mug from the tray. He looked again at Babette. "This really is a beautiful piece. I'd love to buy it—should I pay you or the artist?"

Zuriel grinned as he lowered the tray. In all his years of working for the Grahams, no one had ever offered to buy anything directly from him. He didn't want the money; of course, he had no need for earthly possessions. But Babette's response might prove interesting . . .

She didn't hesitate. "Zuriel has been some gracious to us, but he's your friend. If you want the teapot, I'm sure you can buy it directly from him."

Zuriel wrapped his arms around the tray and hugged it to his chest. Despite the financial strain on her family, Babette had retained a generous heart.

"I'll think about the teapot," Bedell said, moving toward a row of paintings draped in plastic. "May I look at these?"

"Be my guest."

Bedell took a perfunctory sip from the coffee mug, then set it on the edge of a shelf, dropped his camera bag, and began to flip through the standing frames.

Babette lifted a brow as if to ask, "What gives?"

Zuriel shrugged.

"Very soothing seascape," Bedell murmured, eyeing a scene Charles had painted last summer. "But what's this card at the bottom?"

Babette let out a sharp laugh. "My husband is not only an artist, but an incurable storyteller. He likes to include a short story or essay with each painting. He says it makes the paintings more personal."

"My dear lady," Bedell murmured, squinting downward at the painting, "if a picture paints a thousand words, why would anyone add to such art? This card is unnecessary, redundant."

Behind Bedell's back, Babette winked at Zuriel.

"What a tasteful portrait," Bedell said, studying another painting. "Most exquisite."

"All our paintings are tasteful," Babette answered, casting Zuriel a worried glance. "After all, I have a five-year-old son. I look for artists who deal as much with shadow and implication as with, um, anatomical detail."

Bedell cast a quick grin over his shoulder. "I understand, Madame. A wise decision, no doubt."

He moved to another rack of paintings, lifted the plastic, then stiffened. "Eureka," he breathed, "I have found it."

Zuriel and Babette looked at each other as she asked, "What did you find?"

"This—this incredible piece," Bedell whispered, his voice a hoarse rasp in the room. "Such colors! Such honesty! Such . . . there is no word but passion! It is stark and primitive, yes, but this is the most genuine work I have seen in years."

With curiosity snapping in her eyes, Babette walked over and peered past Bedell's shoulder. Zuriel felt his stomach drop when her gaze caught and held his. "Oh," she said, her voice flat, *"The Puffin."*

"It is a masterpiece!" Bedell pulled it from the rack with both hands, then carried it to the display easel at the front of the room. With the afternoon sun brightening the window, Zuriel had to admit Georgie's painting was attractive.

"I have a client in Boston," Bedell was saying, one finger pressed to his mustache, "who would be thrilled to add this to her collection. She loves the Maine seashore, you see, and hasn't seen a real puffin in years. I'm certain I could sell this to her."

"Really?" Babette's voice was a whimper in the room.

"I'd stake my life on it." Bedell ran his finger over the bold *G* in the lower right corner. "And the artist is—?"

"Georgie," Babette whispered, her voice fainter than air.

"Zhorzh-ay," Bedell corrected. "I should have recognized his work immediately. In any case"—he pulled a checkbook from his inner coat pocket, then turned to Babette—"I'd like to take this painting to Boston. Let's see—suppose I offer you ten for it?"

Babette's face fell. Zuriel knew she'd probably spent five times that amount on the frame.

"I really can't part with that picture, I'm sorry." She pushed a hank of hair from her brow and gave him a sad smile. "It was a gift. It really shouldn't be in the gallery at all, but our roof was leaking, so I moved it—"

"All right—ten now and five more when I sell the painting. That's fifteen, and at that price I'll be lucky to break even."

"I'm sorry."

Zuriel stepped between Babette and the art dealer, effectively cutting off their conversation. Mindful of his heavenly mission, he lowered his gaze to study Babette's face. "Think of George." He bent closer to whisper in her ear. "He wanted you to sell that picture. If you do, no matter what the sales price, he'll know he did something to help his family."

She looked away, maternal love and pride struggling on her face. "All right," she said, sighing. "I'll sell it. But only because Georgie wanted me to."

"Zhorzh-ay," Bedell said, scrawling on his check. "And to whom should I make this check payable?"

"The Graham Gallery." Babette rolled her eyes at Zuriel, then flashed him a wicked grin that said *ten dollars is better than nothing.*

Zuriel grinned back, knowing Georgie would think the amount a princely sum. Ten dollars could buy a lot of saltwater taffy at the Mercantile.

As he stepped forward to wrap the painting in brown paper, Zuriel heard the satisfying sound of paper ripping from a checkbook. Babette took the check and dropped it on the desk, then opened the drawer and fumbled for the ball of twine they hadn't used in over a month.

"We hope you like the painting, even if you're not able to resell it," she said, freeing a chain of paper clips from the twine. "George will be thrilled to hear that we sold his first painting."

Pierce Bedell's smile nearly jumped out from under his mustache. "This was his first? What luck! This will add tremendous value!"

Babette's face twisted in concern. "You do understand, don't you? The Puffin was painted by a boy."

Bedell laughed as Zuriel finished wrapping the painting. "My dear lady, we are all boys at heart. We are all children in a sea of life's experiences."

"No, I mean . . ."

Babette's voice trailed off as Bedell took the wrapped painting, tucked it under his arm, then glanced at his watch. "My heavens, the ferry will be leaving. Guess I won't make it out to that blasted lighthouse after all. But that's fine. I've found something far more valuable."

Slinging his camera bag over his shoulder, he settled his cap back on his head, then waved a cheery farewell. "Call me if you acquire another Zhorzh-ay. My number's on the check."

Babette waved him out the door with a perplexed expression on her face. "Thank you very much."

As the bells over the door jangled in farewell, Zuriel handed Babette the ball of twine, then put away the roll of brown paper. She chuckled as she dropped the twine back into the desk drawer. "Georgie will be thrilled to hear he made his first sale," she said. She picked up the check and waved it in the air. "Maybe we should frame this for him."

"That'd be nice." Zuriel pulled the protective plastic back over the rows of paintings. "And every time he sees it, he'll remember how God answered his prayers."

"His prayers?" Babette said, glancing at the check in her hand. "For an entire ten—oh! Z, this check is for ten *thousand* dollars!"

Zuriel felt his mortal heart pound in an odd double beat. Ten thousand? Was this the Lord's provision . . . or a mistake?

"It can't be," Babette whispered, sinking onto a stool. Her face had gone pale, and the hand holding the check trembled. "He misunder stood. But I was honest, wasn't I? I told him Georgie was the artist. I said Georgie was only a boy."

"Ayuh, you did." Zuriel moved to the French doors, not sure whether he should comfort Babette or chase Pierce Bedell. His orders had been simple: meet the man on the ferry, and escort him to the Graham Gallery. Nothing more specific than that.

So . . . what did the Lord want him to do now?

Babette sat motionless, the check in her hand, as wave after wave of shock slapped at her. Ten thousand dollars! Pierce Bedell was a fool—no, an angel! She couldn't keep this—yes, she could—but she shouldn't. Either the fellow had misunderstood, he didn't know what he was doing, or he was a pretentious dilettante who wouldn't know a Klimt from a Klump.

"Zuriel," she whispered, her heart doing a strange little dance in her chest. "Run after him. No—I'll go. I should go."

Her leaden feet reluctantly obeyed her command and carried her through the foyer, over the porch, and past the front gate. In the distance she could see the ferry, the man on the dock, even Captain Stroble's blue coat. With any luck, she'd be able to catch Bedell and explain that he'd bought a child's painting. With even greater luck, he'd laugh and say he'd done exactly what he intended to do.

Fat chance.

Bedell's dark figure moved from the dock to the boat deck, and Babette hurried, the check fluttering in her fingers as the wind blew through the nap of her sweater. Now the captain was aboard, too, and soon the boat would be pulling away . . .

She broke into a run at the intersection of Ferry and Main, then cried out as a shaggy shape leapt from the shadows of the Mercantile's deep front porch. Her shins encountered something soft, then Babette went flying forward, her elbows striking the cobblestones with a heavy scrape.

For a moment she lay on the ground, terribly conscious of the fact that she must look ridiculous, then her eyes opened. Her fist still grasped the check—at least she hadn't lost that along with her dignity.

"Glory be, Babette, are you all right?"

Elezar Smith, Vernie's helper at the Mercantile, came running out of the building, the storm door slamming behind him. Before reaching her, though, he stopped to examine a mass of white fur in the road. "Tallulah? You okay?"

Babette made a wry face as she pushed herself up to a sitting position. Only in Heavenly Daze would a man be as concerned for the de Cuviers' mutt as for a lady.

Brushing a layer of sandy grit from her sweater, she called, "I'm fine, Elezar." She winced as her fingers encountered a sore spot at her elbow. "Tallulah and I were on a collision course, that's all."

"That Tallulah can get under your feet, and don't I know it." The tall man knelt and ran his fingers over the old dog who lay on her side, four legs and a pink tongue extended. At the touch of the man's fingers, Tallulah opened her button eyes and whimpered, then waved one forepaw in a helpless gesture.

"My goodness, I think the old girl might really be hurt." Elezar's walnut complexion took on a shade of concern. "Wonder if I should carry her over to see Dr. Marc?" He squatted in the road and crossed his arms, one finger over his lips as he considered the situation. "Olympia's going to be mighty upset if Tallulah gets hurt right when Mr. Edmund's doing so poorly. I don't know if she could handle losing them both at once."

"Let's not panic yet." Babette groaned as she stood, then she bent with her hands on her knees and looked at the whimpering dog. Brightening her voice, she called, "Tallulah? Would you like to go inside and get a cruller?"

As if by magic, the terrier lifted her head. The forepaw that had been waving helplessly only a moment before served her well enough now, and before Babette could straighten her aching muscles, the dog had righted herself and begun to prance toward Birdie's Bakery, her plumed tail waving like a flag over her back. When Elezar and Babette didn't immediately follow, she turned and looked at them, her mouth opening in a toothy doggie smile.

Elezar removed his cap and scratched his head, grinning. "If that don't beat all."

"I've seen this little actress do her injured act before," Babette said, wincing again as she gently squeezed her sore elbow. "She'll do anything for a cruller."

"I suspect I'd better keep our end of the bargain." Elezar stood and moved toward the door. "I hope Birdie has some day-old doughnuts left for this little missy."

Leaving the spoiled dog and her friend, Babette turned and looked toward the sea. As she feared, the ferry had pulled away from the dock and was already plowing through the crushed diamond sea. Nothing she could do but go home and leave a message on Mr. Bedell's answering machine.

As she turned to go, she saw Elezar standing by the center post of Vernie's front porch. He was watching her, a look of marked concern on his face.

"You must think me ill-mannered, tending to a dog before looking after a lady," he said, his tone apologetic. "Truth is, you didn't look much hurt."

Babette forced a smile. "I'm afraid the only thing hurt was my pride."

"So everything's fine with you and yours?"

Babette opened her mouth, intending to give him a polite, reserved answer, but her true feelings spilled out in a rush. "Actually, Elezar, things aren't so fine. I think I've just made a major mistake—my brain or my ethics or something went to sleep on me, and for a moment I lost my bearings. I was running to catch the ferry to set things right, but—well, you saw what happened."

Elezar nodded, one corner of his mouth twisting upward. When he spoke again, his voice rang with depth and authority. "Listen to your heart, Babette. If the Spirit of God is speaking, you listen carefully."

What did that mean? Her heart was filled with confusing impulses and emotions, so how was she to know which ideas came from God and which were born of her own selfishness?

Babette raked her hand through her hair, then smiled a polite farewell. "Better get going," she said, gesturing toward her house. "I've got things to do."

Sitting alone in the art gallery, Zuriel stilled his spirit and listened to the sounds of life in the house. Upstairs, Charles worked on his latest manuscript, the heavy click, clack, ching! of the old typewriter sending a staccato vibration through the walls. From another room, Zuriel heard the sound of childish singing—which meant Georgie was painting again. The boy loved to paint, and Zuriel truly believed the Lord had given him a unique gift. Like his father, Georgie saw stories in every object, but he turned those stories into art through the medium of paint and paper.

Like a bird who warbles when he builds a nest, Georgie sang as he created. Babette had once told Zuriel that Georgie's pediatrician asked her if the boy ever sang around the house. "All the time," she'd answered, wondering at the significance of the question.

"Then he's a happy child," the pediatrician told her, "because happy children sing."

Zuriel smiled at the doctor's insight. Sometimes humans amazed him with their perspicacity. They grasped so many truths, but others, including some of the most basic and eternal, eluded them. He would never understand why so many humans could believe that human life developed from nothingness, yet refuse to accept the more logical truth that God created man from clay and the breath of life.

At the moment, he was struggling to understand how a family as happy as the Grahams had become so . . . compartmentalized. Ever since the end of the tourist season, each of them had seemed to go in a separate direction—Charles to his writing room, Babette to her kitchen, Georgie to his schoolroom at the Kennebunk Kid Kare Center, then to wherever little boys liked to roam after school. The Scriptures clearly taught that a threefold cord could not be easily broken, but the members of this family had become so independent that any one of them could snap at any moment.

At the sound of footsteps on the porch, Zuriel stood and moved toward the front door. A moment later Babette entered the foyer, and from the distressed expression on her face he knew she hadn't been able to catch the ferry.

"Had a little accident," she said, apparently reading the question on his face. "Tallulah and I had a collision on Main Street. Neither of us are hurt, but tomorrow I'm going to have a bruise the size of Wisconsin on my elbow."

"But Mr. Bedell—"

"Got away." She lifted one shoulder in a shrug. "I'm going to leave a message on his answering machine. If it has a time and date stamp, at least he'll know I tried to reach him as soon as possible."

She stepped into the gallery, then stood behind the tall work desk and picked up the phone. Turning to Zuriel, she said, "Don't tell Georgie we sold his painting." She lowered her voice. "Because I'm going to have to take it back."

"I won't say a word," Zuriel promised.

Moving stiffly, as if the action caused her pain, Babette smoothed the crinkled check on the polished desk, then dialed Mr. Bedell's telephone number. Zuriel stepped back into the gallery and pretended to check the pottery inventory as she placed the call, then he heard her speak in the strangely artificial voice people always used when addressing an answering machine: "Hello, this is Babette Graham, from the Graham Gallery. I really must speak to you, Mr. Bedell, about the painting you bought today. Will you call me as soon as you get in? Thanks very much."

She lowered the phone back into its cradle, then blew out her cheeks. "It's done," she said, cocking a brow at Zuriel. "It may cost us a new roof, but we've done the right thing."

Zuriel smiled, glad that she had obeyed the voice of her conscience, but a little confused by the day's latest development. He'd been sent to escort Mr. Bedell to the Graham Gallery so Georgie's prayer could be answered. He did, and it was. So what was Babette doing now, and how would her actions affect Georgie?

Tugging on his beard, he turned to the window, anxious to see what changes the next few days would bring.

After Zuriel left the gallery, Babette walked to her desk in the kitchen. She slipped Mr. Bedell's check into an envelope, then placed the envelope atop the stack of roofing bids, wishing that Bedell's ten thousand dollars could cover her financial needs as easily as she could cover her bills with his check.

Strange, that she'd been handed ten thousand dollars when she needed almost that exact amount to replace her roof. Odd that the money had come from a painting Georgie wanted her to sell. In simple, childlike faith he had given her an offering, and his offering had brought in exactly what she needed . . .

She froze as a sudden thought struck her. Was Pierce Bedell's visit an odd coincidence . . . or heavenly provision? She had never in her life experienced a miracle quite like this one, but there was a first time for everything.

Perhaps it would be wrong to return the money. After all, she'd begged God to meet their needs, and he had promised to take care of his children. Hadn't Pastor Wickam recently reminded them to be like lilies of the field, not worrying about food or clothes because the heavenly Father would take care of them?

She could easily cash the check and say nothing. Why not? The man wanted a puffin painting and he bought one, and she'd been honest with him. She hadn't even wanted to sell the painting, but her reluctance only seemed to increase his eagerness to buy. She would never need to say anything further about it, because Pierce Bedell, whoever he was, obviously knew nothing about the real art world. He was probably a graduate from a liberal arts college who'd taken one class in art appreciation and now fancied himself an expert. But he wasn't, obviously, because he'd assumed the puffin painting was something spectacular while he'd passed over Charles's excellent seascapes as if they were little more than art on black velvet . . .

If he was truly ignorant, maybe she ought to protect him from himself . . . but could she do it at the expense of her family?

How would she ever know what to do?

CHAPTER FOUR

Babette spent the entire weekend battling her conscience. As tense as a bowstring, she snapped at Georgie when he spilled milk at the breakfast table, and she kept her distance from Charles even on Sunday. She didn't want to discuss the puffin matter with him—first, because he might tell her to return the money, and second, because she couldn't bring herself to tell him that his five-year-old had sold a puffin picture for more than Charles had ever earned on a single painting.

Not even Zuriel was safe from her crusty mood. On Monday morning he suddenly stepped around the gallery corner, startling her so badly that she dropped the beautiful teapot in her hands and screamed out her frustration. Five minutes later, she had to apologize for screaming and destroying one of his best pieces. He was helping her sweep up the broken pottery when the gallery phone rang.

She froze.

"Answer it," Zuriel said, his face displaying an uncanny awareness of her mental state. "It might be Mr. Bedell."

Babette lifted the phone and held it to her ear. "Good afternoon, this is the Graham Gallery."

Zuriel leaned forward as Babette's face paled. The caller had to be Pierce Bedell. Few people called in the off-season, and none of the usual suspects would make the color drain from Babette's face.

He rose from his stool, about to leave and give her privacy, but she covered the phone with one hand. "Please, stay," she mouthed the words. "I may need you."

Relieved, Zuriel sat back down and lifted a brow when Babette pressed the button to activate the speakerphone.

"Mr. Bedell," Babette said, setting her mouth in a determined line as she crossed her arms and faced the phone, "I'm glad you called. I wanted to be sure you understood the background of the puffin painting. I told you the artist was a boy—what I didn't tell you is that the boy is my five-year-old son, Georgie Graham."

For a moment, the static hum of the speakerphone was the only sound in the room, then Bedell's piercing laugh ripped through the stillness. "Your son? Why, that's delicious news! Marvelous! You have the artist on the premises, so you can easily have him paint another!"

Babette's blue eyes widened. "You—surely you don't want another one?"

"My dear, that's my good news. I do want another puffin. I sold the first painting, for twic—well, for an amount that adequately covered my expenses. I was planning to bring a check for the balance when I return to your quaint little island this week, and I was hoping you could find another painting for me."

Babette eyed the phone as if it were a bad smell. "But—isn't this fraud or something?"

"Of course not!" Bedell laughed again. "Fraud is when you claim something is what it isn't. I told the buyer the Puffin was a charming primitive. Which it is."

"But you said it was painted by Zhorzh-ay somebody or other."

"Zhorzh-ay, Georgie, what's the difference? We're still referring to the same person—a boy. A prodigy. How delightful!"

Babette looked at Zuriel, a frown hovering above her eyes. "I don't know about this, Mr. Bedell."

"Call me Pierce, please. If we're going to be in business together, we should dispense with formality."

She drew a deep breath. "I'm just not sure whether this is the right thing to do."

"My dear lady," Bedell's voice dropped to a pleasant drawl, "let me tell you a true story. My sister, a housewife from Ohio, went to a yard sale and bought a pair of salt-and-pepper shakers. While she was there, the man of the house offered to sell her a few other salt-and-pepper shaker sets, with only one catch—she had to buy the entire collection for one dollar per set. His late wife, it seemed, had collected salt and pepper shakers her entire life."

Like any good storyteller, Bedell paused. Babette took the bait. "What happened?"

Bedell laughed. "The man took her to a specially-built trailer stuffed to the ceiling with five thousand sets of salt-and-pepper shakers. My sister didn't have that kind of cash, so she approached me, and together we bought the late wife's collection. Then my sister began to sell salt-and-pepper shakers on eBay, the Internet auction site, and soon she was getting hundreds of dollars for single sets of salt-and-pepper shakers. The other day she sold a simple pair of goldfish shakers for six hundred dollars."

"They must have been valuable," Babette whispered, a note of disbelief in her voice. "Fine porcelain or something."

Bedell chortled. "There was absolutely nothing special about them. But people got caught up in the frenzy, and the price escalated. The last time I checked with my sister, she'd earned over $40,000 from selling these things, and she still has a garage full of shaker sets she hasn't even unpacked."

His voice dropped to a conspiratorial tone. "Remember this, dear Mrs. Graham. Value has nothing to do with worth, but it has everything to do with perceived worth. And art can easily be perceived as priceless."

"I suppose," Babette whispered, her gaze meeting Zuriel's across the room, "there's no rhyme or reason to it."

"You're absolutely right."

Zuriel felt his heart twist as Bedell cackled again, then promised to visit soon . . . to pick up another puffin painting.

"Birdie, will you look at this?" Bea, her glasses perched on the end of her nose, wandered into the sitting room late Monday morning.

Awakened from a nap by the sound of her sister's voice, Birdie sat up and cleared her throat. "What is it, Bea? I'm busy."

Bea peered over the rim of her glasses. "I can see that," she said, her voice dry. "Are you awake enough to help me with this? It's another angel letter that came general delivery to Heavenly Daze. It's from a child"—Bea lifted her brows—"who wants a baby sister. Listen."

While Birdie blinked sleep cobwebs from her eyes, Bea read the letter.

Dear Angel,

I don't believe in Santa Claus or the Easter Bunny but I do believe in angels. Mom says she can feel your spirit sometimes. I can't, but I burnt my finger the other day, so maybe that's why.

I am nine years old and the only kid mom and dad have, which sometimes causes a problem. I have been praying for God to send another baby to my mom and dad so they won't have so much time on their hands. Mother needs someone other than me to worry about. She can be a pain sometimes. I am writing to you to make sure God hears my prayers. Will you please ask him to help me? My name is Skip Patterson and I live in Detroit, Michigan. Tell him its S-K-I-P P-A-T-T-E-R-S-O-N on Lombard Street.

Thank you very much.
Sincerely,
Skip Patterson (on Lombard Street. In case there's another one.)

"My, my." Birdie removed her glasses and polished the lens. "Such a sweet letter. I suppose you'll need to write him right away. But what are you going to say?"

"That I'll pray for him, of course." Seating herself at the writing desk, Bea reached for pen and paper. "Two angel letters in less than a week. Why are people suddenly thinking of Heavenly Daze as a celestial substation?"

"I imagine it's for the same reason folks think the North Pole is Santa's address."

"The North Pole has elves to help with the work load," Bea pointed out. " I don't.'"

Birdie stiffened in her chair. "Now, Beatrice. Surely you can write a couple of letters to precious little kids."

"Two letters, ayuh, but if the mail gets heavier, I don't see how I'll keep up."

"We'll cross that bridge when we come to it, Sister. No use borrowing trouble." Birdie slipped her glasses on, hooking the rims over her ears. "I think I'll go to the library this afternoon, visit with Faye a little while. Do you need anything from Ogunquit?"

"More stationery," Bea murmured.

Birdie dressed warmly for the ride across the bay, pulling on a heavy wool coat and leather gloves. The boat had a heated cabin, but the ride across the inlet would be windy.

"Better wear a hat," Abner told her as he bagged bear claws for her to take to Captain Stroble.

"Thank you, Abner. I will."

Baker and proprietor parted outside the store, and Birdie set off for the landing.

Crossing Main and Ferry, she spotted the inelegant boat moored at the dock. Cormorants flew overhead, darting in and out of the water in search of a tasty morsel.

"Afternoon, Birdie." Captain Stroble greeted her with a smile as she crossed the gangplank.

"Afternoon, Gus." She handed the distinguished looking man the bakery bag. "Thought you might enjoy these with your afternoon coffee."

Brightening, the captain took his pipe out of his mouth, his eyes scanning the goody bag. "Much obliged, Birdie. You know I can't pass up Abner's pastry."

When the ferry docked in Ogunquit, Birdie pulled her collar close and headed into the wind. By the time she arrived at the library on Shore Road, her lips were numb with cold.

Faye Lewiston, the current head librarian, flashed a friendly smile when Birdie walked in. "Birdie, girl, get yourself in here and get warm."

Familiar scents washed over her: the lemon oil of the polished floor, the mingled dry scents of leather and paper, and Faye's distinctive rose perfume. In years past she had spent many a day among the tomes and periodicals, and sometimes she missed her old haunt. She missed sharing her morning coffee with Faye and discussing important things like the prospect of getting a new computer system to assist the reading public. Extra money wasn't easy to come by, but still it had been fun to dream of new reading tables and an enlarged reference section.

Faye stepped from behind the circulation desk, her rubber-soled shoes brushing against the tile floor. Birdie drew her into a quick embrace. "How are you, Faye?"

"Fine as frog hair—and you?"

"Wonderful."

Adjusting a lightweight sweater casually draped around her shoulders, the elderly woman frowned. "What brings you out on such a blustery afternoon?"

Birdie felt her mouth quirk in a smile. "Thought I might see what you had left over from the used book sale."

"I don't rightly recall what's left," Faye admitted. "The boxes are in the back room. Do you want to look through them?"

"That would be nice, Faye." Birdie followed the petite woman into the private room where stacks of books and magazines littered the floor.

Faye stopped before an empty space and tapped her fingertips together as she glanced around. "Looking for anything in particular?"

"Children's books."

Faye turned to stare at her.

"For a friend," Birdie explained.

"Well," Faye bent to study a box, "I believe they're all mixed together, but you're welcome to go through anything in here."

After shrugging out of her coat, Birdie hung it on the hook she'd used for over twenty years, then stepped back and sighed. "Look at that—my coat looks right at home there, Faye."

"That it does," Faye answered, chuckling. "But you can't have my job. You gave it up for cookies, remember?"

Still smiling, Faye returned to the front when a patron rang the bell.

Birdie sank to her knees and set about scavenging the cardboard boxes, pulling out worn copies of *The Adventures of Huckleberry Finn, Black Beauty,* and *Betsy-Tacy and Tib.* Pulling up a chair, she reread a couple of Grimms' fairy tales, delighted with the fanciful illustrations.

An hour later, her feet propped on a storage bin, she helped Nancy Drew discover *The Secret of the Old Clock.* Before she knew it, she heard Faye closing up for the day, switching off lights in the early fall dusk.

"Faye, do we have any McGuffey's readers lying around?"

The librarian came into the back room carrying a handful of paperclips. "The school system donated a whole stack last spring," she said, pitching the paper clips into a bin. "But what in the world do you want with kindergarten material? Are you teaching little Georgie Graham to read?"

"Georgie?" Birdie laughed. "That boy can read nearly as well as I can."

She pressed her lips together, unwilling and unable to say that Salt Gribbon would be the recipient of her generosity. But how was she going to get the material to him without violating his privacy? After all, a man like the captain was bound to be sensitive about his inability to read, and she wouldn't hurt his feelings for the world.

Faye rummaged through a shelf and came up with a handful of *McGuffey's Eclectic Primers.* "How many do you need?"

"One will do." Birdie confiscated the book, her eyes eagerly scanning the pages. The material was elementary and illustrated—perfect. Now, to get the primer in the captain's hands without causing him to suspect she knew what he was doing. Self-educating wasn't the easiest way to learn to read, but she supposed it was better than doing nothing at all.

"This will be great," she announced, adding the book to her growing stack.

By the time Birdie left the library, she'd bought twenty dollars worth of reading material. Some books she would keep and dole out as Salt progressed, but she'd deliver the elementary reader right away.

She was the only passenger on the six o'clock ferry. The water was choppy and the wind sharp enough to cut through a body.

"Bundle up tight," Captain Stroble called as the boat bumped the dock. She waved as she hopped off, then shifted the heavy sack of books to her left hand as she braced herself for the cold walk home.

As she passed Frenchman's Folly, she couldn't help noticing that a warm light glowed in Edmund de Cuvier's sick room. Birdie imagined Caleb and Olympia keeping the deathwatch. A tough time for them, surely.

She shook her head, huddling deeper into her coat as she toted the heavy books up the hill. Her thoughts shifted from the sober image of the de Cuviers to Captain Gribbon's pleased expression when she delivered the books. "Now, Birdie," he'd say in his clipped New England accent, "you shouldn't have gone to the bother."

"Don't get yourself all frothed up, Cap'n Gribbon," Birdie would say right back. "Weren't no bother a-tall."

Some thought the cap'n a little crabby, but Birdie suspected a heart of gold beat beneath all that bluster and blow.

The wood stove burned brightly as Birdie entered the house through the back door, and the smell of clam chowder hung thick in the air. Bea turned in the kitchen, wielding a wooden spoon. "You must be near frozen, Sister. I'll get you a cup of hot coffee."

Birdie set the sack of books on the kitchen counter before stripping off her coat and gloves. "Frozen clean to my toes, I reckon. I need something to get the blood circulating." She moved toward the fire. "It's fearsome out there tonight."

"Ayuh, cold as a well digger's ankles." Bea poured coffee into a thick white mug, then added cream and a teaspoon and a half of sugar. "Been at the library all afternoon?"

"Ayuh. Faye and I had a nice visit."

Taking a pan of cornbread from the oven, Bea eyed the bulging book bag. "Got you some reading material?"

Birdie pretended not to hear the question. Bea wouldn't approve of her buying books for the captain, and she didn't want to begin an argument she couldn't win. She cast about for a new topic, then asked, "Have you ordered the Thanksgiving bird yet?"

The diversion worked like a charm. Bea snapped her fingers and headed toward the desk to write herself a note. "Thirty pounder again this year?"

"Of course, we can always freeze the leftovers."

Smiling, Birdie picked up her cup of coffee and went into the sitting room, then sank wearily into her recliner. Beyond the frosted windowpanes, the wind whistled around the eaves, banging the shutters, but Birdie was warm as a puppy and about as happy.

Charles listened in stunned silence as Babette told him the story of Pierce Bedell and the puffin painting. She had called him and Zuriel into the kitchen, then, over steaming bowls of vegetable soup, she proceeded to tell the most incredible art tale he'd ever heard.

Despite his elation at the thought of money, parts of the story bothered him. The idea that someone would pay $15,000 for a child's painting was ludicrous, and the realization that Babette had conducted this transaction in secret disturbed him. But they desperately needed a new roof, and by the time she pulled Bedell's check from a blank envelope and slid it across the table, Charles was ready to forget his petty annoyances and consider the possibility that good fortune had smiled upon them.

Dense silence filled the kitchen as Zuriel and Babette waited for his reaction. "Well," he finally said, drawing a deep breath as he placed the check on the table, "they say truth is stranger than fiction. I suppose this proves it." He slid the check back to Babette. "Cash it, though, before you call the roofers. Let's make sure this thing won't bounce."

Babette took the check and folded it. "Bedell said he sold the painting already. I'm not certain, but I think he may have sold it for double what he paid us."

Zuriel grunted. "Quite a markup. One hundred percent?"

"Standard in retail," Babette countered. "That's fine, I can't begrudge him a profit. I just want to be sure we're doing the right thing."

"It's incredible, but it feels right." Charles leaned over and squeezed Babette's shoulder. "You'll get your new roof."

"And the remaining five thousand will come in handy as an emergency cushion this winter." Her face brightened as if his approval had lightened her load. "I won't have to worry if the weather turns cold and we have to crank up the thermostat."

"Wait a minute." Leaning back, Charles brought one hand up to scratch at his jaw. "You said he wants another painting, right? That makes another fifteen thousand we can count on."

A look of discomfort crossed Babette's face. "I don't know. Georgie's other puffin paintings aren't as good as the one I framed."

"He can paint more, can't he? The kid's always painting puffins. Last summer all he talked about was puffins swimming, puffins flying, puffins in the nest—"

"I think," Zuriel said, breaking in, "that George might be a little put out with puffins. I haven't heard him mention them in a while."

"The boy's a born artist; he can paint whatever he sets his mind to painting," Charles countered, smacking the table for emphasis. "So he can paint more puffins." He looked directly at his wife. "And we can use that next five thousand for a top-of-the-line computer. I can finally toss out that old typewriter and get a computer to write this book. The book will practically write itself if I get a good machine."

Babette's blue eyes narrowed. "Do we really need a computer?"

"Of course we do." Charles crossed his arms and jerked his chin downward in a decisive gesture. "These days you can do practically anything with a computer: You can do the accounting for the gallery. You can do payroll, track inventory, and sell art on the Internet. You can even build us a Web page! We can increase our sales and reach the entire world, Babs! Here we can only sell six months out of the year, but with a Web page, we can sell year round, and to people even in Timbuktu! We need a computer!"

Babette said nothing, but slowly, nodded, visibly acceding the argument. He had her, and he knew it. And though she might not realize her need for a computer now, she'd soon wonder how they ever ran a business without one.

"Okay," she said slowly, "we'll use the next five thousand for a computer. And we'll sell one more puffin painting—I think I have one in the drawer that's suitable for framing. I can mat it right away and have it ready when Mr. Bedell comes later this week."

"And the next $15,000?" Charles asked, hoping she'd suggest a wide-screen TV . . .

"Will be our emergency cushion," she said, her tone flat and matter-of-fact. "We need one. The money will go into savings, and it will stay there unless we desperately need it." She looked from her husband to Zuriel. "And then I'll be able to sleep at night."

Charles nodded, ruefully accepting the fact that Babette would not be swayed from this conviction. And since he'd given her the responsibility of handling their finances, he'd have to give her the right to do her job.

"All right." He smiled, feeling a great deal cheerier than he had when Babette began her story. "One more puffin painting, and we'll be set. Now"—he looked at the steaming soup and picked up a cracker—"call Georgie, and let's eat supper. I'm starving."

CHAPTER FIVE

Two days later, Babette held up the newly-framed puffin painting and regarded it with a critical eye. The other puffins in the drawer weren't nearly as good as this one and the first, but she did have to admit this piece possessed a colorful and youthful exuberance. Perhaps Georgie really was a prodigy. After all, his father was an artist, and maybe such things could be inherited . . .

Who knew?

The front door jangled a welcome. She looked up in time to see Pierce Bedell, dressed in a new coat that looked like cashmere, enter through the French doors. "Madame Babette," he called, crossing the polished floor in three smooth steps. He took her outstretched hand and kissed it, his mustache tickling the skin near her wrist.

"Mr. Bedell."

"Pierce."

"Of course, Pierce." Gently, she pulled her hand out of his grasp. "Welcome back."

With a flourish, the art dealer swung his briefcase (butter-soft calfskin, Babette noticed, unmarked and clean) onto the counter, spun the locks, and opened it. From a folder he pulled a slip of paper and flashed it before her eyes. "The remaining deposit on the first painting. Five thousand dollars."

Babette focused on the check, devouring it with her eyes. She'd lain awake the last two nights, half-afraid the ferry would sink and they'd never see Bedell again. Charles had ordered his new computer on credit, and Babette knew she wouldn't feel any peace about his high-tech purchase until this five-thousand-dollar check was safely deposited in their account at the Key Bank of Ogunquit.

"Thank you, Mr. Bedell." She accepted the check and slipped it into her zippered cash bag. "And I have something for you."

His dark gaze shifted toward the painting on the display easel. "Ah, I see it already. And I do believe this one is more stunning than the last."

Babette couldn't stop a half-smile from lifting the corner of her mouth. "You really think so?"

"Madame, I know so." Bedell moved to a position directly in front of the easel, then held up his hand like a movie director framing a camera shot. "Look at those colors! They seem deeper than watercolors—"

"That's because some of them are oils," Babette pointed out. "Georgie tends to use whatever he can find around the house."

"Even better!" Bedell clapped his hands. "I see . . . a successful incorporation of watercolor delicacy and oilistic texture. Look how the white speck embellishes the bird's eye! Notice the way you can see water purling on the beach in the background!"

Babette leaned forward and frowned at the painting. Odd that she'd never noticed any of those things. Then again, she wasn't artistic.

Laughing softly, Bedell pressed his fingertips to his chin. "How ingenious, having the simple beach serve as a foil to the colorfully plumaged bird. Yes, this is genius. Your son, Madame, is something special."

Straightening, Babette shrugged modestly. "We've always thought him bright and inquisitive."

"And my clients will be very grateful for the opportunity to own his work."

He pulled another check from his pocket, this one already signed and made out for $15,000. Babette gasped at the man's confidence. "Are you sure you can sell it? Wouldn't you rather take this on consignment—"

"My dear, I already have a buyer. In fact, I have buyers lined up to buy more puffins. The owner of the first painting—a lady in Boston who wishes to remain anonymous—immediately entered *The Puffin* into an art show sponsored by the *Boston Globe.* Already your son's work has won rave reviews. Here, I brought this to show you. It's from yesterday's paper."

The briefcase opened again, then another folder appeared. From it Bedell withdrew a folded newspaper, then snapped it open. Babette gaped at the headline over a column on the left side of the front page: "Puffin Painting Prodigy Packs a Punch and Parallels Picasso!"

"Oh, my," she murmured, sinking to her stool.

"Keep that copy," Bedell said, snapping the locks on his attaché. "Read away. I'll wrap the painting myself, if you don't mind, and hurry to catch Captain Stroble before he takes the ferry back to the mainland."

Murmuring her agreement, Babette picked up the paper. She was only half-conscious of Bedell's movements as he wrapped the second puffin painting in brown paper and twine. Her thoughts were too busy following the words of Howard Crabbe, art critic for the *Globe:*

> *Boston's art community was rocked today by the appearance of a new artist—a newcomer represented by Pierce Bedell, a private art dealer headquartered in Portsmouth. The artist is a young man known only as "George," and his signature is a bold, cocky* G.
>
> *The cause of this weekend's commotion was a single simple painting of a black bird common to Maine seashores and properly called* Fratercula arctica, *or common Atlantic puffin. George's puffins, however, are unlike any of those seen along Maine's rocky shores. The puffin of George's imagination has stark, stalklike legs, enormous eyes, and a face that seems to smile grimly at the environmental destruction of the puffins' habitat and hereditary nesting places.*
>
> *Professor Milford Higgenbottom, of Harvard University, discovered evidence of strong environmental concerns in the controversial piece. "In this painting," he told a crowd of onlookers at the gallery, "I see a dire concern for mother earth and all things natural. Look at the slender, almost reedlike legs—the artist is pointing to the thin thread of life which binds the bird to*

earth and all of us to each other. Look at the colors on the beak—the blue of the sky, the white of a cloud, the orange of the sun. Are these not the colors of nature? Can we live without air or water or sunlight? Indeed not."

Amelia Scarborough, a visiting professor from Oxford, echoed Professor Higgenbottom's views. "In London, of course, we are much more aware of environmental matters, yet you will never find a puffin on England's shores. But in the composition of this piece, I see myriad messages. Like the Impressionists, the artist seems to be working en plein air *to capture spontaneous impressions of a timeless world. Notice that the sun is an orange blob in the distance. For this artist, obviously, the sun and all it cheers is the signifier of an eternal organic cosmos, yet he hints at another world outside our own temporal existence. This is an extension of the Pre-Raphaelite 'truth to nature' concept through which artists seek to render the temporary as permanent by the use of structured patterning of creation, color, and concept."*

"I don't know who this young artist is," Higgenbottom added, "but I cannot wait to observe his career as he passes through the angst of early adulthood. His maturation will bring us closer to our own souls and mother earth."

Stunned, Babette looked up and caught Bedell's gaze. "You're kidding," she said, dropping the newspaper to her lap. "Do these people know who—or what—they're talking about?"

"They are talking about the art world's latest prodigy." Bedell grinned and tucked the new painting under his arm. "And you, Madame, are the mother of a genius. Keep him painting. Call me when you have other puffins—I can sell as many as the lad can produce."

"I'll see what I can do." The words slipped from Babette's mouth before she could think. Surprised at her own audacity, she stammered a correction: "That is—if we need to continue. But thank you, Mr. Bedell—I mean, Pierce."

"You're welcome, Madame. And I certainly hope you will continue. The world is clamoring to see more from your son."

After jauntily tipping his hat in her direction, Bedell left the gallery. Watching through the window, Babette saw him duck his head into the wind and hurry toward the ferry, leaving her alone with Georgie's first published review.

Birdie looked up when the bakery door opened, then grinned when she saw what the wind had blown in: Babette and Georgie Graham. Babette's blue eyes were shining, and wide-eyed Georgie immediately focused on the plump round sugar cookies on the top shelf of the display case.

Abner lifted his brows to Babette in a silent question, then grinned when she nodded.

He leaned on the counter. "Hey, Georgie! In the mood for a sugar cookie?"

"Yeah!"

"Only one," Babette cautioned. "You'll spoil your supper."

Abner wrapped the cookie in tissue and handed it over the counter, then reached out to affectionately ruffle the child's hair. Birdie walked away from the cake she was decorating and smiled at Babette. "He's growing like ragweed."

Babette sighed. "I know. We can't keep him in clothes." Her eyes scanned the display case, then rested longingly on the éclairs. Rich creamy filling spilled from the delicately browned and chocolate-covered pastry. Ordinarily, Babette bought two and gave one to Georgie. Today she bought six.

"Half a dozen?" Abner asked, surprise registering on his pleasant features.

"Six, please," Babette repeated, looking a little smug.

As Abner set about boxing up the special treats, Birdie stepped closer. "Celebrating?" she asked, knowing it was nosy of her but unable to resist. What was the sense in living in a small town if you couldn't feel free to ask about your neighbors? "Don't tell me." She clapped her hands. "Did Charles sell his book?"

Grinning, Babette shook her head. "Nothing like that, just splurging a little."

Birdie accepted this news in silence. The islanders knew money was tight at the Graham's. But Babette wasn't likely to spend money frivolously, and six éclairs wouldn't break anybody's bank. It was good to see the young woman loosening up a bit.

"I think you'll find the éclairs extra good today," she said, turning back to her cake.

Georgie grinned. "Everything Abner bakes is super good."

Abner beamed, adding a couple of extra pastries to the bag. Then he reached for a loaf of fresh cheese bread and laid it on the counter beside the bag of éclairs.

"Oh—," Babette exclaimed.

Winking, he leaned closer. "I baked twice what we'd need today. Please, do me a favor and take this off our hands."

Babette glanced at Birdie for approval. As if Abner needed it!

Chuckling, Birdie pulled out a box for Vernie Bidderman's cake. "Tell that young husband of yours to stop in and visit. He needs to get away from that typewriter now and then."

"I will. Thank you, Birdie!" With a final smile, Babette grabbed her package and Georgie's hand, then hurried him toward the door.

"Mom," the boy protested, just before shoving the last of the cookie in his mouth.

The bakery door closed, choking off a frigid blast.

Right after the Grahams left, Birdie yanked the CLOSED sign into place, then reminded Abner of Edith Wickam's order for the next morning. The pastor's wife needed two dozen glazed and a dozen chocolate sour cream doughnuts for the ladies' auxiliary ten o'clock meeting.

"I'll take them when I go," Birdie offered, "and you might want to throw in some of those cinnamon crusted bagels—you know, for those of us who are watching our figures."

"Yes, Birdie. I always do."

Walking back through the living quarters, Birdie's eyes darted to and fro, checking to be sure the coast was clear before she tiptoed into her bedroom for the bag of library books. Bea was nowhere in sight. Good. Birdie didn't want to answer a lot of questions.

Intermittent sunshine made the walk to Puffin Cove tolerable. Ferry Road took her past the Mercantile, the Graham Gallery, and the Lobster Pot on one side, the bed and breakfast, the church, and the tidy clapboard parsonage on the other. The last two buildings on Ferry Road were relatively new structures, both brick red and bone ugly: the public restrooms and Floyd Lansdown's pride and joy, the Heavenly Daze Municipal Building. The rigid and unimaginative structure held the municipal office (a desk, chair, and telephone) and one jail cell (used only once, as far as Birdie could recall, when an inebriated tourist pulled a live lobster from the restaurant's tank and proceeded to threaten the other customers with its claws).

She sighed with relief when she passed the modern buildings. The remainder of Ferry Road had been left as God made it—wild, windswept, and rocky. Beige grasses moved as the wind blew, and soon they'd be covered over in snow. Beyond them, black stones lined the shore, where the feather-white sea pounded incessantly. The leeward shore of the island was not as suitable for human habitation as the windward side. Captain Salt Gribbon was the only person she could even imagine living in this starkly desolate place.

Gribbon had taken up residence in the historic lighthouse about the time Bea had returned to the island. The town mayor, Floyd Lansdown, hired him to operate the light. Rumor said Gribbon had remodeled the old monument into comfortable living quarters, though Birdie suspected the skipper's idea of comfort differed greatly from the average person's. Besides, since Gribbon assumed the job of light keeper, no one had ever been inside the lighthouse to judge the Captain's lifestyle. The old man kept to himself and had lately begun to aggressively guard his privacy. Other than regular trips to the bakery and a monthly stop at the municipal building for his paycheck, he shopped in Ogunquit and steered clear of the other islanders.

Until a few months ago, Pastor Wickam had regularly made the long walk out to Puffin Cove to invite Salt to church. Lately the minister hadn't expended the energy, saying that Salt Gribbon knew there was a service every Sunday morning, rain or shine. He was a grown man, and he certainly didn't need Winslow Wickam to remind him of what his own town had to offer.

Birdie clutched the collection of books to her bosom and thought about the two dozen molasses cookies she'd added to her little care package. Surely the captain wouldn't object to an occasional neighborly visit.

Wind whipped the waves around the rocky point, sending an icy Atlantic spray crashing along the shoreline. Birdie smiled when she spotted a lone cormorant sitting on a rock drying his wings. He seemed a solitary old bird, just like the man she was going to see.

In the distance, an Ogunquit fishing fleet was returning from one of its last trips of the year. Their tall-masted ships mingled with the smaller boats of lobstermen who were busy running traps for the second time that day.

The tall stone lighthouse appeared deserted as Birdie approached. Even in the light of midafternoon, the structure looked almost sinister, jutting up from the rocks like a warning finger, urging her to turn back.

Shaking off a shiver, she approached with slowing steps, clutching at the bag of books and cookies. At the end of Ferry Road she paused, cupping her hand over her eyes to stare up at the light tower, which had kept many a lost seaman safe from a watery death. A chill wind tugged at her scarf and chafed her cheeks.

Should she go up and knock on the door? Had Salt seen her approach? Probably not, since he hadn't come out to greet her or throw rocks.

Her heart hammered as she took another step forward. Maybe she shouldn't have come unannounced. But he didn't have a phone, and when he was in the bakery, curious eyes were always twinkling in her direction. She'd waited two days to gather her courage, and if she didn't proceed now, she might never again find the nerve.

Her grip tightened around the bag in her arms. She was acting like a nervous schoolgirl! Why was she so jittery? She was bringing books to an old sea dog, not singing a solo in church. There was no earthly reason why she should be feeling spleeny about walking up to knock on an old man's door.

Fortifying her nerve, she quickened her pace. In less than a moment she stood in front of the lighthouse, in front of a rugged wooden door someone had painted bright red.

The color of a stop sign.

Or a warning signal.

Lifting her hand, she pecked at it with a knuckle.

A moment later she knocked with her whole hand.

When no one answered, she reared back, about to pound for all she was worth, but at that moment the door opened. She pitched forward, fist upraised, and nearly knocked Salt Gribbon to the ground.

Catching her, with surprising strength he steadied her arm and set her upright, then half-closed the door, blocking her entrance.

Cold blue eyes bore down on her. "What do you want?"

Birdie opened her mouth but nothing came out. Her throat worked and her eyes fixated on his stern gaze while her mouth opened and closed like a speared cod.

"Well?" he demanded.

"I—"

He planted his solid frame between her and the door, his aggressive stance leaving no doubt about what he thought of the intrusion. She was clearly not welcome.

Her heart slammed against her ribs. "I—," she began again, feeling faint.

"Speak up woman," he roared.

Spurred into action, she flung her bag at him. "Books," she said, but the word came out in a squeak.

Steel blue eyes focused on the bag against his chest. Frowning, he thrust his hand into the sack and pulled out the McGuffey primer. His frowned deepened.

"It's a book," she explained, shivering.

"I can see that."

"For you," she added, feeling sick to her stomach. She shouldn't have come. She had better things to do with her time than bring books to a man who clearly didn't want company. What on earth had made her think he would welcome a visit from her when he'd told the world he wanted to be left in peace?

Whirling, she stalked off, keeping her head down as she shoved her fists into her coat pockets. Mortification stung her cheeks.

Why oh why had she made such a fool of herself? She could feel Salt Gibbon's eyes boring a hole in her back. She'd never felt more idiotic, not even when she was seventeen and her daddy caught her kissing Floyd Lansdown down at the beach.

Live and learn—she could almost hear Bea now. Oh dear, if Bea ever got wind of this . . .

Her footsteps quickened, carrying her away from the lighthouse in a breathless lope.

Stepping into the lighthouse, Salt Gribbon placed Birdie Wester's bag on the old pine table and emptied it. More books, just like she'd said, and a bag of cookies—his favorite. Why?

Frowning, he focused on the titles.

The Adventures of Huckleberry Finn, McGuffey's Eclectic Primer, Betsy-Tacy and Tib.

His eyes pivoted back to the children's primer.

He glanced up at the winding staircase as fingers of apprehension gripped him.

Birdie knew.

How in the world?

He scratched his head. No matter how, she knew. Probably been snoopin' around when he was over in Ogunquit picking up supplies. He always told the kids to stay in the lighthouse and out of sight, but a six- and seven-year-old couldn't always be trusted.

He tugged at his beard. How long had she known? And why hadn't she said anything?

He had been so careful. He'd made the trip to Wells undetected, using his own boat in broad daylight so no one could say he had abandoned his post. Once on shore, he'd taken a bus to Wells, then gone to his son's apartment and found him missing. The kids were skittish and shy, probably scared to death of the bearded stranger who came in and pounded the wall in frustration.

When Patrick returned and searched for Brittany and Bobby—assuming he cared enough to look for them—he would have found them gone. Salt had left a note so Patrick wouldn't do anything as foolish as calling the police, but in the past three months Patrick had never contacted Heavenly Daze, either.

He was probably relieved to be rid of the kids.

Julie, their mother, hadn't even cared enough about her children to stick around. Having never married Patrick, she obviously didn't feel any binding ties. Salt wasn't sure of the details, but from what he'd picked up over the years he knew she'd moved to England when Brittany was three weeks old, leaving both children with a drunken father. Patrick had then immersed himself deeper into the bottle. Nothing Salt said or did could convince his son that he was neglecting two precious lives. Two years ago he had begged Patrick to let him have the children, but Patrick refused.

"You're sixty-eight years old. An old man," he'd slurred. "Get out of my life, Pop. Leave me and my kids alone!"

The passing months had made Salt two years older, but as long as he had his mind and his health he wasn't about to stand by while his grandchildren were mistreated. Patrick, he'd decided, would never shape up on his own. Until he reached the point of wanting help, he wouldn't accept it.

So, after watching Brittany and Bobby suffer from the neglect of an alcoholic parent who wouldn't work more than a week at a time, Salt had done the only thing a responsible grandparent could do—he'd taken the matter into his own hands and gone to Wells to fetch the children. He wasn't unaware of the trouble he could find himself in, and he knew he'd done wrong in the eyes of the law. But what Patrick was doing was far worse.

Now Salt eased himself into a chair, once again considering the ramifications of his actions. If Social Services found the kids here, they'd have plenty to crow about. He was seventy years old, living in rustic conditions, and some would say a lighthouse wasn't an appropriate home for children. But he would fight with every God-given breath to keep the children, regardless of red tape, rules, and regulations. Who better to raise a pair of kids than the grandfather who adored them?

For three months now, he'd kept the children hidden in the lighthouse and ended each day with a muttered prayer that their presence would remain undetected. He knew they couldn't hide here forever, but each day they lived under his roof meant one more day they lived in peace. With him they had food to eat and warm clothing. At night they said their prayers with him, and in the daytime they played with the puffins along the shoreline.

But now Birdie Wester knew his secret. Trouble was comin'; time to batten down the hatches.

Rising from his chair, he slid the door's deadbolt into place, determined to lock the world out.

Flat on his back beneath three antique quilts, Charles lay in the midst of a quiet so thick the only sound was the rhythm of Babette's breathing. Despite her stillness and the dim outline of her back, he knew she wasn't asleep, and he suspected she knew he knew. He wanted to talk, but the topic of Georgie's puffin paintings would destroy the semblance of peace in their bedroom. Still, the matter hung in the air like a hatchet, a threat hanging over them all night until one of them acknowledged it.

Finally, he broke the silence. "I can understand why you think the idea is silly," he said, his words rumbling in the darkness. "That review is the most exaggerated and overblown piece of foolishness I've ever read. But shouldn't we think a little more long term? If Georgie is as hot as everyone thinks he is, maybe we should take advantage of this moment. We have no way of knowing how long he'll be interested in painting, so we can't afford to waste this opportunity."

The mattress creaked as Babette rolled onto her back. "Strike while the iron is hot, you mean."

"Exactly."

"But they're just childish paintings."

"They're paying for your new roof, aren't they?"

For that Babette had no comeback. Charles had heard her on the phone with Handyman Roofing ten minutes after Bedell left, so that ninety-nine hundred dollars wouldn't even have a chance to warm their pockets. Even after the sale of two paintings, they were in almost the same financial state they'd been in before the puffins—except now the roof wouldn't leak on his new computer when it arrived.

The room swelled with silence as the shadows shifted and she folded her hands across her chest. "What did you have in mind?" she finally asked.

Turning onto his side, he propped his head on his hand. "Well, there's Georgie's college to consider. I figure we'll need to set aside at least eighty thousand for that."

She groaned.

"And more, if he wants to go to graduate school," Charles continued in a rush. "Tuition is rising, and there's no way to know how expensive things will be when he's ready for the university."

"Eighty thousand?" Babette's voice was whispery soft and tinged with tension. "That's 5.3 puffin paintings."

Charles struggled to do the math in his head, but she'd always been faster with figures. "Well . . . eight puffins would see him through college and graduate school. And if we put the money in one of those special college accounts, it could earn tax-free interest while Georgie is growing up."

The sheets rustled slightly, and Charles knew Babette was probably clicking off objections on her fingertips. "Okay," she said, "eight more puffins, then we'll quit, okay? I really don't feel good about this, Charles. I mean, that review won't matter in the long term, considering that it was mostly a bunch of pompous professors trying to outtalk each other, but don't you think they'll feel foolish when they learn that Georgie is a little boy?" She sighed heavily. "I mean . . . what will the *Globe* print when the entire truth comes out?"

"I don't really care what anyone else thinks," Charles answered, stiffening. "No one asked them to rattle off all that pretentious gobbledygook. If the art critics look foolish, it's their own fault. Besides"—he gentled his tone and reached out to run a finger along her shoulder.—"they'll probably proclaim our son a genius if only to save face. Those kinds of people never admit they're wrong."

She squirmed, but whether from his touch or the idea of selling more paintings, Charles couldn't tell. "Still," she said, "I'll be relieved when it's all over."

"There's something else we should think about"—Charles brought his hand up to the soft curve of her cheek—"our retirement. In eighteen years Georgie will be out on his own, and we'll still be relatively young—in our midfifties. Do you want to spend the rest of your life here, shoveling snow and repairing the roof, or would you like to move to Florida and relax in the sunshine? If Georgie painted only a few more paintings, we could invest the money and have plenty to retire on by the time he's through college and grad school."

A short silence followed, in which his words seemed to hang in the darkness as if for inspection, then Babette said, "That's a lot of paintings, Charles. If we're going to retire that early, we'd need at least a million dollars in investments. And you can't ignore the financial risk—the markets go up and down, and who knows what the future will bring—"

"You can figure it out." He moved closer, cupping her face. "You always do, honey."

And then, before she could object further, he kissed her into silence.

CHAPTER SIX

On Friday morning, while the crew from Handyman Roofing stomped and hammered overhead, Babette sat at her kitchen desk, a collection of papers spread in front of her. After researching various mutual funds, investment strategies, and college savings programs, she had designed a Graham Family Financial Plan:

Goals:	*Puffin paintings required at 15K each:*
G's college and grad school	*8*
Emergency cushion	*1*
New golf cart	*.1*
New clothes for 16.6 years	*1*
Retirement fund	*66.666666*
	TOTAL: 76.766666 puffins
	77 Puffin Paintings!

She rechecked her figures, then held up her steno pad and studied the numbers. Her goals list contained nothing extravagant or unreasonable—Georgie's college education was important, as was their emergency fund. They needed a golf cart, which would be far less expensive than buying a car like people on the mainland, and she hadn't gone overboard on her clothing allowance, figuring that one painting alone could clothe the three of them for 16.6 years—nearly long enough to get Georgie through school.

Her retirement plan resulted from simple and sound financial planning. Everyone knew you couldn't depend upon Social Security to provide for retirement, so they'd have to fund their own golden years in Florida. A neat little townhouse in St. Petersburg, with a community tennis court and a view of the beach at sunset—surely that wasn't too much to expect from a retirement plan. The puffin paintings would provide investment capital up front; the rest of their nest egg would come from interest accumulated over the years.

She dropped the steno pad and breathed a huge sigh of relief. Her plan made sense. The thought of selling seventy-seven additional puffins made her dizzy at first, but a quick call to Pierce Bedell had set her mind at ease. Like every trend, he told her, the puffin craze would start slow and rise in a bell curve, then taper off. Because all trends rose and fell in such a predictable pattern, they had to get out as many puffins as soon as possible. Seventy-seven original Georgie puffins would not saturate the market, far from it. In fact, Bedell assured her, if the pictures continued to attract attention, he might be able to license one of the more popular paintings and sell a series of prints. "Imagine," Bedell said, his voice filling Babette's ears and imagination, "Georgie's puffins could soon be selling in every Wal-Mart in America. Then we will be wealthy beyond our wildest dreams."

For an instant Babette was tempted to ask exactly how wealthy Bedell intended to become, then she bit her lip. On her desk lay a copy of the contract he had faxed that morning. In solid black letters the contract stated that "Babette and Charles Graham, legal guardians and representatives of George Graham, agree to deliver ____ original puffin paintings to Pierce Bedell, art dealer, for $15,000 each, to be paid upon delivery of the paintings. In the event they can not provide the aforementioned number of paintings within a six-month period, the contract will be canceled and all moneys for undelivered paintings returned."

Babette lifted her pen and wrote "77" in the blank space. Georgie could create that many paintings; she'd seen him paint half a dozen in an afternoon. She wouldn't even need six months. If Georgie were properly motivated, she could deliver seventy-seven paintings before Christmas. After Bedell had accepted them, she and Charles and Georgie could relax and enjoy the most prosperous Christmas they'd ever known.

The thought of Christmas brought a wrinkle to her brow. Why not have a truly extravagant Christmas? They could close up the house and go to Florida—maybe take in Disney World and Clearwater Beach and the Kennedy Space Center. They'd fly down, spare no expense, and enjoy the first vacation they'd ever funded without painfully pinching pennies. Just one more puffin would pay for everything . . .

She picked up her pen and adjusted the number. Seventy-eight puffins before Christmas. Georgie could do it. After all, he had her to help.

Standing at the bakery window, Abner sipped from his coffee cup and watched as Buddy Franklin trudged down Main Street with a large gray mail sack over his right shoulder. Abner smiled at the young man's plodding pace. Buddy never got in a hurry, usually taking twice as much time to accomplish a task than anyone else.

A patient sort of lad.

Ten minutes later Buddy arrived at the bakery, tracking mud across Abner's clean linoleum.

Squish, squish, squish.

The mail sack hit the floor with a solid sound, then Buddy took a deep breath. "Mail."

Abner viewed the huge sack quizzically. "For Bea?"

Buddy shrugged, red creeping up his narrow cheeks. "Ain't she here?"

Abner bent to open the sack. As mistress of the tiny post office, Bea usually received a single tray filled with mail on the noon ferry. Abner couldn't recall her ever receiving an entire sack, so there had to be a mistake—

He pulled out a handful of letters and examined the addresses. "Angel mail?"

Buddy bent low, his face inches away from Abner's. As Abner turned, their gazes collided.

Buddy flashed a grin. "Cool, huh?"

Cool, but disturbing, Abner decided as he climbed the steps of Heavenly Daze Community Church later that afternoon. When Bea saw the sack of mail—with every letter asking for a response—she'd thrown up her hands and told Birdie it would take a month to answer all those letters. "I may be an angel assistant," she'd said, her head bobbing, "but I'm not superhuman. I can only write so fast."

Winded after his brisk walk, Abner sat down in the church vestibule to catch his breath. That's where Gavriel found him, huffing and puffing under Winslow Wickam's portrait.

Tsking, Gavriel brought his hands to his trim waist. "Perhaps, brother Abner, you have been sampling your own cooking too often?"

Blushing, Abner patted his ever-widening girth. "I fear you're right, brother."

The angel captain, who materialized only when needed, sported a head of long white hair and eyes as rich as the chocolate Abner put in his cakes. Abner tended to think the senior angel possessed an unfair advantage—his mortal body didn't have to endure as much as the others'. Of course, if the truth be told, Abner had forced his body to endure all sorts of delicious treats, sinfully rich cakes, scrumptious cookies, and oh, those spice pies he was baking for the holidays . . .

But he'd come to the church on business.

Standing, Abner gestured toward the quiet of the sanctuary, and Gavriel nodded. Once they were seated on a back pew, the two angels bowed their heads, communing with the Lord before they set about the business of speaking with each other.

When they had finished their prayers, Gavriel leaned one arm on the pew back and turned to face his friend. "Is there a problem at the bakery?"

Abner shook his head. "No, not the bakery. But it seems the post office is suddenly being deluged with 'heavenly' requests. Do you know anything about this?"

Gavriel adopted a thoughtful expression. "I'm not aware of anything, and the Lord has given me no specific instruction in this area. What sort of requests are these?"

Abner looked toward the window. "Some are amusing, but most are heartbreaking. So far all the letters have come from children who are desperately seeking hope. In today's mail I read a couple of pleas for baby brothers and sisters and a dozen appeals for daddies to come home. There was one from a six-year-old looking for his lost canary, another begging that his severed leg be restored so he could play baseball. Bea and Birdie are doing their best to keep up with the volume, but if it keeps coming by the bagful, well, I don't know if they can do it. Heavenly Daze barely qualifies as a post office. If this angel mail keeps up, Bea will have to hire outside help."

Gavriel stroked his chin. "Apparently there is a reason for the increased activity—spiritual interest, perhaps? Then again, perhaps people are beginning to confuse Heavenly Daze with the North Pole."

"I don't know how things like this get started."

"Often by eager retailers capitalizing on people's needs."

"Needs?"

"The need to believe in something greater than themselves. That's why people turned the true story of Saint Nicholas into Santa Claus, a mythical demigod capable of fulfilling children's greatest desires. People who believe themselves too old or too sophisticated for Santa beg angels to dole out favors like sticks of peppermint candy."

Abner shook her head. "There's no need to go to extremes. People have only to ask the Father to meet their needs."

"Yes, but not every human knows the Lord as Father . . . and many who do have too much pride to bring their needs to him." Gavriel's eyes grew distant. "'Seek and you will find; knock and the door will be opened.' It's so simple, yet they do not act as if they believe it." He lowered his gaze, refocusing on Abner. "I'm not sure what spurred this present surge in mail—probably a tidbit in some travel magazine. But Bea's efforts are commendable, and perhaps the Lord wants the citizens of Heavenly Daze to help. In due time we will know."

"Of course." Abner nodded. "And all things will work together for good. I'm not doubting; I was only curious."

"No harm in asking, Abner; the Father wants to share his heart with his servants. I would advise you to encourage Bea to continue her efforts. Meanwhile, I will speak to the Father about this strange situation and seek instruction." His face lit with a smile. "Who knows? Perhaps Bea will have to petition the postmaster general for larger facilities in order to handle all the mail."

Abner chuckled. "I'll continue to do all I can to assist Bea and Birdie. And the activity may stop as suddenly as it began. Thank you, Gavriel. I feel much better about the situation."

Gavriel reached out to touch Abner's arm. Warmth, goodness, and joy surged between them. "It is my job, brother, and I am delighted to serve you. And I ask you to look for opportunities to serve the Grahams as well."

"The Grahams?" Abner frowned. "Is something wrong at their house? Babette and Georgie were in the bakery this week—"

Gavriel stopped him. "Dark powers are at work, brother. Zuriel has asked for special prayer support at this time."

"Of course."

"And keep Salt Gribbon in your thoughts."

"The light keeper?" Abner knew Gavriel looked after Salt, but he rarely interceded in the old man's life because Salt rarely asked for help. "Is there a problem at the lighthouse?"

Gavriel sighed. "Always."

"Then I will pray—fervently."

CHAPTER SEVEN

Flush with a sense of completion now that the house had a beautiful new roof, on Monday morning, November 12, Babette set up Georgie's easel in the gallery, then pulled a large calendar from the desk and taped it to the French door. Beginning with the current date, she framed each Monday through Saturday with a bright red marker, purposely skipping Sundays and Thanksgiving. After all, no one should have to work on Sunday, and they all deserved a holiday.

She drew the last box around Saturday, December 22, then looked over her work. Thirty-five bright red boxes shone on the glossy paper, so Georgie would have thirty-five days in which to create seventy-eight original puffins.

She smiled when she heard the squeak of the stairs. "In here, Georgie," she called, turning toward the foyer. Her son peered at her through the glass gallery door, his eyes puffy and his hair still tousled from sleep.

"Whatcha doing, Mom?"

"Come here, Son; I've got something to show you."

He shuffled forward, nearly dropping the ragged blankie in his right hand. He'd slept with that flannel blanket since infancy, and she'd never had the heart to suggest that he toss the tattered thing away. But now that he was about to enjoy his first real job, perhaps the blankie would go the way of his teddy bear and pacifier.

"Look at this, Georgie." She gestured toward the calendar, then knelt to meet him at eye level. "See these boxes on each date? Every day when you come home from kindergarten, the days marked in red are going to be workdays for you and me. We're going to make some money, enough for a golf cart and some really important things. Then, after thirty-five workdays, we're going to celebrate Christmas at Disney World in Florida." She gave him the biggest grin she could muster. "Doesn't that sound like fun?"

Shock flickered over his face like summer lightning. "Disney World?"

"Ayuh." She reached out and drew him close. "We're going to have a lot of fun. And all you have to do is paint puffins like the one you made for me to sell."

He pulled out of her grasp. "But you already sold the puffin."

"I know, dear. And it was very helpful. In fact, the woman who bought that puffin liked it so much that she told lots of other people about it. Now they want a puffin painting, too."

Georgie shrugged. "Can't they paint their own puffins?"

Babette reinforced her smile. "I don't think so, honey. Some of them have never seen a puffin, and they like the way you paint them. So every afternoon after school, you and I will come in here and you will paint puffins. We need you to paint 2.2 puffins a day to meet our goal."

The heavy lashes that shadowed his cheeks flew up. "I don't know what a tutu puffin is, Mom."

Babette laughed. "Aw, sweetie, it's just a number. I meant that you'll need to paint two pictures and get started on the next one. That's all. We want you to paint puffins like you always do."

Georgie digested this for a moment, then turned and moved toward the kitchen, his blanket dragging on the floor.

"Okay, Georgie?" Babette called. "Can we get started today after school?"

No answer.

"I've got your easel in here where the light is good. And we can use Dad's big paint box; he said it's okay. You can paint with any colors you want."

From the kitchen, she heard the banging sound of the cabinet, and knew Georgie was pulling out his Frosty Flakes.

Sighing, she stood. He hadn't exactly warmed to the idea, but that was okay. There would be plenty of time for painting later.

At noon, after Georgie had returned from the Kid Kare Center and feasted on a fine lunch of clam chowder and a tuna fish sandwich, Babette called her son into the gallery. One look at his face told her he was no more inclined to paint now than he had been that morning. Anticipating this, she had hoped Charles would be able to help her persuade the boy, but that blasted computer had arrived at ten. Charles had been upstairs tinkering with it ever since.

Crossing her arms, she struggled to present her son with a pleasant, let's-get-down-to-business face. "Okay," she told him, "it's time to paint. Are you ready?"

Georgie crinkled his nose, and Babette counted to three, a handy exercise in controlling her temper. "If you don't like your easel in here," she said, her tone clipped as she faced her reluctant son, "where would you like me to put it?"

Georgie screwed up his face in thought. "Dad's office? So I can see the new computer?"

She nearly guffawed aloud. Charles wouldn't appreciate them barging in on him, but fathers and sons should spend quality time together . . .

"Fine." She grabbed the easel with one hand and tucked the blank canvas beneath her arm. "Grab the paint box, then, and follow me upstairs."

She'd crossed the foyer and climbed half the staircase before she realized Georgie wasn't behind her.

"George Louis Graham!" she yelled, not caring if she disturbed the great and mighty writer upstairs. "Get yourself up these stairs right this instant!"

With Charles's paint box weighing him down, Georgie dragged himself to the bottom of the staircase, then looked up at her. "I don't feel like painting," he whined, his voice grating on her nerves. He rubbed his free hand over his belly. "My stomach hurts."

Laden with the awkward easel and canvas, Babette gritted her teeth. "If you don't paint today," she muttered, her brain racing through the calculations, "you'll have only thirty-four painting days before Christmas. That means you'll have to do 2.29 puffins a day. And if you get lazy, Georgie, we won't be able to go to Disney World at Christmas!"

Georgie dropped the paint box, a frown puckering the skin between his brown eyes into fine wrinkles. "I don't feel like going to Disney World. I feel like watching TV."

While Babette teetered precariously on the stairs, Georgie turned and ran toward the den beyond the kitchen.

Babette sighed and leaned against the wall. Earning the family fortune was not going to be as easy as she had first thought.

Birdie hunkered deeper into the industrial-sized mixing bowl, ignoring the note of desperation in Abner's plea.

Covered to the elbows in soapy water, she kept scrubbing and singing: "When the roll is called up yonder . . . I'll be therrrreeeeer!"

"Birdie!"

Heaving a sigh, she dropped the sponge and straightened, then felt her heart tighten. Salt Gribbon stood behind the counter and must have entered the bakery sometime during her concert. From the embarrassed look on Abner's face, she reckoned he'd heard at least two choruses.

After shooting Gribbon an exasperated look, she lowered her voice and turned to her helper. "Can't you get his bread, Abner?"

"Yes," Abner silently mouthed, "but he wants you to wait on him."

"He can't have me," she whispered back.

"Then he won't leave," Abner said, his face brightening to the shade of a cherry tomato.

After the embarrassing exchange of last week, Birdie was in no mood to go another round with the scrappy skipper. But here he was, behaving as if nothing had happened, looking for his weekly bread and cookies and insisting that she wait on him. She! Why, she owned this bakery, and she didn't have to lift a hand for anyone if she didn't want to.

Absently touching a hand to her hair, she toyed with the idea of refusing to serve him. If he wanted his bread and cookies, he'd have to let Abner get them or do without.

Then again, she was running a business and she couldn't cut off a customer because of personal feelings. She lifted her gaze and peeked at the old goat. The set of his square jaw told her all she needed to know. He was as stubborn as a barnacle and he wasn't about to leave until she personally filled his order.

Downright mule-headed, that one. He deserved to stew in his juices, but maybe, as an act of Christian charity, she ought to turn the other cheek and give the man his cookies.

"Seriously, Birdie, you need to take care of him," Abner pleaded. "I have pies in the oven and they need to come out."

"Oh, all right." Squaring her shoulders, Birdie paused in front of a shiny aluminum baking tray to make sure her lipstick was still intact, then marched up to the counter with a bright smile pasted on her face.

"One loaf of rye and two dozen molasses cookies coming right up," she called, injecting a falsely cheerful note into her voice. "Will there be anything else this afternoon, Cap'n?"

Gribbon stood behind the counter, his arresting blue eyes focused on her. She shivered, wondering what he was thinking—no, she didn't want to know; it would only upset her. She'd been upset enough by her own recent actions.

She bent to wrap the cookies, grateful for a chance to look away. Buying those books for Salt Gribbon had been a mistake. One she wasn't likely to make again.

She hurriedly bagged the bread, avoiding his burning gaze. Stepping to the register, she rang up the sale. "Two dollars and twenty-four cents." Silence stretched between them as he fished in his pocket and counted out change. He laid two dimes and four pennies on the counter, then added two dollar bills.

"Thank you." She gave him a prim smile, then put the money in the register and closed the door. She wheeled on her heel, about to return to her dishwashing, but his iron-edged voice stopped her in her tracks.

"Birdie, let's go for a walk."

A walk? Her heart tripped. Events were taking a serious turn: a walk was more personal than, say, a talk. She'd only talked to him before, never walked with him.

What should she say?

"You're about through here, aren't you?" His voice was lower now, and there was no denying it held a note of pleading. Even Bea would have heard it.

She glanced at the clock and saw that it was a few minutes past two. Abner could take care of what little business there'd be between now and closing. Still undecided, she turned and looked at the man. When his eyes captured hers, she couldn't think of the simplest excuse.

"Why . . . okay."

"Bundle up tight. It's breezin' up outside."

Before Birdie knew what hit her, she was buttoning her coat and winding a heavy wool scarf around her neck. From the corner of her eye she saw Abner grinning as he took three pies out of the oven and set them on the cooling rack.

Avoiding his gaze, Birdie lifted her chin. "I may not be back before you close, Abner. Make certain the front door is shut tight—the thing popped open on me yesterday."

"I'll do that, Birdie."

"Thank you."

Sly as a cat, Abner stepped into her line of vision and winked. "You be a good girl."

Flustered, Birdie reached for her keys and dropped them in her pocket, then meekly followed Gribbon out of the store. An unannounced and unchaperoned walk was highly unusual; Bea would have a cow if she found out. Of course, in this day and at her age she shouldn't have been concerned about taking a simple little walk with a man, but something in her clung to the old ways . . . and Salt made her more than a little nervous.

Stuffing her hands in her coat pockets, she matched the captain's stride, step for step. Neither of them spoke as they headed up Main, then turned onto Ferry Road and walked north toward Puffin Cove. Despite the sunshine, the wind was sharp and from the southwest.

She lifted her eyes to the church steeple, which reached up and above its historic neighbors with a kind of easy majesty. Next to the church stood the parsonage, and Edith Wickam had hung an autumn wreath on the front door. The effect of the colorful wreath against the dark green door was utterly—

"Charming," she said aloud, then bit her lip. Heavens, suppose Salt thought she was talking about him! She walked a few more paces, her eyes wide and her nerves tense, but either he didn't notice her slip or he was content to ignore her.

Just like a man—ask a woman out for a walk and not say a blessed word the entire outing.

They walked on, past the Lobster Pot and the municipal building, and then it hit her—for some reason Birdie couldn't fathom, she was enjoying this unexpected diversion. Social activities on the island were as scarce as feathers on a fish. With the few exceptions of church functions, most islanders kept to themselves during the winter months.

They turned slightly into the wind and kept walking toward the lighthouse. It would have been more comfortable to talk in the civilized part of town where the road was smoother, but this was Salt's walk, not hers, so she kept quiet.

Wind whipped across the island, colliding with the incoming waves and shooting a cold spray across the rocky shoreline. Overhead, a watery sun skipped in and out of lowering clouds. The island was in for another snowstorm by nightfall. Birdie thought about turning around and going back; the path was cold and the company even colder.

She took another stab at conversation. "Feels like sleet."

"Ayuh."

The silence began to pluck at Birdie's strained nerves. Talkative by nature, she didn't know how to handle conversational lapses. She found herself grasping for topics.

"Thanksgiving's right around the corner—will you be visiting family?"

"No."

"Will family be visiting you?"

He paused, turning to give her a penetrating, almost frightening look. For an instant she wondered if he'd brought her out here to beam her with a rock and teach the others a lesson.

Watching him, she saw something almost like bitterness enter his face. "Why did you bring those books?"

"Because . . . I want to help." She felt color creeping up her cheeks, a flush that had nothing to do with the weather.

"You'll help me by staying away."

"Away?" She bristled, falling into step when he resumed his pace. "I was trying to do you a favor, Salt Gribbon."

"Don't need any favors from you, woman. Nor anyone else."

Birdie was running now to keep up with his long-legged stride. If she'd known he'd react so negatively to those books she would have kept them to herself.

"If you want to return the books—"

"Don't want to return 'em."

Then what did he want? Simply to berate her for an act of kindness? Birdie crossed her arms, offended and bewildered, and stopped dead in the middle of the road. "Salt Gribbon," she fixed him in a steely gaze that would match any of his own, "you have to talk to me. Speak!"

Pausing, his eyes scanned the horizon with seasoned experience. "Backing wind," he murmured.

Birdie frowned. "Backing what?"

"Backing wind is an ill wind. Storm approaching."

Birdie focused on the choppy three-foot swells and huddled deeper into her coat. This time of year weather could disintegrate from bad to worse in a matter of minutes. From the corner of her eye she studied Salt and wondered about the sights he'd witnessed over the years. Rumor held that he'd been a longliner—a fisherman who went out at sea longer than most but returned with more catch. Longliner fishermen sometimes came into the bakery, and she heard them talking about working twenty-hour days for as long as two to three weeks, then falling numb into bunks to sleep round the clock on the long trip home. All to meet a quota.

She nodded toward the sea. "Guess you've spent your fair share of time out there?"

"Ayuh." She expected that would be the extent of his conversation, but then he surprised her. "Let's sit a spell."

Guiding her into a windbreak behind a tree, he sat down and motioned for her to follow suit. She settled on a rock beside the tree and found that she could see for miles. Out on the blue Atlantic, ships bobbed against the horizon while gulls caught the updrafts and soared high above their heads.

Contentment washed over Birdie, and suddenly she was glad she came. Out here a body's problems seemed insignificant, easily swallowed up by the rolling surf. She could understand why the sea obsessed men. Such beauty and power tended to put things in perspective.

Salt was a man of the sea, as elemental and rough and powerful as the breakers crashing on the shore. He didn't walk or talk or think like a shore-hugger . . . and in that lay his appeal.

They sat, each of them deep in thought, staring out across the waters. What she'd considered awkward lapses in conversation now seemed moments of comfortable and quiet companionship. Birdie found herself enjoying the moment.

"Ever been in a bad storm?" she asked.

"Ayuh. Many." He turned to look at her, his stance softening. "Working a school of cod one time when a gale blew in. The fish were closely packed, and we were having a hard time keeping our distance from other boats. Fishing grounds can be small and close to the shore, so a man is stationed at each end of the boat to cut anchor cables should another boat bear down on 'em. That night, without warning, the stars disappeared and snow started to drive down on us horizontally. I looked up and saw a craft heading straight for us, so I yelled for the line to be cut. But by the time the men sliced through the heavy cables, we were hit astern. Both vessels went down. Water closed over us." He shook his head, apparently overcome by memories of the night's horror. "When I surfaced, the night was so dark I couldn't see my hand in front of my face. Waves buried me for a minute at a time, and I couldn't get a clear breath. Every few minutes I had to retch the sea from my lungs. The winds were howling and the sea was covered in foam—spindrift. All around me I could hear my shipmates yelling, trying to save themselves. After a while I lost strength; I could hardly keep my head up. Then I went under."

He paused, and Birdie waited, her heart constricting with compassion. In all her years, she'd never been in a situation even close to what Salt was describing.

"The instinct not to breathe under water is so strong that it overrides the need to supply air to the lungs," he said, his eyes staring out across the water. "I struggled, thoughts shrieking through my mind: I was too young to die; I had a wife and four-month-old son waiting for me at home. I could see my mother shaking her head, railing over my senseless death. Then, through the grace of God, I came back up, sucking air, puking water, and crying like a frightened boy. A piece of flotsam passed and I grabbed out and held on. Somehow I reached out for five more of my shipmates, and then a tuna boat came up to pluck us out of the churning water. Saved us from dyin' of the cold."

They fell silent, with only the sounds of the breakers against the shore to break the heavy quiet. Birdie stared at the sun-spangled sea, thinking of the men who lost their lives that night, men calling out for help that did not come soon enough—

"God is good," Salt said quietly. "I don't know why he saved me and allowed the others to die, but I'm grateful."

Birdie's blood ran thick with guilt. He'd suffered so much in his life, and she'd intruded upon the boundaries he'd set up to protect himself. What did it matter that he couldn't read? A man could be wise in other ways.

"Salt," she said, the words coming out in a tumble, "I'm sorry about those books. I was out of line and nosy and intrusive and unkind—"

"No." He stopped her with an uplifted hand. "I overreacted, Birdie. I sometimes say things unkindly. I appreciate the books, but I'm going to ask that you keep the reason for them quiet."

She met his worried gaze with a compassionate smile. Of course he would be concerned that others would laugh if they knew he couldn't read. None would, but she supposed she might feel the same way if the situation were reversed. "I'll not tell another soul, Salt."

"I don't want you to tell Bea. She . . . gets around the island too much, if you know what I mean."

"I certainly do." Birdie loved her sister, but Bea couldn't be trusted with sensitive information. She wasn't a gossip, at least not intentionally, but information leaked out of Bea like a sieve. Birdie learned long ago if she didn't want something made known, she didn't dare mention a word of it to Beatrice.

As Salt looked away Birdie detected a red flush creeping up his neck. Why, he was ashamed of his lack of knowledge! Her heart went out to him.

"I figured it was the only thing I could do," he said.

"Yes, but working alone isn't always the best way," she gently pointed out. "I could help."

Frowning, he turned back to look at her.

"I could come to your place and help out—"

"No!"

She blinked.

"No." He tempered his voice. "I don't want you or anyone else snooping around the point. It's too dangerous."

It was her turn to frown. "Dangerous?"

"I want this kept quiet, Birdie. You are the only one who knows—and I'm mad at myself for being so careless. I didn't want anyone to know—no one can know. Do you understand?"

"Of course." Tentatively, she reached out and patted his broad hand. "You've nothing to be ashamed of—this situation happens to all kinds of people."

He lifted a white brow.

"You're not the only one who's had to do this," she went on, "it happens more often than you'd think. Actually, you should have done it sooner. And you shouldn't be ashamed to ask for help."

His scowl deepened. "I don't need help to do this, Birdie. I'm not too old, no matter what they might say."

"Of course you're not! I knew a man who did it when he was ninety-seven!"

Salt's jaw dropped. "He was ninety-seven? With his grandkids?"

She laughed. "No, he used the kids down the street. And they were happy for the experience. Their parents were grateful."

Salt stared at her, drawing back. "Well," he said after a long pause, "I appreciate the books, but I don't need them."

"Then tapes. There are wonderful tapes—"

"No tapes or books! Are you daft, woman?"

"Then home correspondence. I'll deliver the material to you personally. No one will ever know what you're doing."

Surprise siphoned the blood from his face. "There's a home correspondence program?"

"Of course, wonderfully informative material, clearly outlined, step by step."

He stared at her. "Step by step?"

She nodded. "With tapes and videos and expert lecturers. You could have a diploma in no time."

He turned away, disgust flaring his nostrils. "Don't need no diploma."

"Please, Salt, let me help. I'm quite good—I was a librarian for over twenty years."

"What's all this got to do with kids?"

"Kids?" She smiled, perplexed by the way his mind wandered. That was odd and potentially troublesome. "Well . . . I suppose people in your situation often find themselves reading lots of kids' books. But you don't have to. There are adult-level easy readers, too."

Abruptly standing, Salt pulled his collar tighter against the rising wind. "No books, no home correspondence courses, no tapes, and no diploma. I'll do this myself. All I need from you is your promise not to gab my secret around the island." His eyes darkened. "I mean it, Birdie, no one can know. If they find out I'll be forced to leave."

Leave? The gormy cuss was being a little melodramatic.

But he was set on teaching himself to read. Without books. Or tapes. Or home correspondence courses. She'd like to know how he planned to accomplish that!

But Salt's inability to read wasn't her problem. If he was too proud to accept help, there was nothing she could do. The only clear course at the moment was to lay low until he admitted defeat. Eventually he would realize he needed help and she'd be around to extend a hand of help.

"You have my promise," she said, smiling up at him. "I won't breathe a word to anyone."

"Thank you."

"You're welcome."

Opening his coat, he withdrew his bakery bag, then offered her a cookie. She accepted it and they ate the sweets in silence.

"Abner bakes a mean cookie," she ventured.

"Ayuh."

"The best in the State of Maine, if I can say so without seeming uppity."

Salt's eyes studied the deteriorating weather on the horizon. "Getting colder; we need to be going."

They walked back in companionable silence, but Birdie's thoughts were all aflutter with confusion. Teach himself to read? The man had to be crazy as a backhouse rat.

Babette felt like breaking into a round of the "Hallelujah Chorus" when, after supper, Georgie went to his easel without being asked. While he had watched TV and babied his upset stomach, she'd reconsidered her plan and decided that Georgie's reluctance to paint had to be rooted in her change of his routine. He usually painted in his bedroom or in the den, so while he went out to call Zuriel to supper, she carried the paint box and easel to the den, set up a blank canvas across from the television, and quietly left the room.

After eating two grilled cheese sandwiches and three chocolate chip cookies and downing two glasses of milk, Georgie returned to the den, Zuriel slipped out to his cottage, and Charles went back upstairs to learn about RAM and ROM and other computer alphabet soups. Babette quickly cleaned up the kitchen, then moved to the den doorway to watch Georgie paint.

On the television screen, animated crime-fighters blasted criminals with ray guns as high-pitched screams filled the air. Georgie stood before his easel, his brush in his hand, but his wide eyes were focused on the television. As Babette watched, he dipped the brush in orange paint, then smeared it across the blank canvas in a distracted motion.

"No, Georgie, not like that!" Hurrying forward, she took the brush from his hand. "Whoever heard of an orange puffin? You have to do the body like the others—black and white, with color only on the beak. Remember?"

Georgie blinked, then his gaze hardened. "I want to paint my kind of puffins."

"We have to paint these like the others." Babette withdrew a clean brush from the paint box and offered it to him. "Now dip this in the black paint and see if you can paint over the orange. Try not to waste the canvas—I had to order more, and the new shipment won't arrive for another week, at least. Remember—these things cost money!"

The frown between Georgie's brows deepened into a scowl.

Unable to understand exactly what he was supposed to do, Georgie glared at his mother. Paint puffins like the others? Why? He didn't like those kinds of puffins any more.

"I don't want to paint black puffins."

"You have to paint them black, dear. That's what color they are."

"I want orange puffins."

"God tells the puffins what color to be. And you're not God."

He dropped the brush onto the easel tray, then crossed his arms over his chest. "I don't want to paint today."

"You have to paint, Georgie. A couple of puffins a day until Christmas, that's all."

Why was his mom being so mean? He stamped his foot on the floor, then looked away. Christmas took forever to come, so he'd be painting forever and ever and ever . . . unless he could change her mind.

Deliberately, he fell into the beanbag chair in front of the television set. "I want to watch cartoons."

"We have to work. After work, you can watch whatever you want."

He closed his eyes. "I want to go out and see Zuriel."

"Zuriel is working, too. You know how hard he works at his pottery. Your dad works. Your mom works. Now you can work, too, and grind your own bait, just like the old-timers say. And everybody will be glad when we get to go to Disney World."

Georgie lifted one eye and squinted at his mother. He wanted to see Disney World, but he didn't want to paint puffins. Not today. Maybe not ever.

"I want to play outside."

"It's too cold."

"Then I want to watch Nickelodeon."

His mother's pretty face hardened. "Young man, you will work today. After your work, you can play inside and watch TV until bedtime. But no play until your job is done. And your job is painting puffins."

Georgie chewed on his lip, considering the idea of a job. He used to think having a job would be fun. After all, his dad seemed to enjoy his jobs of writing and painting, and sometimes his mother said she enjoyed her job in the gallery—though lately she frowned a lot more than she smiled. But if having a job meant painting when he'd rather be playing, a job was not something he wanted to have.

He tried another approach. "I want to watch Dad and his computer."

"George Louis Graham." His mother's voice had that final, flat tone that meant she would not argue any longer. "You will paint puffins, or you will go to your room and stay there for the rest of the night. Fish or cut bait, Son. Make your choice."

Georgie lifted his chin, tightened his grip on his arms, and pulled himself out of the beanbag chair, stomping loudly on his way through the foyer. A rhyme formed in his head, and he chanted it at the top of his lungs as he climbed the stairs:

"Puffins stink!

Puffins clink!

Puffins poop on our bathroom sink!"

But later, as he lay on his bed and stared at the crinkly plaster ceiling, he thought he might be angry with his mother and not puffins. And when the shadows lengthened and finally swallowed up the room and neither his mom nor dad came in to tell him to brush his teeth and say his prayers, Georgie thought he might even be a little frightened.

Outside the Graham Gallery, Zuriel stood in the alley that led to his cottage, enjoying the serenity of the twilight. The dark sky seemed to hover just above the village, and streamers of night were gently falling over the sleepy houses of Heavenly Daze. The brisk air was cool, and already the evergreens at the side of the house wore a sweater of crisp frost.

He walked slowly toward his cottage, his boots crunching the dried autumn leaves, his heart heavy with thoughts and prayers for the folks he was privileged to serve. A nudge of the Spirit caused him to look up, and his heart tightened when he saw Georgie at the window. Their gazes met and locked, and even in the dim light Zuriel could see the sheen of tears upon the boy's face. After a long moment, Georgie turned from the window without a wave and the light disappeared.

Georgie's unhappiness seemed to cast a shroud over the house, no less tangible than the layer of frost that would coat the dried grass by morning.

What were Charles and Babette doing to their son? Remaining beneath the boy's window, Zuriel pulled his hands from his pockets and rubbed them together, the cold stinging his skin. Did they know Georgie was unhappy? Had they taken the time to notice?

He debated going into the house on the pretext of looking for something else to eat, but Babette had already fed him a hearty supper. Besides, he wasn't supposed to pry. His job was to serve these people, and at the moment they didn't seem to want his help.

A human might have worried—but Zuriel had long ago learned to resist that particular sin. Trusting the situation to the Lord, he shoved his cold hands into his pockets and trudged back to his little house.

His kiln stood open, the lid raised, and upon entering he could tell that its heat had fully dissipated into the room. The clay objects he had fired were finally ready to be removed from the oven.

He walked to the kiln and lifted out the first piece, a spiral bowl he had thrown in two stages, then carved when the piece was leather hard.

The design featured a simple star, cut into the piece with a wire loop and repeated around the bowl in a never-ending circle.

He smiled in satisfaction. The piece should bring a good price for the Grahams, and the natural design spoke of the Lord Creator, as all art should.

With the finished piece in his hands, he flinched as someone pounded on the door. "Z?" Babette's voice came through the frosted windowpanes. "Can I speak to you?"

He placed the bowl on his table, then crossed the small room in three long strides. Babette stood on the stoop, shivering and without a jacket, but with a sheet of printed paper in her grasp. Not seeming to mind the cold, she thumped the page with the back of her hand.

"I found this on the Internet! I can't believe it! Trouble is, I can't do anything about it because I signed a contract!"

Zuriel stepped back, wordlessly inviting her in, then closed the door and sank to his workbench. "Suppose you begin at the beginning?" He folded his hands and nodded toward the paper. "What is that?"

"This?" She waved the paper again, then held it aloft. "This is an article from the *Boston Globe*—an article Pierce Bedell did not show me. I would never have known about this if not for that blasted computer. Charles was doing an Internet search on puffins, and he stumbled across this."

Zuriel lifted a brow. "I still don't understand."

"Bedell!" Babette slammed her hand to the paper again. "No wonder he was so eager to buy our paintings. I'm not sure what he got for the first one, but this article says the second puffin sold at Sotheby's last weekend for $55,000. That's more than a 366 percent markup!"

Zuriel's gut reaction was indifference—what did money matter, after all? The Lord provided for his children, and Charles, Babette, and Georgie had never lacked for the things they needed. As far as he knew, they had never gone without clothing, shelter, or medical care . . .

But this news about Bedell had obviously astonished Babette.

His eyes widened in pretended surprise. "Fifty-five thousand dollars?" he said, allowing a grin to cross his face. "That's wonderful news!"

Her mouth curled into a smile that was not particularly attractive. "Wonderful?" She snarled the word. "It's not wonderful; it's . . . dishonest. The typical markup on gifts and fine art is 100 percent. By that standard, we should have made twenty-seven thousand on the second puffin painting, so Bedell owes me twelve thousand bucks! What's more, if his prices keep increasing, he'll owe us more and more as time goes by."

Zuriel pressed his hand to his mouth in a moment of contemplation, then pulled it away. "But didn't you agree to sell all the paintings for a certain amount? It wouldn't be fair of you to—"

"That was before I knew what he was doing." Babette flushed to the roots of her hair. "I didn't know he was making this kind of money. It just"—she waved her arms in a flurried gesture—"it seems unfair, that's all."

Zuriel scratched at his beard. "You didn't think it was unfair when he paid fifteen thousand for the first painting and took all the risk. He didn't have any assurance he could sell the first picture."

"He sure thought he could sell it." Babette sank into the small guest chair with a sudden plop. "I don't think he was taking any great risks."

"And what is your risk?" Zuriel made an effort to keep his tone gentle. "You sold a painting your son gave you to sell. You lost nothing, not even your son's respect, because he wanted you to sell it. And the Lord has always provided for you, so what have you to lose?"

Babette's flush deepened to crimson, and she would not meet Zuriel's gaze.

"The Word of God warns us," he continued, "about letting the cares of this life, the lure of wealth, and the desire for nice things choke out the joy of the Lord."

"Somehow it doesn't seem right," she muttered, staring at the empty potter's wheel. "Not fair. And now I've got to make Georgie paint seventy-eight puffins, and today he didn't even want to look at the easel."

Zuriel tugged at his beard, finally understanding the scene at the window. Georgie was like any other five-year-old human boy. He could be led, but he couldn't be forced . . . not to create, anyway. Creation overflowed from a peaceful and joyous heart, never from coercion.

"Babette," he said, keeping his voice low, "you cannot force an artist to paint. Let him choose his own pace and his own pictures. Then you will not be disappointed."

She looked at him then, her eyes dark and disbelieving. Had she listened to a word he'd said?

"Did you"—he softened his tone—"talk to Georgie about this when you tucked him in tonight?"

"Charles tucked him in," she said, waving her hand in a distracted gesture.

Zuriel scratched his beard, knowing full well that Charles hadn't left his computer room since supper. Georgie had been overlooked by both his parents, and neither of them knew it.

"Thanks, Z," Babette said, standing. She crumpled the paper in her hand, then tossed it in the corner wastebasket. "But I'll deal with Georgie in my own way. I'm his mother, and he's supposed to obey me. The Good Book says that, too."

The door opened, letting in a blast of frigid air that shivered Zuriel's spine, then she was gone.

CHAPTER EIGHT

. . . and so, Angel, if you could bring me a blue sock I would be real happy. They were my favorite socks. And could you bring Mom a new dryer? One that doesn't eat socks? She says that sock eating dryer is driving her nuts.

Thank you,
Holly Madison
2664 Swallow Lane
Wichita, Kansas

Bea folded the letter, then glanced at Birdie and Abner and sighed.

"Wichita?" Birdie frowned as she set a bowl of bread dough beneath the commercial mixer. "How in the world did somebody in Kansas hear about Heavenly Daze?"

"Good news travels fast," Abner said, grinning as he pulled a tray of cookies from the oven.

"Some of the letters are from far-flung places," Bea said. "But here's one with an Ogunquit postmark." She pulled out a pink envelope, opened the letter, and began to read:

Dear Angel,

Can you please help us get enough money to pay our utidly bill? My mama's been sick and she can't go to work much. It's cold in our house, and the fridgerator is old and worn out like my mom. Ha. She makes a joke like that all the time. When it's snowing we have to wrap in blankets and sit around our hot plate to keep warm, then we drink hot milk from a fridgerator that's supposed to be cold. Ha. In church (Grace Unity Church), my teacher said there are angels waching over us all the time. So if you're waching, Angel, we need help.

I love you.
Raleigh Akerman

Lifting cookies off the tray, Abner shook his head, his face lined with concern. "Poor child."

"It breaks my heart." Birdie flipped the mixer switch, thinking about the appeal as the motor whirred. Such a simple request—warmth. A body was entitled to be warm in the winter.

Bea slid the second letter back into its envelope and laid it on the counter, atop a growing pile of unanswered correspondence. She eyed the mail with a calculating expression. "I don't understand," she shouted above the mixer. "It's almost as if some divine decree has gone out and Heavenly Daze has suddenly become a celestial post office."

Birdie looked up as the door opened and Vernie Bidderman came in. Stomping her boots on the rubber mat, she grinned, her large, uneven teeth shining in a weather-lined face. "How be you, friends? Is that chocolate chip cookies I smell?"

"Hot out of the oven," Abner confirmed. He slid a cookie on a plate, then set it on the counter.

Sniffing appreciably, Vernie unsnapped her down plaid jacket. "Saw Annie getting off the ferry a few minutes ago."

"Annie?" Birdie shut off the mixer, grateful for the sudden quiet. "Now what would Annie be doing in Heavenly Daze on a Thursday?"

Vernie shrugged and lifted a cookie from the plate. "Maybe she's taking a long weekend. Those tomatoes look a bit peaked when it snows."

"Maybe," Birdie mused, "or maybe Edmund's worse."

"Be a terrible thing for Olympia to lose him so close to the holidays," Vernie said.

"It's going to be hard on her anytime," Bea corrected.

Her mouth full of cookie, Vernie nodded, then swallowed with an effort. "No denyin' that Olympia loves Edmund." Her eyes shifted to the pile of letters on the counter. "Don't tell me—more angel mail?"

Bea nodded, her expression grim. "If it keeps up I'm gonna have to have help. I've answered over twenty letters this week alone. I'm running out of things to say."

"Heard Buddy Maxwell's looking for work." Vernie took another bite of cookie.

Bea propped her chin on her knuckles. "Thought he was going to buy the Lobster Pot."

Vernie swallowed, then wiped her mouth with the back of her hand. "Lately he's realized he doesn't have a hope of getting that kind of money. Alst I know is he's a professional moocher. I don't think he wants a steady job." She grinned. "Might have to actually do some work."

Birdie glanced at her sister. "You could hire him to help answer letters."

Bea shot her a sour look. "I'm not that desperate." She picked up the stack of letters and disappeared through the back hallway as the door opened. Dr. Marc came in on a rush of cold air.

"Morning, Dr. Marc," Birdie called.

"Good morning, Birdie. Brrrr!" The doctor rubbed his hands together. "Do you have any of that flavored coffee?"

"Coming right up." Birdie poured a cup of raspberry decaf and handed it over the counter. Dr. Marc accepted it, smiling gratefully. "Don't know if I'll ever get used to these Maine winters."

"You don't get used to them, Doctor; you learn to live with them," Abner said.

Vernie sidled toward the doctor. "How's Edmund this morning?"

Dr. Marc shook his head. "Won't be long now."

Sighing, Birdie pulled the mixing bowl off the stand and sniffed appreciatively at the mix. Nothing beat the scent of yeast bread, and in a few hours, this entire place would smell of it. She grimaced as a sudden thought struck her. "Vernie," she turned to face her friend, "you did order my Thanksgiving bird, didn't you?"

Vernie scowled in indignation. "Of course I ordered your bird: thirty-one plus pounds, at sixty-nine cents a pound. Got a good buy on toms this year."

"And the sage?"

"Birdie Wester, when have you ever known me to forget to order anything?"

Not once, Birdie silently conceded. Vernie Bidderman prided herself on efficiency; anyone with a lick of sense knew they could depend on Vernie for supplies. Most of the islanders shopped in Ogunquit for staples, weather permitting; prices were better and the selection beat the Mercantile any day. But during bad weather Heavenly Daze had to depend on Vernie for essentials, and she hadn't failed them yet. You could call Vernie in a blizzard and ask for Epsom salts, and you'd find your order bagged and waiting by the time you managed to track through the snow to the Mercantile. Though she specialized in candy and tourist trinkets in season, folks agreed you couldn't beat the Mooseleuk Mercantile in a pinch.

"Used the last of my sage when Bea got a craving for cornbread dressing this summer," Birdie said, carrying her bowl to the flour-sprinkled work counter. "Been meaning to pick up a tin at the Grocery Mart but I keep forgetting."

Vernie stiffened at the mention of her competitor across the bay. "Your sage will be waiting for you when you want to pick it up." She pointed to the sour cream doughnuts. "I'll have a couple dozen of those and a dozen glazed, Abner. Are they fresh?"

"Yes, ma'am." The baker sent Birdie a look that said *be patient.* "Our pastry is baked fresh every morning."

"Hmm, well, make that two dozen glazed. MaGoo will eat what I don't."

Abner wiped his hands on a white cloth. "Coming right up, Vernie."

"Vernie, that cat is getting as broad as a boxcar," Dr. Marc commented. "What does he weigh now?"

"Land, who knows? Must be up around forty-five pounds by now. Alst I know is that I nearly put my back out every time I lift him."

Birdie smothered a smile as she thought of the cat next door. Tourists made a point to stop by the Mercantile to see if rumors about the glandular feline were true. Unless the cat moved—and MaGoo wasn't fond of physical exertion—folks thought they were looking at a huge black-and-white doorstop.

She glanced at the doctor. "Your son going to make it to the island for Thanksgiving?"

Dr. Marc lowered his coffee cup and nodded. "That's his plan, unless an emergency keeps him away."

"A doctor's life is never his own," Vernie said. "I sure hope young Alex makes it—Annie's coming home every weekend now."

"I know." The corners of Dr. Marc's mouth lifted with amusement. "Hope to get those two introduced one of these days."

Heads turned in unison when the door opened and Buddy Maxwell stomped in.

Squeak. Squeak. Squeak.

Big muddy boots approached the display counter.

"Morning, Buddy," Birdie said, eyeing the puddles forming beside his boots.

Red suffused the young man's cheeks as he hung his head with a sheepish grin. "Whatever."

"What can I get you this morning?"

Buddy studied the case. "What's that thing?"

Birdie wiped her hands, trying to follow Buddy's pointing finger. "Fried blueberry pies."

His finger inched down the glass, streaking it, no doubt.

"Those are bear claws.

"Cinnamon crullers.

"Vanilla iced cake doughnuts.

"Doughnut holes." She glanced at him sharply. "You taking a survey?"

His flush deepened. "I'll have two cinnamon rolls, I guess."

Bea reappeared in the kitchen, still holding the handful of letters. "I've been thinking."

Birdie put two warm cinnamon rolls in a sack and handed it to Buddy. "Beatrice, you know that's dangerous."

Not taking the bait, Bea waved the pink envelope from Ogunquit. "I have an idea."

Birdie rang up Buddy's order, then turned to face her sister. "What's your idea?"

Brightening, Bea said, "Seems like a utility bill isn't a big thing. We could take part of our tithe money and send it to this child."

"Now, Beatrice," Birdie cautioned, "that's a generous thought, but taking tithe money away from the church doesn't seem exactly fair. Without tourist donations, the church budget gets real lean during the winter."

Bea shook her head. "I know that, but it would only be this once, and I'm sure Pastor Wickam would approve if he knew about the need." She glanced at Abner and Dr. Marc. "We could all chip in and send this poor woman a couple of hundred dollars. She could pay the utility bill and maybe get her refrigerator fixed. What do you think?"

Abner took to the idea right away. "I'd be willing to contribute."

Birdie wasn't convinced. "Now, Bea, if we start giving away money there'll be no end to the letters. You and I aren't rich."

"But this is such a small request—and folks in Ogunquit are almost like family." Bea gazed wistfully at the envelope. "No one has to know where the money comes from. Besides, having her need met will bolster little Raleigh's faith."

Birdie shook her head. "I don't like it, Bea. I have no objections to helping, but that little girl said she and her mother attend church. Surely Grace Unity has a benevolent program to assist members in need."

"Maybe . . . or maybe the mother is too proud to ask for help, so little Raleigh is depending on angels."

Birdie glanced up to see Abner nodding his head. "You approve of this plan?"

"The family needs help," he said quietly. "And why are we here, if not to extend a hand to those in need?"

"Bea's right," Dr. Marc added. "Often pride does blind a person—especially a single parent. The shadows of past mistakes can make it hard to ask for assistance."

"But," Birdie stuttered, "we'd be misleading the child if we pretended to be angels!"

Smiling, Abner wiped his hands on his apron. "We are the Father's hands on earth. Perhaps Bea can word the letter in such a way that the little girl will understand that God's people answered her request."

Bea's head bobbed enthusiastically. "I could do that—I'm sure of it."

Dr. Marc spoke up. "Why not donate the money to the church in Raleigh's name and have the pastor deliver it?"

All eyes swiveled to focus on the doctor.

"Ayuh," Birdie mused. "It might work."

A smile found its way through Bea's mask of uncertainty. "Please, Birdie? We can't cure cancer or bring fathers back to families, but we can scrape up enough money to make sure a little girl and her mama are warm this winter."

Smiling, Abner added his vote of confidence. "I'm sure there are others in Heavenly Daze who would be willing to chip in. And as far as taking money away from the church, we are the church. We are God's people, commanded to help our brothers and sisters." The baker turned to Buddy, who'd been listening with his mouth slightly open. "Don't you agree?"

Red-faced, Buddy shrugged. "Whatever."

"Well . . . all right," Birdie conceded, wondering if she would live to regret this decision. Answering the letters with hope and comfort was one thing; giving money away was quite another. They were inviting trouble, for certain, but she wouldn't be able to sleep nights knowing that young Raleigh dinglefuzzie and her ailing mother were lying in a cold bed and drinking spoiled milk out of a faulty refrigerator.

"All right." Birdie trained her gaze on her sister. "But donate the money anonymously and instruct the little girl's pastor to personally deliver it to her mother. Hopefully, the child will assume her church has come to the rescue."

Bea expelled a whoosh of relief. "I'll get on it right away." She turned to leave, then hesitated at the threshold. "It wouldn't hurt to write and tell Raleigh that God has heard her prayers, would it?"

"No, that wouldn't hurt." Birdie gave her sister a smile. God had heard the prayer, so she had no qualms about allowing the child to believe that truth. She turned back to her waiting bread dough, then jerked around as another thought struck her. "Bea?"

Bea leaned back through the doorway. "Yes?"

"Exactly what do you plan to do about the sock-eating dryer?"

Buddy glanced up, frosting shining on his upper lip, apparently bumfuzzled by the question.

Shrugging, Bea's grin widened. "Why, send a pair of new blue socks. What else?"

As the door closed behind Bea, Birdie picked up the coffeepot to refill the doctor's cup. "I'm still a little uneasy about this. If we attempt to meddle in other folks' problems there'll be trouble, mark my words."

"Now, Birdie," Dr. Marc said as she poured, "who could possibly object to a few concerned souls trying to help a needy mother and her daughter? Aren't you always saying that folks don't neighbor like they used to? And this is the season for giving thanks, a time when we should reflect upon our blessings and share with those who are less fortunate. Two or three utility bills and a part for a refrigerator—those are needs we can handle."

Holding the coffee pot in midair, Birdie checked her thoughts. Dr. Marc was right, of course. Who in Heavenly Daze could possibly object to a random act of compassion? Setting the pot back on the warmer, Birdie dismissed her objections. This was the month for grateful hearts, so she was worrying needlessly.

Thursday afternoon, three days and seven puffin pictures behind schedule, Babette decided to change her tactics. The enticement of Disney World hadn't done much to persuade Georgie to pursue puffin painting, but now, in hindsight, she thought she could understand why. Georgie had never been to Disney World, so he didn't know what he was missing, and an after-Christmas trip must have seemed like a lifetime away.

Punishment hadn't worked, either. For the last two days, after Georgie came home from kindergarten and ate lunch, she had offered her son the choice of puffin painting or confinement to his room. Inevitably, he had chosen his room, coming out only for supper and bathroom breaks.

She had been so upset and disappointed she couldn't bring herself to say bedtime prayers with him. Charles had fulfilled that duty. For the last two nights she had listened from the hallway as her son asked God to bless Dad, Mike and Dana Klackenbush, the ailing Mr. Edmund, and Zuriel. Babette couldn't help but notice that her son made no mention of her or the puffin project.

Determined to change her approach, on Thursday afternoon she fed Georgie an egg salad sandwich and bean soup, then put away the dishes and told him to wait at the kitchen table. While he sat there, his head on his folded hands and his foot rhythmically kicking the table legs, she went upstairs to Charles's office and picked up the pages she'd prepared.

Returning to her reluctant son, she spread the papers on the kitchen table. "Do you know what this is?" she asked, pointing to a photograph. "It's a pug puppy. They are adorable little dogs—clean and neat and small. They're good watchdogs and great companions. They are also one-person dogs, so if you're a very good boy, this will be your very own dog. He can even sleep in your bed."

Georgie's countenance lit up. "Really?"

"Really." She sank into the chair next to him. "I found a lady in Ogunquit with a litter of puppy pugs. We will call and get one of these dogs for you tomorrow if you promise to paint three puffins every day for the next two months."

The light in Georgie's eyes dimmed, and for a moment he didn't speak. Then, as his chin quivered, he pushed away from the table. "Puffins stink," he said, standing. "Puffins clink! And I want to go to my room and think."

Babette felt her own eyes fill with tears of frustration, but at that moment Charles came down the stairs, his stockinged feet pounding out a th-thump rhythm over the wooden treads. "Hey, Georgie," he called, coming into the kitchen. "Just the man I wanted to see."

Georgie looked up, a question on his face.

"Hey, buddy." Charles knelt next to Georgie and squeezed his upper arm. "Did your mom tell you about the puppy? I'm ready to go get it tomorrow, if you'll give the word."

"Charles—," Babette began.

"You know what else, Georgie boy?" Charles barked out a laugh. "Your dad's going to be a published author!"

Frowning, Babette drew in a quick breath. When had this happened? She hadn't heard the phone ring, and Bea hadn't yet come by with the mail . . .

"Ayuh," Charles said, releasing his son. He turned and smiled at Babette. "For only 1.3 puffin paintings, I can pay to have my book printed at SelfPublish.com. I'll order five thousand copies, and we'll sell them on our Web page."

Babette groaned. "No, Charles, a thousand times no. What if we end up with an attic full of books we can't sell?"

"But we will sell them, honey." He sank into the chair Georgie had vacated. "Don't you know about what happened with *The Christmas Box*? The fellow who wrote that little book self-published it first. He was selling it in a local bookstore, then an editor found it and bought the rights for a million bucks or so, and then it became a runaway best-seller and a TV movie. The author's gone on to do other books, too—"

"That doesn't mean your silly book is going to sell."

The moment the words slipped from her mouth, Babette knew she had made a colossal mistake. Charles had suffered brutal appraisals from a host of agents and publishers; he didn't need to hear harsh comments from his wife.

He pulled away as abruptly as if she'd slapped him.

"Charles," she turned toward him, trying to soften the blow, "I'm sorry, the book isn't silly. I know you take your writing quite seriously. But, honey, look at the comments you've received. The only people who've been encouraging are those who want your money. Everyone else—the people who actually pay other people to write—has told you to stick to your day job." Sighing, she ran her hands through her hair and shifted her gaze to the window. "I wish you'd listen to them."

Charles's face had gone as red as a stop sign. "Well. I'm glad you finally told me what you really think."

"I don't think anything." She raked her hand through her hair again. "I don't know what to think. All I know is you're a much better painter than writer. Bless your heart for trying, babe, but you're not cutting it. And you could do a lot to ease the financial pressure on this family if you'd paint in the winter instead of working on those useless books. You could paint puffins and take the pressure off all of us."

"Financial pressure?" His eyes widened into glittering ovals of denial. "Who put us under financial pressure? You did. You had to have the roof fixed, and you made up that funky little budget."

"You ordered the new computer!"

"You told me I could! You were bribing me to go along with your little puffin scheme!"

"The scheme wasn't my idea!" She spat the words at him. "You're the one who wanted the computer. You said we could handle this. But obviously we can't."

He glared at her, his gaze burning and reproachful. "We could, you know. If you weren't trying to browbeat Georgie into painting those putrid puffins—"

"Browbeat him?" Breathless with rage, she thrust out her hand and grabbed Georgie's arm. "I'm not browbeating him," she said, struggling to keep her voice under control. "I've tried discipline. I've tried positive motivation."

"Bribes."

"Okay, bribes. But this boy is like you—stubborn and set in his ways."

"Puffins stink!" Yanking out of her grasp, Georgie stepped away, his brown eyes blazing in the center of a paper-white face. As his body trembled, he looked from Babette to Charles, then pointed to the ceiling and proclaimed, "I WILL PAINT NO MORE PUFFINS!"

While Babette and Charles stared at each other in horrified silence, Georgie turned on his heel and ran out the back door.

Around the corner at the bakery, Birdie hurried to fill the pastor's order while the clergyman, Winslow Wickam, leaned on the counter.

"I must say," he said, his brow furrowing, "I am a little concerned that funds will be diverted from the church—albeit for a worthy cause. I'm certainly not averse to helping out, you understand, indeed not—but must we pull the funds from the church budget?"

Birdie wrapped the bagel in tissue, then dropped it into a bag. Word of little Raleigh's plight had spread faster than a bad rash.

"Now, Winslow," she soothed, handing him the bag, "you're a thoughtful and God-ordained man, so surely you can see the need here. The mother and daughter can't pay their utility bill."

Winslow's head bobbed with sympathy. "I have no qualms about helping with the need, but perhaps we should have the Ogunquit church take up a special offering. After all, our church has utility bills, which are especially high in the winter."

"And run the risk of offending the folks from Grace Unity? We don't know if they are even aware of the family's need, and my guess is they aren't. If it weren't for the letter, we wouldn't know about the little girl's unfortunate circumstances. No." Birdie leaned her chin on her palm. "We can't tell those people they need to take care of their own. That would seem uppity."

"Well, we certainly can't imply that an angel is answering the need."

Birdie's thoughts drifted to something Abner had said earlier: *We are the Father's hands on earth.*

The bakery door opened. Amid a flurry of cold air and the sound of stomping boots, Floyd and Cleta Lansdown came in.

Birdie smiled. "How be things at the bed and breakfast today?"

"Doin' nicely, thank you," Cleta answered, her voice clipped.

Birdie asked from mere politeness, for this time of year business at the bed and breakfast was slower than an oak's growth. Nearly all the commercial establishments in Heavenly Daze slowed or closed during the winter months because tourists were scarce.

Birdie paused, thinking of the odd little mustached man who'd paid at least two visits to the Graham Gallery. Maybe Charles and Babette had found a regular customer.

Floyd grunted something, flipping his earmuffs to the crown of his hat. Floyd must have something on his mind—never a good thing. Cleta usually did the talking for the couple, but today she held back and tossed an expectant look in her husband's direction. The head of the household gave Winslow an abrupt nod.

Pastor Wickam returned the greeting. "Afternoon, Floyd and Cleta."

"Afternoon, Pastor." Cleta stationed herself beside Floyd, her smile vanishing as her lips pulled into a thin line. While Birdie watched, Cleta's nostrils flared and red crept up from her throat. She stared at the pastor with eyes like two burnt holes in a blanket.

Uh-oh, that look meant trouble. Birdie had seen Cleta's battle stance before.

She blew out her cheeks, then made an effort to lighten the mood. "What can I get you this afternoon, Cleta? Just took some fresh loaves of sourdough out of the oven."

Cleta shook her head, then gouged Floyd with her elbow.

"Don't need no bread," Floyd said. "Came to discuss this utility bill business. Pastor, we don't want no money taken from the church."

"Now, don't go getting yourself all exercised about this," Pastor said, glancing at Birdie. "We were just discussing the matter."

Sighing, Birdie picked up a bottle and shot a stream of Windex on the glass countertop.

"It's nothing to lose sleep over, Floyd," she said, ripping off a paper towel. "Bea and I have decided to personally respond to an angel letter—just one—from Ogunquit. The family is having trouble paying their utility bill so we thought we'd pitch in and help."

"So you and Bea are using your own money?"

Birdie wiped the counter in long strokes. "A little bit of our tithe—not that it's anything you need to be concerned about."

Floyd shook his head. "The tithe is God's money," he said, his voice booming like thunder. "If you take it away from our church, you're siphoning funds from our budget. You're stealing from the church!"

By the inflexible set of Floyd's jaw, Birdie knew she and Bea were in for a fight. As head deacon of the Heavenly Daze Community Church, he often took too much upon himself. She could stand and face him, or she could be a little creative . . .

She gave him a meek smile. "Maybe we ought to have a bake sale instead."

"Guess we could," Bea said, coming out of the back room. Birdie turned in surprise, wondering how much her sister had heard. "But this time of year there's only the locals and I doubt we'd earn enough to make a drop in the bucket. It makes a whole lot more sense to let Birdie and I send the money and save us all from added poundage. After all, we're using part of our tenth to help a sister in need, and I don't think the good Lord would fault us for that."

Cleta nudged Floyd, whose expression remained thunderous.

Birdie looked at Bea. "Then maybe a craft sale."

Bea shook her head. "Same problem, not enough customers this time of year to warrant the bother. Floyd, you know as well as I do that most islanders are living on a limited income in the winter. If we ask them to dig a little deeper into their pockets, they're going to say they give at church and that's enough."

Birdie turned to look at Cleta. "We can't forget that Christmas is coming up."

"And folks have already turned their pockets inside out to provide funds for the Women's Circle," Bea continued.

"But," Floyd said, his dark eyes blazing, "if we all started cutting our tithe for this and that, we won't be able to send our monthly support to Missionary Boggs and his family in Zimbabwe."

Good point, Birdie conceded. Her eyes flicked to Pastor Wickam.

Winslow took a moment to wipe his mouth with a napkin, then said, "It's not that I'm against helping this family. The need is certainly there, but the church's furnace is about to give out, and we'll not be able to hold services this winter if we can't heat the building."

Cleta jabbed Floyd.

"Ayuh," he said, giving Birdie a pointed look. "No heat, no services."

All this excitement was giving Birdie a headache. Pitching the paper towel in the waste can, she glanced around the corner. Abner was in the storeroom, his forehead creased in thought as he counted bags of flour and sugar.

"Well," she said, turning back to face the opposition, "no use getting our colons in a kink over this. All right. Bea and I will try to come up with funds apart from our tithe money."

Winslow looked decidedly relieved. "Edith and I will chip in. We don't have a lot to spare, but maybe if I ate fewer pastries . . ."

Birdie clucked at him. "If you cut out the pastries, you'll be cutting back on my ability to give, Pastor. You'll have to think of something else to give up."

Silently, she wondered how much the pastor and his wife could contribute. Though the parsonage was provided by the church, the Wickams had other expenses like everyone else. And Winslow's salary was barely adequate.

Cleta rammed Floyd.

"One more thing," Floyd added, after giving his wife a nasty look.

"Yes?" Sighing in exasperation, Birdie lifted her head to see what else the Lansdowns could possibly find to complain about.

Clearing his throat, Floyd fixed his gaze on the strudel tray. "We don't think it's wise to answer those angel letters. If folks think they can write to Heavenly Daze and then angels will solve their problems, well, it just ain't fittin'. It'll turn into one big, ugly mess. The island will be overrun with folks looking for a handout, crime will increase, and we'll have to start locking our doors at night. On top of that, we'll have to arm ourselves and hire security guards. The septic system won't be able to handle the overload, and we'll have to build a bigger post office to handle all the mail. Before long, we'll have folks fighting in the streets and we'll be on the six o'clock news in Portland."

His gaze narrowed as he stared at Birdie. "I don't want our town to be on the six o'clock news. It won't be good for the legitimate businesses here."

Cleta punched him.

"Is that what you want, Birdie?" Floyd continued. "Do you want Heavenly Daze to turn into Las Vegas?"

Winslow's eyes widened. "Oh my. Las Vegas . . . gambling and show girls. We certainly can't have that."

Floyd gave a succinct nod. "Ayuh."

"Ayuh," the pastor added absently, sending Birdie a worried look.

Las Vegas? Birdie had never heard anything so silly. Purposefully, she turned her back to the crowd and untied her apron, signaling the end of the conversation. Good grief, a simple act of compassion was turning into a three-ring circus.

"Excuse me, folks," she said, pulling off her apron. "But it's near two o'clock. We're closin'."

Taking the hint, the Lansdowns buttoned their coats, then trailed Pastor Wickam out of the bakery.

Birdie tossed her apron onto the counter, then pressed her face to her hands. Las Vegas? Honestly! Floyd needed to keep his predictions of gloom and doom to himself.

Shaking her head, she walked to the front door and turned the sign.

"Try it like this, George."

Pretending not to notice the tracks of tears on the boy's face, Zuriel picked up the lump of raw clay, formed it into a tight ball, then tossed it from one hand to the other. "What you want to do is create shock waves that will distribute the moisture evenly," he said, handing the ball back to the boy. "Clay must have water all the way through before we can mold it."

Georgie sniffed, wiped his dripping nose on his sleeve, then picked up the clay and slowly tossed it from hand to hand.

"That's good." Zuriel patted Georgie's shoulder, feeling the boy's small, frail frame beneath his crusty palm. "Now we're going to wedge the clay. Have you ever seen your mother knead a loaf of bread?"

Georgie shook his head almost reflexively, then shrugged. "I dunno."

"I'll bet you have." Zuriel picked up another piece of clay and pressed it to the sturdy tabletop, then bent and folded it back upon itself. Leaning forward and pushing against the clay with the heels of both hands, he demonstrated the art of wedging. "We don't want to flatten the clay too much," he said, watching from the corner of his eye as Georgie began to imitate him. "You never want to beat the clay down or push it too far. That's not a good thing."

Children shouldn't be pushed too far, either. He glanced out the window toward the house, where lights gleamed in the kitchen window. Odd, that neither Babette nor Charles had come out to check on Georgie or take him up to bed. It was nearly eight o'clock and past the boy's usual bedtime.

"George," he asked, stepping back to watch the boy work the clay, "your folks know you're out here?"

Another sniffle, then: "I don't care."

Zuriel stroked his beard. "Something happen today? I'm glad you spent the afternoon with me, but you've never been allowed to stay out this late on a school night."

Another stroke of the sleeve across the nose and a sudden rush of tears. "Puffins stink. Puffins clink. Puffin people are great big finks."

"Oh." Zuriel picked up his lump of clay and began to wedge it, matching his pace to the boy's. "I'm glad you like pottery. I love making things. I love the feel of the clay in my fingers and the coolness of the water over my hands. And when the pot comes through the firing, I love holding something strong and beautiful . . . and I'm happy to know I helped make it."

Georgie sniffed again, wiping his nose with his hand this time, leaving a smear of gray mud across his upper lip. "Whaddya mean, you helped?" he asked, his brown eyes flashing toward Zuriel. "I thought you made your pots by yourself."

"God helps me." Zuriel lifted his lump of clay from the table, smoothed it one more time, then set it on the bat above the potter's wheel. "God is the great Creator, and all good gifts flow through him. When I make a circle or a sphere or a star, I'm only copying the things he has already made. I feel his Spirit when I'm working . . . and when I do my best, I know the Creator is pleased."

Wiping his nose again, Georgie moved toward the wheel, his eyes intent upon the clay. Zuriel moistened the mound with a damp sponge, then set the switch to its slowest speed. As the wheel turned, he used both hands to push the ball to the center of the bat and pressed it to the surface.

"Did you know we are jars of clay?" Zuriel remarked, his wet hands centering the earth. He picked up the sponge again, then dribbled water over the lump. "God created the first man out of earth, which is another word for clay. The Bible says humans are like clay jars in which the treasure of God is stored."

He lifted his muddy hands and held them aloft. "You want to try?"

Georgie nodded.

"Wet your hands in the bucket, then place them on the mound, like I did. Relax, and let the mud mold itself to your fingers."

And while Georgie lowered his hands to the lump of earth and smiled in the joy of creation, Zuriel studied the living clay jar before him and wondered when the boy's parents would come to their senses. Lately they had become far too concerned with earthly possessions. Their true treasure was the priceless soul of their child.

He lowered his gaze, accepting the knowledge that something had created schisms within this human family. Babette and Charles were good parents, but apparently tonight neither of them was up to the challenge of comforting their son. Again.

"I'll save this for you, sport," Zuriel said, lifting Georgie's wrists and sliding the small hands off the clay. "I'll wrap it in plastic, and tomorrow you can pick up where you left off . . . if you want to. But for now, I think maybe we should clean you up and get you ready for bed."

Holding his wet hands stiffly before him, Georgie looked up with eyes soft with hurt. "Will you say prayers with me, Z?"

"Sure I will," Zuriel said, pointing the boy toward the sink in the kitchen area. "Anytime."

CHAPTER NINE

Hunched in her robe, Babette stared at the steaming cup of coffee between her hands and considered the state of the universe. Right now things seemed pretty cold on Planet Graham. Though she'd heard sounds of life in the galaxy of Georgie's room, he hadn't come downstairs. And though she could hear the groaning of the shower pipes, Charles hadn't uttered a word since their disastrous fight of the day before. Somehow, from out of nowhere, a thundercloud had moved into the household and slammed them all with a bolt in the heart. If not for Zuriel, who'd stepped in and taken care of Georgie . . .

She closed her eyes, desperately wishing she could turn back time and take back the words she'd spewed yesterday afternoon. She and Charles rarely argued—he was usually too easygoing to fight—but yesterday she had thoughtlessly attacked the dream he held most dear to his heart. Worst of all, they had argued in front of Georgie, who in his entire lifetime had never heard them utter a harsh word to each other.

Her memory flitted back to an afternoon in July when they'd taken the ferry over for a day of shopping in Ogunquit. As they rode the trolley car back to Perkins Cove, they'd begun to banter about whether or not they should stop for ice cream. Charles wanted to, Babette didn't, and after a couple of playful exchanges Georgie clapped both hands over his ears and screamed, "Stop!"

The trolley car driver, a sweet older fellow, slammed on the brakes so hard that Babette's purse went flying from her lap. Every eye in the vehicle turned to Georgie, who slowly lowered his hands and regarded his parents with a somber expression. "I don't want to choose," he said.

"Choose what, bud?" Charles asked.

"Who I'll live with," Georgie answered, "when you get a divorce."

While Charles put his arm around Georgie and tried to explain that he didn't have to worry about divorce, Babette smiled stupidly at the other trolley passengers, then tried to distract them by pointing out the world famous Lobster Pound restaurant.

If a snappy discussion about ice cream had nearly convinced Georgie that his parents' marriage was doomed, what had last night's genuine battle done to him?

Groaning, she buried her face in her hands. She wasn't fit to be a mother or a wife. Charles might never forgive her for being so cruel, and Georgie . . . what must he think of her? If not for Zuriel, who watched over Georgie like some kind of guardian angel, last night could have been even worse.

She heard footsteps on the stairs and tilted her head, analyzing the sound. The steps were light and tentative—they had to belong to Georgie.

Brushing her hands through her hair, she pasted on a calm face, then stood and moved to the cupboard.

"Good morning, sweetie," she called as he came into the kitchen and slid into his chair. Her voice sounded artificially bright in her own ears. "Want some orange juice with your Frosty Flakes?"

She turned in time to see him shake his head. Georgie's lower lip jutted forward, his gaze focused on the salt-and-pepper shakers in the center of the table.

She forced a smile into her voice. "Want some toast? I have those blueberry preserves you like. They're expensive, so we'd better not let them go to waste."

Again, nothing but head shaking.

She set the cereal before him, then leaned against the counter as he picked up his spoon and began to eat. Upstairs, the bedroom door slammed, then Charles's heavy footfalls creaked the steps.

Turning away from the kitchen doorway, she sought something to do and settled for tightening the twist tie on a loaf of bread.

"About ready, bud?" Charles asked, coming into the kitchen. He paused to tousle Georgie's hair.

Georgie ducked away from his father's hand, then slid out of his chair. "I want to go to school now."

Babette lowered her head, feeling the pressure of Charles's eyes upon her back. Ordinarily they'd be looking at each other, sending a series of invisible signals, a silent communication they'd grown adept at understanding over the years . . .

But the lines of communication were down today.

"Better hurry then, hon." She reached out to pat Georgie's shoulder but nearly missed him as he grabbed his backpack and moved past her without a word.

Pressing her lips together, Babette clung to the back of a chair as her husband and son left the kitchen.

At nine o'clock, after Charles had returned from taking Georgie to kindergarten and silently ascended to his writer's garret, Babette stood in front of her husband's large easel in the gallery. She'd been wrong to expect Georgie to work like an adult. She'd been unfair to impose such a burden upon him, and today she would do all she could to remove that obligation.

One of Georgie's poorer puffin paintings lay on the table next to her, surrounded by jars and tubes of paint she'd pulled from Charles's paint box. Babette tied her kitchen apron behind her back, then picked up a clean paintbrush and regarded the blank canvas.

How hard could painting like a five-year-old be? She could do it, especially since she had one of Georgie's paintings to guide her. Tilting her head, she considered the canvas. Georgie might be a talented little boy, but half of his artistic genes came from her. So even if she'd never painted as much as a ceramic plate, she could produce at least six or seven puffins a day.

She dabbed the brush in a jar of ebony tempera, then drew it across the canvas, boldly approximating the shape of the puffin's head and wing. Satisfied with the result, she dabbed and painted again, coloring in the tail feathers, wing, and the white speck that marked the eye.

Dropping her brush into a glass of water, she stepped back to evaluate her work. Not bad. Not great, but perhaps it would look different when the paint dried and she added a few details. When she was finished, she'd sign a big *G* to the lower right corner, but this time it would stand for "Graham," not "Georgie."

So she could sell them to Pierce Bedell with a reasonably clear conscience.

An hour later, Babette stared at the wasted canvas and admitted defeat. The shape that had looked promising at the beginning had somehow become cluttered and sloppy. Her puffin looked more like a sick puppy than a bird. The orange feet were grossly out of proportion, and the multicolored beak attached to the black head looked more like a Halloween mask.

She dropped her brush into the water jar, then grabbed at the apron strings at her back. She only had a few minutes to put these things away and dispose of that awful canvas. If Georgie came home and saw what she'd been doing, he'd think she was cheating.

Which she was.

Shuddering in sudden humiliation, she pulled the apron over her head. She was about to toss it onto the table when Charles's frame filled the doorway. "Babs—," he said, then he halted, his strong jaw dropping as he stared at the painting on the easel.

"I was—" She felt herself blushing as she looked at the monstrosity she'd created. "I felt bad about putting so much pressure on Georgie. I thought I'd try to paint some puffins myself . . . so he wouldn't have to."

Charles's expression clouded. For a moment she thought he'd say something sarcastic, but then he slapped his hand to his cheek and laughed. "You thought—," he began, then he leaned against the doorframe and grabbed his knees, bending double in laughter. "That's"—he spoke through snorts and cackles—"the silliest looking picture I've ever seen!"

Babette bit the inside of her lip and gathered her apron into her fist. If he didn't stop laughing, she would throw it at him in a minute . . .

"That," he said, wiping tears of laughter from his eyes, "looks like a penguin on steroids!"

Babette felt her mouth twist. She moved closer to the door, then turned and stared at the painting from his vantage point.

What she saw brought a smile to her own lips. "I've got to admit," she said, crossing her arms, "he does look a little . . . hunky."

"Oh, honey." Charles's arm fell loosely over her shoulder. "I'm sorry, but you're not a painter. You have many gifts and talents, but this"—he pointed toward the easel—"is not one of them."

She shook her head, amazed that he couldn't see the irony in his words. He was an excellent painter, so why did he persist in trying to write the Great American Masterpiece?

"I can't do it," she said, turning to face him. "So why don't you help? You could paint a couple of puffins just to motivate Georgie. If you only started one, Georgie would pick up a paintbrush. That's why he paints, anyway. He wants to be like you."

For a moment she thought Charles might soften, but a muscle tightened in his jaw as his arm fell from her back. "I can't paint right now, Babs. I've got to finish my book."

"You can't take even a little break? For a day or two?"

He shook his head. "No. And don't worry about Georgie. Give him some space, and he'll paint again when he's ready."

"What if he doesn't want to paint until after Christmas?" Babette put her hands on her hips. "What if he waits until the trend has passed? You know today's hot commodity can become tomorrow's Talking Elmo or Pokémon. If he doesn't paint while he's in demand, we may as well quit now. No one will care if he waits too long."

Charles turned toward the kitchen. "We can't quit," he called, "we need the money. Besides, Georgie won't wait too long."

"How do you know?" Babette followed him, nipping at his heels like a terrier. "And yet that's not what concerns me most, Charles. I'm worried about what Georgie is becoming. He never used to be belligerent or surly or pouty, but he's become all of those things in the last few days. In the last couple of days, he's been deliberately disobedient—he refuses to paint those puffins! He never used to give us this kind of trouble."

Charles moved to the cupboard and reached for a glass. "Georgie's fine, hon. Leave him alone."

"How can I?" She swept her hand through her hair, wishing it were proper to knock some logic into one's husband's head. "I will not raise a hooligan or a delinquent, and I'm afraid that's what we're doing. But he's so stubborn! I've never seen a kid so strong-willed."

"I was a strong-willed child." A self-satisfied smile crossed Charles's face. "And I turned out okay."

Babette bit back a sarcastic remark, then drew a deep breath. Lead a horse to a mirror and you still can't make him see himself . . .

"Fine." Throwing up her hands, she left Charles alone and sailed away to clean up her mess in the gallery.

At precisely 12:45 on Friday morning, Birdie stepped out of the bakery, her purse in hand. She was running low on buttercream-colored yarn, and the Mercantile didn't have a vast assortment of colors. If she hurried she could make the one o'clock ferry and be home before dark.

She hadn't taken three steps when she spotted the Lansdowns coming her way, accompanied by their daughter and son-in-law, Russell and Barbara Higgs. Vernie Bidderman and Buddy Maxwell brought up the rear of the procession, and every face in the parade was fixed in determination—well, every face except Buddy's, who appeared to have been swept up in the pack.

Birdie tried to cross the street, but Cleta spotted her and flagged her down.

"What is it, Cleta?" Birdie checked her aggravation as she watched the mob approach. She didn't need a crystal ball to know this hunting party was upset. Cleta's face pulsated with passion and Floyd looked as if he could blow a cork out his ears any minute.

The assemblage stopped in the street, then spread out to face her. A tactical maneuver.

Vernie cleared her throat. "We want to talk to you, Birdie Wester."

Birdie calmly consulted her wristwatch. "I'm in a hurry, Vernie. I'm on my way to buy yarn and I don't want to miss the ferry."

"Those old dishrags can wait," Vernie snapped. "We're upset about what you're about to do with this angel problem."

Glowering at her, Birdie snorted. She could put up with most anything, patience was part of her nature, but she didn't tolerate rudeness. Vernie might not fancy the dishcloths Birdie toiled over from May to December, but many a woman on the island appreciated her long hours of labor when they opened a gaily-decorated Christmas present and discovered two of the lovely hand-knitted dishcloths.

Old dishrags, indeed!

She lifted her chin. "We had this conversation earlier, Vernie," she said, injecting a note of steel in her tone. "If you're upset, you need to talk to Bea. She handles the mail."

Vernie shook her head, her strong features solidified in a defiant mask. "Bea won't listen—you know she's mulish."

Birdie checked the time: 12:50. They were going to make her late. "Come to the point, Vernie."

Floyd beat her to it. "We don't want you to answer that letter."

"It's gonna stir up a hornet's nest," Vernie seconded, while Russell and Barbara nodded in halfhearted agreement. Some folks said the Lansdown girl and her husband were backward, but Birdie thought they were just shy of expressing an opinion not originally planted by Floyd or Cleta.

Floyd scowled. "The more we think about it, the worrieder we get."

"Then don't think about it," Birdie snapped. "Let me and Bea do the thinking. And there's no such word as worrieder, Floyd. I dearly wish you'd stop massacring the English language."

"Don't go gettin' highfalutin on me, Birdie Wester."

"You answer that letter," Cleta warned, "and Heavenly Daze will never be the same."

"Nonsense." Birdie straightened her hat. "You're getting in a dither over nothing."

"Old Jacques de Cuvier would roll over in his grave if he knew what you were about to do to his island," Vernie said, her eyes glinting.

"He came here for peace and quiet, and we want the same thing," Floyd added.

"Peace and quiet? You'll get plenty of that when you get to heaven and stand in line for your heavenly reward—if'n you get one, considering that you're telling me to ignore the poor and helpless."

With that parting shot, Birdie set off for the ferry, leaving the troublemakers standing in the street. But troublemakers seldom give up, so she wasn't surprised to look over her shoulder and see them following, still expressing their objections.

"Every Tom, Dick, and Harry in the State of Maine will be coming up here looking for a handout!" Cleta called.

Vernie yelled out, "We'll have to add on to the store and hire more help—you know how hard it is to get good summer help?"

"How are we going to get that new furnace for the church if you give the money away faster than we can bring it in?" Floyd hollered.

Whirling, Birdie confronted the lot of them. "Money—that's what it boils down to, isn't it? That's all you're concerned about, the money. Not the requests—you're not thinking about the people, just your own money!"

"That's not fair, Birdie," Vernie countered. "Somebody's got to mind the store. We're not rich—we live from hand to mouth most months; you know that. If that old furnace gives out, where will we have services? You gonna volunteer your house?"

Birdie stood still as Vernie's question rippled through the group. Well, of course she wasn't volunteering her house! Neither Birdie's place nor the bakery was large enough to hold the congregation. The parsonage was too small, too. The de Cuviers had room to spare, but Olympia had her hands full with Edmund. The Grahams' house was big enough, but that young couple was struggling to establish the art gallery and deal with a wild child, so they couldn't be worrying about hosting church services on Sunday morning.

Birdie focused on the Lansdowns. "What about you, Cleta? You have the bed and breakfast and plenty of room. We could hold services at your house if the furnace blows up."

"Now, Birdie, you know we're remodeling. The whole downstairs is a sawdust mess. We'd be glad to help but we can't."

"What about the Klackenbushes?" Floyd looked to Buddy. "Mike and Dana could help out."

Buddy grimaced, the veins in his throat standing out like ropes. "Whatever," he said, throwing up his hands.

"No," Vernie corrected, shaking her head. "They have that septic line problem, Floyd. No flushing more than once an hour."

Floyd looked thoughtful. "Oh. Right."

The ferry whistle blew.

Consulting her watch, Birdie took a half-step toward the dock. "We'll have to discuss this another time."

Cleta put a bony hand on her hip. "There'd be no need for discussion if you'd use plain old common sense, Birdie Wester."

Birdie turned, leaving the mob behind, but Vernie and Cleta came alongside her, their boots keeping time with her quick steps.

"Don't go meddlin' in other folks' business," Vernie said, a note of pleading in her voice as they stomped over the dock. "We're all upset that a young mother and her daughter are having a hard time paying their utility bill, but there are all kinds of folks in trouble and you can't help 'em all. Some can't pay their car payment, some can't provide enough food for the table, and some have trouble keeping shoes on their kids' feet. We can't answer all those needs, even if we tried. So leave the charity up to the church and leave Heavenly Daze in peace."

"That's the trouble," Birdie said, barely clearing the gangplank before the heavy spiral ropes began to lift from the water.

Conversation halted as Captain Stroble hit the air horn and a deafening blast shattered the cold November afternoon. From out of nowhere Tallulah appeared, making a flying leap from the dock to the boat. Just in time, the feisty canine landed belly down and slid halfway across the polished deck.

Birdie chuckled as the dog scrambled to her feet, paused to shake thoroughly, then shot into the cabin to warm her bones. Birdie followed her in, hoping to finally rid herself of her misguided neighbors.

As the engines revved, the big boat slowly eased back from the dock.

"Don't do it, Birdie!" Cleta yelled above the churning water. "You answer that letter and you'll open the doors to sin and corruption in Heavenly Daze!"

Birdie turned her face to the opposite window. Honestly, Cleta's theatrics could wear a body to the nubbin.

That night, Birdie rested her head on the back of her recliner, a pile of buttercream yarn pooled in her lap. For the first time in years she'd made a mistake and had to tear out three rows. All this mail business had her so upset she couldn't knit straight.

The fire snapped and popped. Outside, a north wind whipped the shutters while in her bedroom Bea snored beneath her electric blanket.

Birdie's mind drifted over the day. She was bone weary of trying to decide what to do about those poor folks in Ogunquit. Two or three hundred dollars was a goodly amount of money, but only a drop in the bucket when one thought of how many people had those kinds of needs.

It should have been simple—send money to provide warmth to a mother and child during a long, cold winter. Bea said they should send the money and quit worrying about what the town thought, but

Heavenly Daze was Birdie's home. How could she purposely upset her friends and neighbors? For Cleta was right; first there'd be one request, then another and another and another until she and Bea couldn't possibly keep up.

But suppose she sent three hundred dollars—why, that equaled two trips to the grocery store, a couple of movies, and a few meals at the Lobster Pot. Compared to a family's need for warmth, it seemed a minimal sacrifice.

She couldn't get the Akermans' plight out of her mind. Raleigh hadn't sent a picture, but Birdie could picture her, dark-haired with a pale face, huddling together with her mother around a hot plate. Maybe she was shivering even tonight—the wind was breezin' up something fierce.

Was Raleigh Akerman wondering why God hadn't answered her prayers?

We are God's hands on earth.

But hands had to be willing to work in order to do any good.

Stirring, Birdie blinked back tears. Then she felt a persistent, reassuring pressure on her left shoulder. She glanced up to see Abner standing beside her chair with a tray of hot tea in his left hand.

Peace, the like of which Birdie seldom experienced, flowed like running water through her heart.

She found her voice. "You startled me—what are you doing here at this hour?"

"I saw the light burning through the window. I hope it isn't too late to pay a visit?"

"It's never too late for you." She smiled, motioning him to the chair opposite her. The fragrant aroma of brewed tea wafted from the steaming teapot.

"I thought you might enjoy a cup of tea before bed."

Sighing, Birdie dropped her head to the chair cushion, closing her eyes. "Thank you, Abner. You always know when I'm troubled. How is that?"

Smiling, Abner poured a cup of tea and added sugar. He extended the cup to her. "Penny for your thoughts."

"Oh, dear." She smiled, balancing the fragile china on her fingertips. "Why does life have to be so complicated?"

"I can't explain, Birdie, but someday you will understand." Settling back into Bea's chair, he sipped his tea, his large hands awkwardly tipping the dainty china cup. Outside, the wind howled while the clock on the shelf above the window ticked away the minutes.

Long minutes, if you were shivering in the cold.

"I don't know what to do about the letter." Softly she explained that her neighbors feared Heavenly Daze would turn into another Las Vegas if people thought money could be had for the asking. Abner listened, occasionally adding an "Oh, my," or "We hope not," but he had no answers.

When she finished, he offered only an observation: "The Lord commands us to love one another. And love often requires sacrifice."

"Yes, but the town's concerns are valid," Birdie admitted. "I love the island's serenity, and I don't want to see it interrupted. And what would we do if the church furnace went out? The old thing is on its last leg."

Abner sipped his tea, then said: "The Lord promises to meet our needs."

"But he hasn't met the Akermans'."

Abner's gaze lifted to meet hers in the mellow lamplight. "He will," he said simply, "through you. And then he'll meet your needs, too."

Birdie blinked. "How can you be sure?"

A thoughtful smile curved Abner's mouth. "When Bea came to live here, did you worry about having another mouth to feed?"

"Of course not, she's my sister. I knew we'd make ends meet somehow. Besides, family should always take care of one another."

"Little Raleigh Akerman is family, too." Abner's grin flashed briefly in the lamplight. "She's a child of God, just like you. And God is your Father, and he's not likely to forget about either of you."

Before going to bed that night, Birdie wrote a personal check for three hundred dollars and slipped it into an envelope. By planning to give her tithe money, she had been, in a way, telling God that she would willingly donate his portion, but she didn't trust him enough to give any of her own. But now . . . well, she'd have to trust him to keep food on the table.

Neither she nor Bea were wealthy women. Bea lived on a small insurance annuity, and Birdie lived on Social Security and income earned from the bakery during tourist season. But she and Bea never failed to have food on the table, a refrigerator that hummed along, and a cozy stove to warm their feet. In all the ways that mattered, they were rich.

After sticking a stamp on the envelope, she addressed it to the Akermans, then enclosed a brief note:

Pay your utility bill and get your refrigerator fixed. God loves you.

Knowing she'd sleep well tonight, Birdie sealed the envelope. The check would reach the family by Monday and their immediate problem would be solved. They'd have something to be thankful for come Thanksgiving, and Birdie could celebrate the coming feast knowing she'd helped someone in need.

Going into her bedroom, she switched off the light, then settled deep into sheets that smelled of fabric softener. Her toes stretched toward the foot of the bed, eagerly seeking the warmth of her hot-water bottle. She and Bea might have to scrimp on groceries until the end of the month, but she'd already paid Vernie for the Thanksgiving turkey, and their cabinets were stuffed with staples. They wouldn't go hungry. If Birdie Wester had learned anything tonight, she'd learned to be confident in God's ability to take care of her.

CHAPTER TEN

Babette made Georgie sit between her and Charles in church on Sunday morning. They filled their usual spots on the left side of the building and smiled at all the usual people: Floyd and Cleta Lansdown, their daughter, Barbara; Mike and Dana Klackenbush; and Edith Wickam, the pastor's wife. After the first hymn, Micah Smith led the congregation in a rousing rendition of "There's a Welcome Here," and Babette made her customary two-step journey across the aisle to greet those who sat on the right side of the sanctuary: Olympia de Cuvier and her niece, Annie; Dr. Marc Hayes; Beatrice Coughlin and Birdie Wester; Vernie Bidderman; and an entire pew of Smiths: Abner, Yakov, Zuriel, and Elezar. Caleb Smith, she noticed, was not present—which could only mean he was home caring for Edmund de Cuvier.

After greeting everyone within handshake distance, Babette returned to her pew, uncomfortably aware that neither Charles nor Georgie had moved from their places. They'd probably shaken hands with those sitting right around them, but those two were like a pair of hard peas in a pod. At some point over the weekend, Georgie must have sensed that his father didn't exactly approve of the puffin plan, so last night Charles, not Babette, had again been invited to lead the boy in his bedtime prayers.

Babette had been fuming ever since. It didn't matter that she cooked, cleaned, and connived for both of them. No matter that she was responsible for the family budget and had no one to help her plan it. None of those things counted, apparently. The males in her life were set against her at the moment, neither one of them was ready to relent, and she could do nothing about it.

At the conclusion of the welcome song, Micah Smith led the congregation in a heartfelt prayer of thanks, then they sat. Babette noticed that Georgie had sidled closer to Charles during the prayer—well, fine. She pressed her back into the pew and lifted her chin, not caring that a measurable twelve inches separated her and her son. Let the world see the gap that had arisen in their family. Everyone on the island was bound to know their business sooner or later.

Reverend Winslow Wickam stepped up to the pulpit, his bald head shining in the light from the overhead fixture. "On this Sunday before Thanksgiving," he said, his voice ringing through the lapel microphone he'd taken to wearing, "I thought we'd do something special." He moved out from behind the pulpit and stood at the edge of the red-carpeted platform, the toes of his shiny black shoes jutting out into space. "I thought perhaps a few of you would like to share some of your blessings with us. After all, God has been good to the people of Heavenly Daze, and he's given us a great love for each other and for this little island." He clapped his hands together and raised a brow as he looked out over the congregation. "Come now, who'll be the first to tell us about something for which they're grateful?"

A twittering rose from the ladies near the organ, and Babette craned her neck at the sound. For days Birdie and Bea had been huddling together about something, but she'd been too involved in her puffin project to ask for details. She'd heard rumors regarding Bea and the mail, but other than a pen-pal boyfriend, Babette couldn't imagine any reason for the sisters to get excited.

"I'll say something, Pastor." Annie Cuvier stood and cast a smile around the small sanctuary. "As most of you know, I had pretty much given up on coming back to Heavenly Daze until a few weeks ago. Now, thanks to Aunt Olympia, the island is beginning to feel like home again—and my tomatoes are hanging in there!"

"Amen!" Dr. Marc shouted from his pew.

From her place, Cleta Lansdown waved her hand. "I'm grateful, Pastor, for a good tourist season. Now that we're settling down for the winter, I think most of us will be well-fed and comfortable. We hosted more visitors than usual last summer, and that's good news for the entire island."

Babette's mouth curved in an automatic smile, but inwardly she cringed. Cleta's bed and breakfast may have done well last summer, but only a few of those tourists had bought fine art. A few weeks earlier, Babette had told Charles that they'd experienced a summer of nickel-and-dimers. Vernie sold tons of saltwater taffy and tourist trinkets and Cleta ran a full house most nights, but fine art mostly went a-begging . . .

"Anyone else want to tell us about something you're grateful for?" the pastor asked. "Tell us about something or someone you really love."

Babette blinked in surprise when Georgie scrambled up on the pew, his heavy-soled church shoes thudding loudly against the wooden bench. She reached out to still him, but he evaded her grasp and called out, "Preacher?"

Every eye turned when Georgie's childish treble rang through the auditorium.

"Yes, Georgie?"

Babette reinforced her polite smile as sympathetic faces turned in her direction. The entire town knew Georgie, and those who didn't adore him seemed to tolerate him. But everyone, from the stern Olympia de Cuvier to sweet Edith Wickam, clucked sympathetically whenever Babette appeared with Georgie in tow.

Squirming beneath the pressure of so many pairs of eyes, Babette turned and studied her son. He was clasping his hands in a fair imitation of Pastor Wickam, warming up the audience. The child ought to consider becoming an actor. He didn't have a timid bone in his body.

She smiled as she caught Charles's eye. This had to be a good thing. In a moment he would tell the church that he loved his parents, or that he wanted to thank God for a Christian home. And then Babette would know that he didn't hate her and he'd forgiven her about the puffins. Everything was going to be okay.

Obviously in a hurry to move things along, Pastor Wickam cleared his throat. "Tell us, Georgie—what do you love?"

Drawing a deep breath, Georgie barreled his twenty-four inch chest. "I LOVE NAKED WOMEN."

Babette's mind went numb as Georgie's words echoed in the church. A fog seemed to fall upon her, transporting her to a dreamlike state where nothing was real, where what appeared to be happening was not really happening, and where children did not blurt out the first thought on their minds . . .

She slowly turned her head and looked to her left through the fog, half-expecting to see the shadowy figure of her grandmother or some other long-gone ancestor, but no, Charles sat beside her, his eyes blazing like dark diamonds. The sound of whispering rose from the pew behind her, and someone said, "It's that art, you know—nude paintings!" Someone else giggled while the pastor's face went a violent shade of eggplant and his genteel wife twisted in the pew to cast Babette a horrified look.

She clapped her hand over her eyes, knowing from the sting of her fingernails that this was no dream. In this nightmare reality, her son really had said what her ringing ears relayed.

In the space of a few moments Georgie had evolved from delinquent to deviant.

Somehow Georgie sat down, and somehow, by the grace of God, Pastor Wickam recovered enough to return to the pulpit and deliver his sermon.

But Babette didn't hear a word of the rest of the service.

Edith Winslow stopped Birdie as she was leaving services Sunday morning. Pressing an envelope into her hand, Edith leaned closer. "Winslow and I wish it could be more."

Shaking her head, Birdie returned the gift. "Thank you, Edith, but the matter's been taken care of." She smiled, patting Edith's arm. "What are you and Winslow doing for lunch?"

"I have tuna salad in the refrigerator," Edith said. "Win plans to stop by the de Cuviers for a few minutes, then we'll make sandwiches, I suppose."

"Tuna, indeed. I have a nice pot roast in the oven. Bea will mash potatoes and I'll make brown gravy. I know Winslow loves roast and potatoes, so come join us, please. We have plenty to share."

Edith broke into a wide, open smile. "Pot roast sounds a lot better than cold tuna. We'll be there, as soon as Win comes back from the de Cuviers."

Birdie moved on, seeing no reason to elaborate on her decision to dip into her household account and send money to the Akermans. Edith's and Winslow's hearts were in the right place, but she and Bea were probably better prepared to supply a monetary need than the pastor and his wife. Besides, she realized with a smile, sharing made her feel good . . . good enough to feel like sharing again and again.

As she moved over the sidewalk, her eyes searched the crowd for a sign of Salt Gribbon. She'd invite him to dinner, too, if he'd ever come to church. Odd that he never attended services. She checked her disappointment. He was probably avoiding her since she'd made a fool of herself over those books. Yesterday he hadn't come into the bakery for his usual bread and cookies.

Though she saw no sign of him, she hesitated in the shadow of the steeple on the off-chance he'd pass by. The Lansdowns and Vernie Bidderman came out of the church, pausing in the doorway to chat with the preacher and the Klackenbushes. That rascal Georgie Graham, full of pent-up energy from having endured an hour of preaching, darted up and down the steps, weaving in and out of parishioners' legs. Bea, who'd stopped to offer a word of comfort to poor Babette Graham, spotted Birdie and nodded as she slipped through the crowd.

Latching onto Birdie's hand, Bea hurried her sister down the sidewalk. "Sister, why are you standing here?" she scolded, the heels of her Sunday shoes scraping the asphalt path. "With dinner in the oven, we don't have time to engage in another spat over those angel letters."

"Doesn't matter, everything's settled," Birdie said, glancing over her shoulder for one last glimpse of the crowd. No Salt.

Sighing, she followed her sister. "Tomorrow morning the Akermans will receive the check, and that will be the end of it. This town can settle down to celebrating Thanksgiving and forget all about folks less fortunate than themselves."

Bea's pleasant face went blank with shock. "Why, Birdie, what a thing to say!"

Birdie shrugged, a little ashamed of her cynicism. But she couldn't help it. She'd done the right thing—after a lot of persuasion, so she was no saint—but the others still seemed content to turn a blind eye to the needs of hurting people.

What would it take to make them see?

After church, the Grahams ate Babette's Crockpot lunch—oyster stew—mostly in silence. Charles kept one eye on his wife and the other on his son, not knowing who would erupt first. When the last of the stew and crackers had been eaten, he pushed back his chair and took Georgie by the hand.

"Let's you and I take a walk out to the lighthouse, bud."

"But, Dad—"

"Mind your father." Babette spoke in a no-nonsense tone, and something in her voice prodded Georgie to obey. Together he and Charles slipped through the foyer, plucked their coats from the rack by the front door, and stepped out into the autumn sunshine.

They walked for five minutes without speaking. Like a fish gasping for air, Charles opened his mouth a half-dozen times, attempting to begin the speech he'd prepared and revised a dozen times during the

Sunday sermon. But the beginning had never quite felt right, and he couldn't bring himself to open the conversation.

He could have hugged Georgie out of sheer relief when his son brought up the taboo topic.

"I guess Mom's pretty mad, huh, Dad?"

"She's not mad, Son. She was embarrassed."

Georgie accepted this news in silence. "But the pastor asked what we love—and I do love naked women. Almost as much as I like whales . . . and puffins."

Charles squinted up at the sky, where a pair of gulls were surfing the wind currents and hoping for a handout. "I love naked women, too—God made women beautiful. But nakedness is a private thing, and not something we're supposed to talk about in public. It embarrasses people."

"Like it embarrassed Mom?"

"Exactly." Pausing on the road, he turned to look at his boy. "Why'd you tell Pastor Wickam you like naked women if you like whales and puffins more?"

Georgie kicked a stone in the path, then shrugged. "I dunno."

"I think I know." Charles resumed his walk. "I think maybe you were angry with your mom, and you knew she'd be embarrassed if you talked about women instead of whales. So that's why you brought it up."

Georgie didn't answer, but his chin quivered as he looked away.

"I don't think you did it on purpose." Charles slipped his hands in his jeans pockets and frowned at the lighthouse in the distance. "Sometimes, when we're angry, we say things to hurt people. If that happens, we need to apologize and ask for their forgiveness. If they forgive us, then we'll be as good as new. Even better, in fact. Because when they forgive us, we understand how much they love us."

Georgie lifted his gaze to meet Charles's. "Did you tell Mom you were sorry? 'Cause the other day you said things to hurt her. You had a fight together."

Charles looked away as his conscience stung. He had hoped

Georgie had tucked that memory away, but apparently he had not.

"We hurt each other that day," Charles said, his voice soft. "And you're right, we need to say we're sorry. And we will forgive each other, because we love each other. And then, you'll see, things will be as good as new."

"You won't"—Georgie's lower lip wobbled—"you won't get a divorce?"

"Not gonna do it."

"Not even if I don't paint puffins?"

Stopping, Charles knelt in the path and placed his hands on his son's shoulders. "Never gonna leave your mom, Son. Never ever. I promise."

Georgie smiled, his features suffused with relief, then he hugged his father tight.

CHAPTER ELEVEN

"A hundred and thirty one letters!" White-faced, Bea stood in the doorway, her eyes wide, her arms filled with angel letters. Several spilled to the floor as she walked to the kitchen, and as Birdie bent to pick them up, she saw how the envelopes were addressed:

Angels Unaware
Heavenly Daze, Maine 09876

To the Heavenly Daze Angels
Heavenly Days, Maine 09876

Any Angel in Heavenly Daze
HD, Maine 09876

To the Whom It May Concern Angel
General Delivery
Island of Heavenly Daze, Maine 09876

Yo, Angel!
Heavenly Days and Nights, Maine 09876

"Oh, my," Birdie whispered as Bea dropped her burden to the kitchen table.

"That's just the top layer," Bea said, stomping back to the bakery.

A moment later she returned, dragging a bulging mail sack. She slid it over the carpet and onto the kitchen linoleum, then dropped the cord. More letters spilled from the drawstring opening. "This all came in on the noon ferry," Bea explained. "And there's more on the way."

Birdie sat down hard in her kitchen chair.

"What are we going to do about this?" Bea lifted her hands. "Every deprived soul in Ogunquit must have heard about the Akerman's letter."

Biting her lower lip, Birdie cringed. "Great day in the morning, how could word have spread so quickly? I just sent the check Saturday."

Stepping over the heap of correspondence, Bea moved to the window and groaned. "Here comes Buddy with another sack—I told him to bring it to the back door. What are we going to do, Birdie?"

Birdie pressed her palm to her forehead. "Stay calm, Bea. Maybe there's been a mistake—all this mail can't be a result of us answering the Akerman's request. That'd be impossible."

At least Birdie hoped it was. Maybe she had been too hasty; perhaps she should have thought a little more and come up with a more indirect way to help the struggling family. But land sakes, who'd ever think one simple act of kindness could result in this madness?

Bea opened the back door, and Buddy stumbled in, the toe of his heavy boot catching on the threshold. The sack in his arms opened and mail flew in all directions.

For the next hour, Birdie, Bea, and Buddy sorted mail around the kitchen table, leaving Abner to run the bakery. In the two sacks of mail there were three bills for the Grahams, a jam and jelly catalog for Vernie Bidderman, a couple of cards for Olympia, and two hundred seventy-five angel letters from all over the nation.

"And one," Bea said, holding up a blue airmail envelope, "from Australia."

"How in the world?" Birdie asked for the twentieth time.

Her musings were interrupted by the sight of Vernie Bidderman on the back porch. "Hallo!" Vernie called, rapping on the glass. "Open up, Birdie, I see you all in there!"

Birdie looked at Bea. "Might as well let her in," she said. "If we're going to hear 'I told you so,' might as well start with our closest neighbor."

She blew a stray hank of hair off her forehead as Bea opened the door. Vernie marched in, but instead of offering a rebuke, she waved a sheet of paper.

"I solved it!" she said, her grin a mile wide. "I knew it had to be something like this."

Bea settled back into her chair. "Will you please speak sense, Vernie?"

Vernie plopped onto the footstool by the stove. "The Internet," she said, lifting a brow as she settled her glasses onto the end of her nose. "I got this note just this morning, via e-mail. Listen."

In a gravelly voice, she began to read:

Miracles are happening in Heavenly Daze! This is not a hoax! It's the honest truth, so pass this e-mail on to everyone you know!

Heavenly Daze, a tiny island off the coast of Maine, is inhabited by angels who will perform miracles for people who have faith enough to write and ask for one! Recent miracles have included tomatoes that grow in the winter, a man who grew a full head of hair overnight, and a dog who was pronounced dead, then got up and walked away!

Legend has it that Jacques de Cuvier, the original founder of the town, prayed that angels would forever inhabit his private island. His request was granted, and invisible angels have inhabited the island ever since.

So if you are missing something in your life, write a letter to the angels today. Just send your request to Heavenly Daze, Maine 09876.

Pass this on to at least twenty people! Bad luck will come your way if you don't!

P.S. This is true! I myself received a note from Bea Coughlin, postmistress of Heavenly Daze, who assured me she was an angel assistant!

Birdie stared wordlessly at her sister. Bea's eyes appeared to be at imminent risk of dropping right out of her face.

"That explains how they got the zip code," Buddy said, shrugging. "I never could remember it myself."

"The Internet." Bea lowered her chin and hissed the words. "A tool of the devil. Lies flying around in cyberspace, sent without a moment of rational thought. Unlike a properly posted letter—"

"That's the biggest bucket of poppycock I've ever heard in my life," Birdie interrupted, staring at the letters. "Why—there are no miracles here! Any man could put on a toupee, and Annie's tomatoes look like they're one leaf away from the compost pile. And what's that nonsense about a dog coming back to life? Who could have started this nonsense?"

"I suppose the dog is supposed to be Butch or Tallulah," Vernie said, grinning. "I'm a little offended they didn't mention MaGoo. I think a forty-five pound cat is a bit of a miracle."

"Some fool tourist must have started this mess," Bea said, nudging the empty mail sack. "We had a smattering of them last month, after all. But for sure there's no miracle here. It's all due to that blasted Internet."

"But the needs . . ." Birdie's eyes drifted back to the letters. "The needs are real. Listen to this one."

Dear Angel,

Can you make me stop feeling so sad? Daddy's gone to live at another little girl's house. I don't know what I did to make him so mad that he'd want to leave me and Mommy and live with somebody else. We miss him so much. Mommy cries and cries and then I start to cry and we can't stop. Can you please bring my daddy back home? I have faith, I really do. I try to think about the times when Daddy laughed a lot and he and Mommy held hands. Angel, please bring my daddy back so Mommy and me can laugh again.

Crissy Stillman, age nine

Birdie shook her head, murmuring a heartfelt, "Lord, help this child" under her breath.

Bea wiped her eyes, then opened another letter. She skimmed a few lines, then rolled her eyes and sent Birdie a smirking smile. "You're not gonna believe this one."

Yo Angel,

How about a motorcycle? I could use a new set of wheels. Like I really believe in angels. Duh.

Jake Foley
4957 Westminster Lane
Salt Lake City, Utah
(In case you try to find me. Duh.)

Birdie ripped open another envelope and read the first two lines. "Dear Angel, I am blind. Can you please make me see again?"

Shaking her head, Bea dropped her letter onto the pile. "Birdie, what have we done?"

The small group sat around the kitchen table, staring at the pile of correspondence. Birdie's heart ached, for herself and for Bea. Unlike the idiot who started the silly e-mail letter, they'd meant no harm; they'd only wanted to spread comfort and help a family in distress. The Lansdowns, Vernie, and Pastor Wickam had foreseen trouble and tried to avoid it, but she and Bea had recklessly pursued the matter, inadvertently encouraging more of this foolishness.

But still—the needs, or most of them, were real. And only God himself could grant some of these poignant petitions.

Birdie shook her head, feeling sick to her stomach. When would she learn not to meddle? First she'd meddled with Salt and his books, and now her impulsive nature was about to create trouble for the whole island.

"Well," Bea said, swiping her bangs off her forehead, "we have a choice. Either we toss these letters and ignore them, or we answer them."

"We can't toss them." Birdie looked at Vernie for confirmation. "Some of these people really need help. We can't send money to everybody, but we can offer a word of encouragement . . . though I'm not sure I'd refer to myself as an angel assistant."

"Definitely not," Bea remarked dryly. "So—why don't we just write a note that says we're praying and God loves them? That's true, and it's innocent."

"Sounds good to me," Birdie said, standing to fetch pen and paper.

"As much as I'd love to stay and help," Vernie said, rising, "I have a store to run."

Buddy stood, too, and gestured toward the door. "And I have to . . . um, go."

Bea rolled her eyes as they left, then sat down and set to work. As the afternoon rolled on, Abner came in and took a seat, silently pitching in to help.

Throughout the long afternoon, Birdie, Bea, and Abner answered letters as simply and truthfully as they could. Only the occasional compassionate pressure of Abner's hand on her shoulder stilled Birdie's chaotic thoughts.

At five o'clock, Birdie put on a heavy coat and left the bakery carrying a shopping bag filled with a loaf of rye bread and two dozen molasses cookies.

Island shadows lengthened as she walked down the alley between the post office and the bakery; it would be full dark soon. She hugged the flashlight in her pocket, reassuring herself before heading into the night. A crisp walk was just what she needed; it ought to clear her head.

She strode toward the cove, intending to cross the salt marsh and catch Ferry Road well past the municipal building. By now everyone in

Heavenly Daze knew about the influx of letters, and right now she couldn't face Cleta or Floyd. Vernie's copy of that preposterous e-mail had proved Birdie didn't cause the deluge, but the embellishment on that silly note indicated that she and Bea might have inadvertently added fuel to the fire.

She paused when she heard male voices. Ducking behind the carriage house where Vernie's helper, Elezar, lived, she saw Buddy and Captain Stroble straining to carry two more burgeoning mail sacks to her own back porch.

Was she only imagining the captain's enough-is-enough look? Probably not. No spring chicken, the captain wasn't used to ferrying this volume of mail. And he'd never had to make two mail deliveries in one day.

Turning quickly lest they see her, she picked up her pace and hurried toward the lighthouse. Maybe she was in a masochistic mood tonight. What else would drive her into Salt Gribbon's territory after a marathon session of answering angel mail? What was she thinking?

Hadn't she had enough humiliation for one day?

She answered her own question—she yearned for a strong dose of Salt Gribbon's no-nonsense approach to life.

In the distance, the large rotating lamp atop the lighthouse swept the cold waters, warning ships away from the jagged coastline. Commercial fisherman and shipping lines knew enough to stay away from the rocks at the north point of Heavenly Daze, but still the beam shone out, lest an ignorant pleasure boater turn his vessel into the rocks. Birdie suspected the job gave Salt comfort—the radiant light shining over the waters must be a sentimental reminder of long ago days when he'd spied the light and realized he'd come safely home.

The tang of briny water hung in the air and she drank it in. A buoy bell clanged as it steadily rode the swells near the shoreline.

Clang, clang, clang.

She matched her strides to the rhythm of the bell and pushed on as lengthening shadows gave way to smoky dusk. Shorebirds flew overhead, soaring into the encroaching darkness as they searched for a place to roost.

Birdie switched on the flashlight and let the beam play over the rocky road.

She lifted her head when a light shone out a window at the midpoint of the lighthouse—Salt's living quarters, she presumed. Had he seen her light? Was he now pulling on his coat so he could step out and investigate the intruder? He'd warned her and everyone else to stay away, and he wouldn't be happy about her visit. But as long as he didn't start throwing rocks . . .

She plodded on, her arguments growing stronger with every step. Salt Gribbon didn't own this part of the island, and he didn't own the lighthouse. He might not care for her audacity, but he couldn't prevent her from coming out to visit one of Heavenly Daze's historical treasures. Besides—she gripped the bakery bag tighter—genuine trespassers didn't bring gifts, and she'd brought a generous rye and some of Abner's best cookies. He could refuse her offering, but he couldn't order her away from Puffin Cove.

The cold air served its purpose and Birdie felt her head begin to clear. The dull ache between her shoulders receded and tension slowly drained away. The sea had that effect on her. Out here a body could rediscover peace and harmony amid the sound of crashing surf.

The lighthouse rose up before her, tall, dark, and forbidding. She looked up, then shivered in a moment of inexplicable panic. What was she doing? Coming out here, acting like a schoolgirl suffering from her first crush. "You old fool," she whispered. "He's going to think you're positively addled."

Veering off the path, she picked her way over the rocky shoreline, stepping carefully over sea-sprayed rocks. The night was full dark now, spangled with a canopy of gleaming stars overhead.

Settling on a large boulder, she opened the bag of cookies and ate one. She'd had no appetite at supper, though the meatloaf Bea had in the oven smelled tempting. Sunday Winslow had remarked that Bea's cooking couldn't be beat, then amended the remark to "Bea's cooking is really great" when Edith's lower lip edged forward in a tiny pout.

Munching on the cookie, Birdie considered the choices she'd made in her life. Maybe she should have married and had children. But she'd always preferred books to men, and it seemed natural for her to go to college and major in library science. Now, at sixty-five, she was living with her choices . . . and with her sister. If anything happened to Bea, she would be utterly alone.

Twenty years ago the prospect of loneliness hadn't given her a moment's thought, but tonight it rested like a shroud around her shoulders. If she had her life to live over, maybe she would have looked harder for a companion, been less picky . . .

"What are you doing here?"

Startled by the voice, Birdie drew in her breath, accidentally inhaling a bit of cookie into her windpipe. Choking, she spat what she could onto the rocks, then grasped her throat with both hands. She stood in panic, then whirled around to meet the wintry blue eyes of Salt Gribbon.

Stepping forward, Salt soundly whacked her on the back. The obstruction popped loose.

Gasping for air, Birdie lowered her lids and glared at him. "You scared a year's growth out of me!"

A wicked grin hovered at the corners of the old sea captain's mouth, and in that moment Birdie realized he must have been quite a scoundrel in his day. She pressed her hand to her belly, aware that a crop of butterflies had awakened and decided to perform handsprings in her midsection.

Salt's grin widened to a roguish smile. "At our age, Birdie, you ought to be thanking me for the excitement."

He sat down as if he'd been invited, then stared out at the sea. Without looking at her, he asked, "What are you doing wandering around the island at this time of night?"

Birdie lifted her chin and gave him a defiant look—which he didn't turn to see. "You don't own this point, Salt Gribbon," she said, feeling proud of her courage. "A body has a right to come out here if she wants." She thrust the bakery bag at him. "Have a cookie."

Opening the bag, he peered inside. "What's this?"

"What does it look like?"

He sniffed the offering appreciably. "Rye bread. Molasses cookies."

She sat on the rock, careful not to sit too close. "I didn't eat supper. Thought I might get hungry on my walk. So I grabbed the first thing I could reach in the display case as I went out the door." She kept her eyes on the feather-white sea, refusing to meet his eyes in the dim light of the rising moon. "Don't try and make anything out of the fact it's your favorite bread and cookies. Your preferences didn't have a thing to do with my selections."

Grinning, he bit into a cookie. "Of course not," he mumbled around the mouthful.

"I wasn't thinkin' of you a-tall."

"Didn't say you were."

"I wasn't."

"Didn't think so."

"Don't flatter yourself."

He snorted, and for a moment Birdie wondered if he was laughing. Salt Gribbon, laughing? Who'd athunk it?

A cold wind blew off the water, but a zillion stars twinkled overhead. Birdie suddenly felt warm and young and foolishly giddy. Age was creeping up on Salt Gribbon, but it hadn't overpowered him, not a-tall. He was still handsome enough to make her heart beat double time.

They sat for a long stretch, neither speaking. Birdie found the companionable silence . . . nice.

She finally brought her hands to her face, exhaling a long breath as she thought about the day's events. "I've done a foolish thing, Salt."

"I'm listening."

Those words weren't a comforting arm or a gentle touch, but at sixty-five, Birdie knew enough to take what she could get.

She spoke slowly at first, then her words tumbled over one another as she told him about the letters, Raleigh Akerman, and that silly e-mail about angel inhabitants. "And now," she finished, "I'm afraid that news about the money we sent will leak out to the Internet—what if this keeps going and growing? We can't send money to every off-islander who writes us."

She stopped, out of words and out of energy, and looked at him. He nodded simply, then said, "You did the right thing."

Birdie nodded, wiping the corners of her eyes with her fingertips. She knew she'd done what the Lord expected, but it was nice to hear support instead of ridicule.

She sniffed. "The letters will continue to come, I fear. There will be more requests and pleas for all kinds of impossible things. We're trying to answer these people by telling them that we're praying and God loves them, but there aren't any angels in Heavenly Daze—only good, kind people who can't perform miracles."

"Ayuh, but maybe by writing a simple letter, the healing is begun." Salt stared at the lapping waters with a molasses cookie in his large hand. "Children will write expressing their wants. They may not get that new bicycle, basketball, or pair of gym shoes, but they'll know someone cared enough to answer. If writing a simple letter to Heavenly Daze brings them the assurance that God is love, what could be the harm?"

"The harm will be that the island could be overrun with people seeking favors from invisible angels," Birdie fretted.

Salt turned to look at her, his rangy features silhouetted in the moonlight. "Is the North Pole overrun with energetic children seeking toy trains and video games?"

Birdie laughed softly. "I couldn't say, having never been to the North Pole. But Heavenly Daze is a lot more accessible, and who knows what could happen?"

"Don't borrow trouble, Birdie. See what tomorrow brings." Salt folded his hands. "The flood of mail might be over and forgotten in a few days."

"Vernie and Cleta won't forget."

"Well, that would be Vernie's and Cleta's problem, wouldn't it?"

Somehow, and Birdie couldn't imagine how, Salt had put the problem into perspective. She'd done what she felt the Lord was leading her to do, so she'd done the right thing by sending the money to little Raleigh. And three or four sacks of mail wasn't a gargantuan task; she and Bea and Abner could handle those letters. She could get Vernie to write an e-mail that said, "No Angels in Heavenly Daze, Pass it On," and maybe the letters would stop. Of course, some folks might find that notion a little unfriendly, but it was better than giving people false hope. And, finally, if their letters could renew hope in a desperate heart . . . well, the whole enterprise would have been worth the stress.

Feeling considerably better, she took a deep breath and sat up straighter. Salt was right; she was borrowing trouble by worrying about tomorrow, and the good Lord clearly said today had its sufficient share.

"So," she said, turning to a more upbeat—she hoped—topic, "how's your situation progressing?"

His brows lowered, meeting in the center of his face as his eyes darkened.

He was defensive as always, but she wouldn't give up. She turned to face him directly. "Are you making progress with your little problem?"

"With what?"

"With . . . your situation."

Did she have to spell it out for him? He was so touchy she didn't dare come right out and ask, but she was dying to know if he'd used the primer.

"Nothing's changed," he said shortly. He stood up, so she followed suit. They lingered for a moment, allowing the sound of the sea to embrace them. The earlier feeling of easy companionship had waned, and Birdie knew the altered mood was her fault.

But she so wanted to help!

"Salt," she began again, "I wish you would let me help you. Abner can watch the bakery a few hours every day—"

"No!" The bark rang with so much authority and prickly defensiveness that she drew back.

But she didn't give up. "Together we could make good progress."

He turned and stalked off, denying her the opportunity to finish her thought. And the stubborn old noodle had left the bag of pastries on the rock.

Oh, no. He wasn't walking away, not this time. She snatched up the bag, then hurried to catch up. If he would allow her to share the burden, she could have him reading in only a few days. What joy awaited him in the world of books, and he'd find so many things to occupy his time in that lonely lighthouse.

She trotted to keep pace with his long-legged stride. He might not want her tutoring services but he was going to accept the rye bread and cookies or watch her feed them to the sea gulls!

"Go home, Birdie Wester. Leave me with my peace."

"I'm going, Salt Gribbon, but I'm leaving you with cookies and rye bread!"

She flung the bag at him, then spun on her heel, snapped on her flashlight, and began the walk home. That old codger was impossible!

Shaking his head, Salt watched her flounce off.

Women!

Why would Birdie Wester want to help him? She had to have her hands full at the bakery.

He couldn't accept her offer of help even if he wanted to. His secret must remain hidden behind the walls of the lighthouse, and no matter how good Birdie was about keeping a promise, if she walked out to the point often enough, suspicions were sure to arise. Floyd and Cleta Lansdown would come to investigate, then word would spread to Vernie Bidderman or that persistent pastor. If even one of them found out about the kids, it wouldn't be long before the authorities from Social Services would come to seize his grandchildren.

His smile died as he watched Birdie disappear into darkness. He couldn't lose those kids. Their future lay in his hands, and he would protect their welfare with every ounce of his strength.

He shoved his fists in his pockets and started to walk up the hill, then remembered the bakery bag on the ground. His smile returned.

Molasses cookies and rye bread.

Walking back to pick up the bag, he snapped a salute toward his visitor's retreating figure.

"You're a right seaworthy vessel, Birdie Wester," he conceded, bending to pick up her goodwill offering, "but the knots in your riggin' are a little loose."

Zuriel had just turned out the lamp and pillowed his head when the tiny hairs at the back of his neck lifted in awareness of a supernatural presence in the room. His eyes flew open, his body tensing to do battle if necessary, then his heart slowed when he recognized the gentle features of Gavriel, the captain of the angelic host assigned to Heavenly Daze.

"Greetings," Zuriel said, sitting up in his bed. His surprise yielded quickly to alarm when he glanced at the clock: 11:14 P.M. Good news did not often come at such a late hour. "Is something wrong?" he asked.

Gavriel's smile dispelled his fears. "No, Zuriel, rest easy. I've come with a message from the Lord."

Zuriel felt his pulse quicken. Strange, that after so many years in a mortal body, the functioning of the physical mechanisms that signaled alarm and excitement still caught him by surprise.

"The Lord wants to see me?" He tilted his head, considering this development. The Lord usually sent messages through Gavriel, who regularly traveled to the third heaven to give progress reports. Though the Spirit, omniscient and omnipresent, moved among them at all times, the routine reporting sessions were an occasion to measure the angels' progress and plot their future course. Gavriel had always been a capable captain, and Zuriel could not recall the last time one of the lower ranking angels had been summoned from Heavenly Daze to the throne room.

He cleared his throat and tried not to look nervous. "Do you have any idea why the Lord wants to see me?"

Gavriel had a diplomat's face—almost anything could have been going on behind his expression of powerful concern. He smiled and shook his head. "I was not given a reason, only the command. You are to report to the throne room immediately." He paused, lifting a golden brow. "Would you like an escort?"

Zuriel bit his lip. Though he once could have covered the great distance between earth and the Highest Heaven in a heartbeat, the angels had not been able to travel unimpeded since Adam's sin gave a foothold to the prince of the power of the air. Satan's fallen angels regularly wreaked havoc in the second heaven, once mightily impeding an angelic messenger sent to the prophet Daniel for twenty-one days. Zuriel was not afraid of Satan's dark forces, for their rebellion had long ago sealed their fates, but he would hate to arrive in the Holy Place disheveled and delayed . . .

"If you wouldn't mind," he met Gavriel's gaze, "I would appreciate your company. It's been a long time."

Gavriel's dark eyes softened with kindness. "I would be honored to travel with you."

He stepped back and gestured toward the door. "Shall we go?"

Swallowing his rising emotion, Zuriel swung his legs out of the bed, raked his hands through his graying hair, then nodded.

Zuriel's soul lifted like the celestial winds that carried them upward faster than the speed of light. His earthly body tingled as it transformed into a supernatural vessel capable of interdimensional travel. As he passed from the physical realm into the spiritual, the atmosphere around him hummed with the prayers of souls on earth and in the heaven above.

Passing through the sharp, thin air, he parsed the sounds much as humans would breathe in a campfire and distinguish wood smoke from sizzling steaks. The prayers of saints rose around him, robust petitions from aged believers on their deathbeds mingling with the sweet faith-filled recitations of children who still saw God as a cross between a loving parent and Santa Claus.

With spiritual eyes, he saw forms gliding past him—heavenly messengers sent to comfort the afflicted children of God and angelic escorts to bring the dying home. His nerves tensed as he neared the invisible boundary separating the earth's atmosphere from the second heaven, but no satanic minions appeared at the perimeter.

He smiled at Gavriel, grateful for the other angel's support. The powerful angelic captain had often traveled this path; perhaps the diabolical ones had learned to refrain from harassing him.

Without a single encounter with evil, they traversed the border of the Highest Heaven. Zuriel blinked, his spirit eyes stunned again by the brightness of the holy Temple. The scents of incense and sweet praise filled the air, and a majestic musical chorus drew him and Gavriel toward the Holy of Holies just as a river's current draws all things toward the sea.

As they descended to the polished marble balcony surrounding the Temple of God, Zuriel glanced behind him and exhaled a quiet sound of surprise at what he saw there.

Gavriel laughed softly. "I understand," he said, his feet soundlessly touching the golden floor. "Sometimes I forget about my wings, too. We can grow too accustomed to mortal flesh."

A group of angels drew near, their faces alight with curiosity and the glorious light of heaven, a sure sign they had not spent much time on earth. Zuriel remembered how in ages past he, too, once looked upon returning messengers with fascination, hoping to catch one alone in order to hear stories of God's work on earth. Now he was the veteran minister, the one to whom an important task had been entrusted.

Tucking his wings behind his back, he followed Gavriel, walking in the wake of looks of honor and respect directed at the angel captain and Zuriel realized with surprise—at him.

He moved in the direction of the music, allowing the swelling strains of praise to pull him toward the One who made all things possible. As he walked, his head lifted to the vast majesty of the eternal heavens in which no sun dwelt, no moon ruled. This place lay in a dimension beyond earthly time and space, for in God there was no beginning and no end, no day or night, no yesterday or tomorrow. The One who was always had been and always would be.

Heaven's music swelled toward them, coming from the twenty-four harpists who sat around the throne of God, playing instruments unlike any ever seen or heard on earth. Behind the harpists, the four living creatures, the highest class of angels, sang, "Holy, holy, holy, Lord God Almighty, who was and is and is to come!"

A rainbow, brighter than the earth's finest emeralds and sapphires and rubies, encircled the throne, and from the center of the circle fire flashed while thunder pealed and rumbled. Immediately before the throne, seven bright lamps on golden stands blazed brighter than a thousand suns.

Waves of holy light radiated from the throne, and Zuriel felt his spirit shrink as he encountered the majesty and glory of God. When in the Lord's presence he never failed to feel small . . . and amazed that the Almighty took notice of him.

All around Zuriel, scores of cherubim waved palm branches before the throne of God, as the sons of men had once waved them before the Lord on his triumphal entry into Jerusalem. Zuriel's eyes, so long accustomed to the timid light of the sun, watered as he beheld the glory of the Lord most high, full of grace and truth.

The Lamb's throne rested upon two pillars, each inscribed in the original seventy human tongues. The left pillar bore the word *righteousness,* the right the word *justice.* Above the throne hovered a pair of the mighty seraphim, their beating wings softly stirring the rarefied atmosphere.

Slowly, Zuriel shifted his gaze to behold the One seated upon the throne. The Lamb of God wore a robe as white as snow, and even his hair gleamed brighter than the hottest star. As his hands extended in greeting, the sleeves fell away, revealing the indentations that marked each wrist—the only man-made marks in heaven.

The Lamb's eyes softened with acknowledgement when Zuriel met his gaze.

"Zuriel, servant of the Most High . . . welcome home."

Zuriel bowed his head, aware of his humble status before the Lord God, then answered over his choking, beating heart. "Thank you, Lord."

As the Lord stood, the harpists softened their music. "Zuriel," Jesus said, moving closer. He smiled, eagerness and tenderness mingled in his expression. "You have done well, faithful servant. We have been watching your work with Charles and Babette Graham."

Zuriel lifted his gaze to study the Savior's face. He found no condemnation there, no rancor or blame. So why had he been summoned from his post?

"You have a command for me?" he asked, finding his voice. "You have but to speak it."

"I have a special concern." Laugh lines crinkled around the Savior's blazing eyes, then his expression stilled and grew serious. "I am especially concerned about young Georgie."

Zuriel blinked in surprise. He knew the Savior held children in high esteem. During his earthly ministry the Lamb had often called boys and girls to his side, even telling his followers that unless they became as little children, they could not enter the kingdom of heaven.

Zuriel lifted his head. "Shall I give Georgie a message from you?"

"Not Georgie." For an instant, wistfulness stole into Jesus' expression. "You must speak to his mother. She holds a precious prize in her grasp, but she has become blind to its value. You must remind her, Zuriel, that anyone who causes one of the little ones who trust in me to lose faith, it would be better for that person to be thrown into the sea tied to a millstone." The Lamb paused, and when he spoke again, his voice was low and urgent. "A son's soul is worth more than any earthly treasure. You must show Babette how she has been blessed."

Zuriel nodded as one corner of his mouth lifted in a smile. "I'll speak to her tomorrow, after the earth's sunrise."

"Even sooner." Jesus' voice cut through the heavenly sounds and scents and sensations until it touched Zuriel's very soul. "In the time you call tomorrow Georgie will need his mother, and she must not be distracted."

Zuriel fell to one knee, bowing again, then felt Jesus' hand upon his shoulder, urging him up. As Zuriel turned to leave the throne room, a chorus of "Holy, Holy, Holy" rose in a crescendo behind him.

At the gleaming entrance to the holy chamber, however, a group of angels approached in a tumult of festivity, their faces shining like meteors streaking across the black night. Zuriel recognized the familiar procession—this was an arrival celebration. A saint had departed the temporal earth, and the angels had gathered to welcome him to paradise.

Anxious to be away, he tugged on his captain's sleeve. "Gavriel, we should go."

"We can watch," Gavriel answered, folding his hands as they paused beside the golden avenue. "You forget, we are beyond time now." His handsome face shone as he smiled. "Many earth years have passed since you've seen one of these, no?" His smile deepened. "You may find this homecoming . . . particularly appealing."

Zuriel wasn't sure what Gavriel's comment meant, but his heart pounded in nostalgic anticipation as the air filled with the ecstatic cries of angels who had shielded another soul from the darts of the evil one. Like spears of flame whistling overhead, first came the warrior angels who had sheltered this human from the onslaught of demons who had shrieked and wailed and tried, ineffectively, to cower the soul already redeemed by the Lamb. The ministering angels, tall, regal beings whose faces had been molded by love, followed the warriors, and behind the ministers came the guardian angels, a mixed multitude of warriors, messengers, and comforting angels who had aided this human on the many occasions of his life—a long life, Zuriel estimated, judging by how many angels approached in that throng. All had been summoned as the man's soul prepared to leave its earthly abode, and now all of them rejoiced to finally welcome this child of God to the fellowship for which he had been created. This human, created of dust and stationed only a little lower than the angels, would now enjoy fellowship with the eternal Lord.

As Zuriel and Gavriel watched from a far corner of the throne room, the harpists' music fell to a reverent hush as the foremost angelic troops settled around the throne. At an unspoken signal, they turned, then the spirit of a human and his angelic escort crossed the threshold of the Holy Place. Zuriel felt a jolt as he recognized the one who had guided this child of God from human death to spiritual life: Caleb, an angelic resident of Heavenly Daze.

The human was present in spirit alone, for the resurrection of his body would not be accomplished until the Lamb appeared in the heavens to summon his Bride. Even so, Zuriel could not mistake the identity of the soul moving toward him. In an awed whisper he breathed the name: "Edmund de Cuvier, of Frenchman's Fairest." No wonder Caleb was beaming!

Gavriel crossed his mighty arms. "I knew Edmund's time was near—how fortunate that we should be allowed to witness his homecoming."

Zuriel smiled, amazed at the change in the man. Though Edmund's faith had never wavered through his illness, his strong spirit had seemed shriveled when Zuriel last saw him on the island of Heavenly Daze. His courage had dwindled with his physical body, and pain had erased all the outward signs of joy. His memory had been muddled by prescription drugs; his enthusiasm sapped by the inescapable knowledge that he would never rise from his sickbed. His flesh, what little of it remained, had gone thin and translucent, mere tissue covering sharp bones and an embroidery of blue veins.

But now—ah, the difference heaven made! Though wrought of spirit and invisible to human eyes, Zuriel could see that Edmund de Cuvier now radiated joy and peace. Clothed in strength and vigor, he fluttered into the throne room like a child testing a new jet pack, then settled before the throne with a look of adoration upon his glowing features.

"My servant Edmund, beloved of God." The Lamb's greeting was as warm as an embrace. "Welcome home."

"My Lord and my God," Edmund whispered, his voice atremble with joy. "How my soul has longed for this place, for you!"

As the living creatures broke out into another hymn of praise to the Lamb who had made Edmund's homecoming possible, Gavriel touched Zuriel's shoulder. "We must go back," he said, levitating from the floor. He tilted his head toward the inky blackness beyond, where stars gleamed like scattered diamonds over an endless succession of galaxies. "Come."

Misty-eyed over the scene he'd witnessed, Zuriel thumbed a tear from his cheek, then rose through the celestial air and followed Gavriel.

After materializing within the privacy of his cottage, Zuriel moved to the window and studied the larger house. A light still burned in the kitchen—which meant that either Charles had wandered in for a cup of milk and forgotten to flip the switch, or Babette was still working at her desk.

He glanced at the digital clock across the room: 11:15 P.M. Babette rarely stayed up this late.

Thoughtfully considering his task, he opened the cottage door and stepped out into the night, the cold air shivering his mortal flesh. After the glorious warmth of the throne room, he suspected even a balmy spring night would have felt frigid.

Hurrying across the yard, he came to the back door and rapped upon it. Shivering, he thrust his hands into his jeans pockets and hoped the Spirit had prodded Babette to remain awake. This message would be easier to deliver if she had been prepared to receive it.

A moment later, the frilled curtain at the door lifted, then her face appeared in the window. Her tense expression relaxed at the sight of him, then the curtain fell and he heard the sound of the latch being lifted.

"Zuriel," she scolded as she opened the door, "what are you doing out here without your coat? You'll catch your death of pneumonia."

He couldn't stop a smile. "I don't think so."

She closed the door behind him, then frowned and pulled her robe together at her neck. "Something wrong? You're not usually up this late."

"Neither are you."

"No." A frown puckered the skin between her brows. "But I can't sleep." She moved toward the stove, where the teakettle was beginning to rattle on the burner. "Want something hot to drink? I've got instant mixes for cocoa, or I could always make tea—"

"Babette, I have a message for you."

Raising fine, arched eyebrows, she looked at him. "Really?" Her voice was dry. "From whom?"

"From the Father."

Lifting the kettle from the stove, Babette made a faint move of distaste. "I knew Charles was annoyed with me, but sending you to carry his messages is too much."

Zuriel coughed slightly as she began to pour water into mugs. "Not Charles. The Father of all who believe. My message is from God."

Babette froze, the teapot in her hand, then threw Zuriel a quick glance of disbelief. "God's been talking to you?"

He smiled, for his fellow angels had often commented on the irony in their situation. These people, who benefited daily from the presence of immortal ministers, often found it difficult to believe in the very God who guarded them. They sang about him, prayed to him, and made all sorts of midnight confessions and resolutions, but when it came down to daily reality, few of them were really willing to trust him with the details of their lives.

"God would speak to you, too," he said, couching his message in terms she ought to understand and accept, "if you would listen."

The frown reappeared between her brows as she began to pour again. "I've had a lot on my mind, Zuriel."

"God knows. That's why he wanted me to give you a message."

She sighed heavily, puffing the bangs away from her forehead, then set the teapot upon a frayed potholder. "You didn't answer—tea or cocoa?"

He frowned at the distraction. "Cocoa."

She tossed him a foil packet, then pushed a steaming mug toward him. While he fumbled with the package, she slid into a chair at the kitchen table and propped her head on her hand. "Okay, let's hear it," she said, ignoring her own cup of hot water. "What does God want me to know?"

Grateful for the opportunity to speak freely, Zuriel dropped the foil packet and sat in the chair opposite her. Leaning forward on his elbows, he caught her weary gaze and held it.

"You," he began, choosing his words carefully, "have been richly blessed with a son. You hold a precious treasure in your grasp, but you have become blind to its true value. Your son's soul is worth more than any earthly riches."

Babette stared at him blankly for a moment, then a spark of irritation entered her blue eyes. "That's it?"

Zuriel nodded.

"Well." She dropped her hand and looked around the room as if searching for something. "Thank you, Z, for that lovely bit of advice."

Watching her, Zuriel weighed the effect of his words. After a moment, the trace of irritation disappeared from her eyes, and her face went blank, almost as if she were wearing a mask. Moving slowly, stiffly, she pulled a teabag from the pottery canister in the center of her table, unwrapped it with jerky gestures, then dropped it into the steaming mug.

"I have never knowingly done anything to hurt my son," she said, her tone defensive. She fixed her gaze on the teabag, trailing it through the water with the string over the tip of her fingernail. "I love Georgie more than anything."

Zuriel did not answer. He had delivered the message and fulfilled his responsibility. How she chose to receive the word of the Lord—well, like angels, humans had free will.

"I think I've been a good mother." Her gaze shifted to meet Zuriel's, then thawed slightly. "Haven't I?"

"I think you're a fine mother." Searching for something to do, Zuriel ripped open his packet of cocoa, dumped the powder into his mug, then reached for a spoon. "Millions of children are far less fortunate than George."

"But you think I've been doing something wrong."

"I didn't say that."

"You implied it."

"I am not a judge. I am only a messenger."

She yanked the teabag up by the string and let it fall to the table with a wet plop. "So, speaking for God—that's more your style."

Zuriel closed his eyes as a blush burned the top of his cheekbones. "God uses whomever he chooses. Whoever is willing."

She snorted softly. "Even Balaam's donkey, right?"

Smiling, he looked at her. "I've heard that was an exceptionally intelligent animal."

"Well, then." After taking a perfunctory sip of her tea, Babette pushed back her chair and tightened the belt of her robe. "I think I'll get started on my baking. I was about to mix up a blueberry gingerbread when you knocked."

Zuriel accepted his cue and stood as well. "You'll want to make some extra for Olympia. I don't imagine she or Caleb will feel much like baking tomorrow."

The thin line of Babette's mouth clamped tight for a moment. "What do you mean?"

Too late, Zuriel realized he'd relayed sensitive information. But he couldn't lie to cover his tracks . . . and Babette would hear the story in a few hours, anyway. She'd probably assume he'd talked to Caleb or Dr. Marc.

He met her questioning gaze with his best look of compassion. "Edmund de Cuvier went home tonight," he said simply. "He's rejoicing before the throne right now."

A tremor passed over Babette's face, then a spasm of grief knit her brows. "Oh, poor Olympia! Though she was expecting it, I know this has to hurt."

"I think," Zuriel spoke slowly, measuring each word, "Olympia will be fine. When a man is suffering the pain of the disintegrating human condition, heaven is a tremendous blessing. Even though Edmund dearly loved his wife, I know he wouldn't exchange his heavenly home for his frail earthly tabernacle."

Despite her compassionate expression, one of Babette's brows lifted. "You know this for a fact."

Zuriel gave her a wry smile. "I do."

"I can tell you've never been married." Shaking her head, Babette moved toward the pantry. "I wouldn't go around town telling folks that Edmund was eager to go," she called as she pulled canisters of flour and sugar from the shelf. "Most people like to think they'll be missed . . . and most wives want to believe their husbands would move heaven and earth in order to remain with them."

Zuriel scratched his beard. Babette had to be tired, or she wouldn't be making such ludicrous statements. Why any child of God would want to linger in a temporary body on a temporary planet . . . the logic escaped him.

After thanking her for the cocoa, he took his mug and stepped out into the chilly night.

Babette sighed as she latched the back door. Zuriel was a wonderful tenant and a talented potter, but sometimes he seemed almost childlike in his naiveté. Though he had to be a good ten years older than her, she often thought he behaved as though he'd spent his entire life in that sheltered little cottage, throwing bowls and vases and pitchers of clay. His strong religious views dominated his viewpoints, but never before had he exhibited the audacity he had tonight—

Speaking for God? How dare he tell her to mind her mothering!

Sudden tears clouded her vision as she pulled her gingerbread recipe from her notebook. She was a good mother . . . at least, she tried to be. She lavished as much love, attention, and discipline upon Georgie as she could, always striving for the proper balance of each. And despite his distracted dreaminess, Charles was a devoted father. Georgie had bucketfuls of love and attention from each of his parents, so what in the world was Zuriel trying to say?

"One-half cup shortening." She read the first ingredient aloud, then moved to the pantry, but the memory of Zuriel's words would not leave her brain. "At least," she told herself as she lifted the shortening from the shelf, "you know Z loves Georgie nearly as much as you do. Maybe he's seen something you've missed."

Her mother had always told her to listen carefully to rebuke. No matter how unfair or unwarranted it seemed, often strong words contained a kernel of truth . . .

Moving slowly, she walked back to the counter and methodically creamed the shortening, added salt and sugar, then picked up an egg. She cracked the shell on the edge of the counter, then watched the white stream toward the bowl as she held the yolk in the broken half-shell. Let the unimportant drift away, and keep what is good. And what had Zuriel said? That she had been richly blessed with Georgie. That Georgie's soul was worth more than earthly riches . . . and that she had become blind to his value.

Utterly ridiculous. Of course she knew her son was worth more than anything on earth. She'd endured sixteen hours of labor to bring him into the world, and she'd gladly endure whatever she must to keep him in the world. She'd give her life for him, her time, her energy . . . She dropped the yolk into the mixing bowl as her thoughts drifted to the puffin paintings. Had her actions of late given Zuriel the impression that she cared more for things than for her beloved son?

Surely not. Everything she did—from the meals she prepared to the puffin-based budget she had designed—she did to benefit her husband and son. Anyone who knew her could see that she was a loving, dedicated mother.

With a quick, sharp motion, she tossed the eggshell into the garbage. She had more important things to think about than Zuriel's well-intentioned words. She needed to make dishes for her family and Olympia's and give serious consideration to Thanksgiving dinner.

After mixing a double batch of her famous blueberry gingerbread, Babette poured the mix into two square pans, sprinkled the top of the batter with sugar, then slid each pan into the oven. After setting the oven timer for sixty minutes, she crossed the kitchen and picked up the telephone. She paused before dialing Frenchman's Fairest, wondering if a midnight call might be ill-advised.

Surely not. With a death in the house, someone was bound to be awake. Olympia or Caleb would be calling the minister, arranging for the funeral director to pick up the body, and overseeing the thousand details one had to consider after someone died.

She dialed the number, then leaned back against the counter as the phone rang. When no one answered on the first or second ring, she considered hanging up, but then a sleepy voice answered: "Hello?"

Babette recognized the voice of Annie Cuvier, Olympia and Edmund's niece.

"Hi, honey." Babette lowered her voice to a sympathetic whisper. "I heard the news. Is your aunt okay?"

"Aunt Olympia?" Annie's voice rose in pitch. "Shouldn't she be?"

"Well—" Babette hesitated. Was it possible Caleb and Olympia were keeping the news from Annie? Of course not, the girl was a grown woman. But she was behaving as if she didn't have a clue about what had happened under her own roof.

"Let me speak to Caleb, honey," Babette said, injecting a note of assurance into her voice. The old butler would know what to do. He knew everything that happened in Frenchman's Fairest.

Annie yawned audibly. "I think he's asleep."

"I'm pretty sure he's awake." Babette forced a note of steel into her voice. Maybe Annie was in shock or denial, and she needed someone to be firm with her. "Just go wake him up, okay?"

The phone dropped to a desk or some other hard surface, and a full three minutes passed before Babette heard anything. Then Annie said, "Caleb's not here! He's not in his bed!"

"What about your aunt?"

"Just a minute, she was sleeping in Uncle Edmund's room . . ."

The phone dropped again, then Babette heard the heavy thumping of bare feet upon a wooden floor. A longer silence followed, then a heartrending wail split the static humming in Babette's ear.

Slowly, she lowered the phone back into the cradle.

Annie hadn't known.

She had obviously gone to her uncle's room to find Olympia and Caleb, then had discovered what Zuriel already knew—Edmund was gone.

To heaven, Z said.

Babette slid into her chair at the kitchen table and brought her thumb to her mouth, clicking the edge of her thumbnail against her teeth as she considered the impossible.

Sleep, when it finally came to Babette, did not bring rest. She dreamed of working in her kitchen, her mixing bowl filled with mud instead of dough, the warmth in her kitchen radiating from Zuriel's kiln instead of her oven. The potter himself sat at her kitchen table, and his electric wheel occupied the center space usually filled with flowers and salt-and-pepper shakers.

Zuriel did not speak in her dream but waited patiently for her to supply the clay. Bewildered by the stiff mud around her wooden spoon, she handed the bowl to him without a word, then watched as he pulled living, pliant clay from the glass.

Babette had watched Zuriel work at his wheel before, so she wasn't surprised when he centered and rounded the clay with scarcely any effort. In the dream, however, his hands seemed to flutter over the spinning earth with a lightning quick touch. When the wheel slowed and stopped spinning, she saw that the piece was not a bowl, but an image—a softly sculptured, deftly molded statue of Georgie.

"But why not a jar?" she asked, marveling at the lifelike creases around the little boy's smile. "The tourists like the stoneware jars. I don't know if I'll ever be able to sell this statue."

Zuriel looked at her then, but something in his appearance had subtly altered. The man sitting there still wore Zuriel's shaggy brown hair and beard, but the eyes were brighter and wiser, scanning her own as if they could see down into her heart and fathom every secret of her soul. "Jars of clay are nothing special," he said, his voice crashing over her with the force of a rogue wave. "Their only purpose is to draw attention to what they contain."

Blinking, she stared at the statue, which seemed to breathe and tremble with life. The potter brought his hand up, extended his thumb, and deftly smoothed a watery streak from the statue's cheek.

Babette felt her heart twist. A tear?

"What," she asked, searching for some purpose in the beautiful object before her, "is this designed to contain? There's no opening, so it can't be a vase. There's no slot, so it can't hold coins."

"Not coins." The potter's hand dropped and gently covered hers. "This clay holds something far more precious."

"What?"

The potter—who, though he wore Zuriel's splotchy overalls and Zuriel's face, definitely was *not* Zuriel—gave her a heart-stopping smile. "This clay, stamped with the image of God, houses the priceless soul of a child. And soon, if you are faithful, it may contain the Spirit of God himself."

Silence settled upon her kitchen, a heavy absence of sound that seemed to leave her in a vacuum, without oxygen, without thought, without sense. Babette fought to breathe in the empty air, struggled to find some meaning in this man and what he'd created in her kitchen. Finally, just as the world went black, she closed her eyes and gasped out the only words her tongue could form: "What do you mean?"

When she opened her eyes, she saw nothing but the quiet shadows of her bedroom, the clock on the nightstand, and a fringe of daylight around the window shade.

It had been a dream, nothing more.

Breathing deeply, she turned to face the sleeping mound of her husband, who snored in the gentle rhythm of the ticking clock in the hall.

If she could get back to sleep, she'd forget everything.

If she could sleep.

CHAPTER TWELVE

By daybreak, the news of Edmund's passing had begun to spread through Heavenly Daze. Charles heard the news from Babette, who said she'd heard it from Zuriel. As Charles stepped out to get the newspaper at the ferry landing, he met Pastor Wickam, who had just come from Frenchman's Folly. "They're all doing fine over there," Winslow said, buttoning his jacket against the cold. "Olympia's upset, of course, but mainly because she fell asleep sitting up with Edmund last night. She keeps insisting she wanted to kiss him good-bye."

"Annie's home?" Charles asked.

Winslow nodded. "She's a big comfort to Olympia, as is Caleb. He's the calm in the middle of the storm right now. Dr. Marc is handling all the funeral arrangements, and I'm to do the service. I think we'll have the service on Saturday."

"If it's just us Heavenly Daze folks—," Charles began.

The pastor interrupted him. "It won't be just islanders. Seems like everybody in the State of Maine knew and loved Edmund, and they'll all want to come pay their respects. We'll have standing room only at the church."

Charles thought of the two blueberry gingerbreads on his kitchen counter—Babette said she made an extra to share with the de Cuviers. Birdie and Bea and Cleta would undoubtedly make something, too, so the folks at Frenchman's Folly would soon have enough food to feed a crowd. A good thing, apparently.

"Anything we can do, Pastor?" Charles asked the question out of politeness, for he knew the women would gather around Olympia and Annie like mother hens gathering in stray chicks. Though Olympia was known for her prickly, independent nature, he didn't think she'd resist comfort at this time in her life.

A resigned smile crossed Winslow's face. "Don't think there's much to be done. They were expecting this, of course, but it still hurts. I imagine they'll have to sorrow until the pain goes away. The visitors will help. Edmund was a generous and kind man, and lots of folks thought well of him."

The welcoming blast of the ferry boat sounded over the harbor, and both men turned toward the sea. "'Bout time," Charles said, checking his watch. "Cap'n Stroble's running a little late this morning."

"Aren't we all." Winslow glanced over his shoulder. "Good to see you, Charles. Say hello to the family for me."

"I will."

As Charles inadvertently let the storm door slam behind him, the sound seemed unusually loud. After crossing the foyer and entering the kitchen, he understood why: Babette and Georgie were at the table eating cereal, but an unnatural silence prevailed in the room. Though Georgie appeared to be absorbed in the back of his cereal box, Charles doubted that anything written on a Frosty Flakes package could hold his son's attention for sixty seconds, let alone several minutes.

Dropping the newspaper on the table, he reached out and scrubbed his son's tousled head. "Morning, kiddo."

Georgie grunted but didn't lift his gaze from the cereal box. Charles glanced at Babette, who merely shrugged one shoulder, then leaned forward to riffle through the paper in her search for the lifestyles section.

Sighing, Charles poured himself a bowl of milk, heated it for thirty seconds in the microwave, then filled the bowl with Nuts 'n Flakes. He had just taken his seat when Georgie hopped up, dumped his cereal bowl in the sink, and dashed upstairs.

"He's still peeved at me," Babette said, her gaze meeting Charles's over the edge of her newspaper. "He thinks I'm going to make him paint puffins."

"Are you?"

Her smile seemed sad. "Not today."

Charles picked up the sports section and scanned the headlines.

"Charles," Babette's hand appeared at the top of the page and pulled it down, "do you believe God speaks to us in dreams?"

The corner of his mouth twisted. "Good grief, Babs, at breakfast?"

He was about to lift the paper again, but something in her expression stopped him. "I need to know," she whispered, her blue eyes piercing the distance between them. "I had a dream last night, and I think it might have been more than a dream."

Resigning himself to the fact that he would not be allowed to read his paper, Charles folded the sports section and set it aside. "What did you dream?"

Looking away, she brought her hands to her temples, rubbing them as if the memory pained her. "I was here, in the kitchen, making clay. Zuriel—at least, I think it was Z—made a little statue of Georgie on the potter's wheel. There was more, but I can't remember all the details."

Charles looked toward the ceiling, pretending to be deep in thought, then lowered his gaze and smiled. "It probably doesn't mean anything, honey. We dream every night, but we forget most of them."

"This one felt different"—she propped her arms on the table—"really different."

Charles shrugged again. "Ask Zuriel," he said, picking up his spoon. "If he was in your dream, maybe he'll have an answer for you."

He sipped the warm milk in his cereal bowl and found the temperature just right.

When Birdie walked into the bakery on Wednesday morning, Elezar and Micah were sitting together, their elbows propped on the table, a spread of hot doughnuts and coffee between them. The two men immediately rose to their feet when Birdie walked by.

"Mornin', Birdie," they said in unison.

"Good morning, gentlemen. Carry on; don't let me bother you." Frowning, she stepped to the window and peered out on Main Street. "Is that Buddy Franklin? What's he doing up so early?"

Clearing his throat, Abner began to wipe the counter. "The captain got Buddy up when he made the seven o'clock run this morning. Seems there was an awful lot of mail, and he needed someone to help haul it up from the dock."

Birdie's hand flew to her mouth. More mail? Merciful heavens! Before noon? Her worst fears were coming true.

"Now, Birdie, don't fret." Abner stepped to the window and patted her shoulder. Their eyes followed Buddy's progress up Main Street, his labored breathing creating frosty breath from his nostrils.

"Abner," she whispered, "this is turning into a nightmare. Somebody's got to answer all that mail."

She turned as Buddy burst into the bakery, then unceremoniously dropped a bulging canvas sack onto the floor. Clucking in disapproval, Abner bent to pick up the drawstring, then dragged the bag past the counter and through the doorway that led to Birdie's sitting room.

She swallowed hard and stared at her once-clean floor. The bag, damp with sea-spray, left a sluglike slick on the linoleum.

Birdie glanced at Buddy, who merely stared at her, his eyes like vacant windows above a crimson nose.

"Thanks, Buddy," she said wearily. "Bea will be dressed in a few minutes and we'll decide what to do with it."

Buddy shrugged. "Whatever."

"Let me get you something warm to drink." Birdie crossed to the counter, then poured a cup of hot coffee into a foam cup. As she handed it to the younger man, she said, "I hope there isn't more—"

"There're nine more," Buddy confided in a rare burst of chattiness.

"More'n I've ever seen on a day, let alone a morning. Captain Stroble's fit to be tied."

"Nine," Birdie mouthed, stunned.

"The others are sittin' in the ferry shack." Buddy took a swig of hot coffee. "And the cap'n says there'll be more at noontime."

Birdie's knees threatened to buckle.

Elezar patted her shoulder as they prepared to leave, but Micah caught Abner's eye and said, "You know where to find us if you need us."

Nodding, Abner escorted his friends to the door. They shook hands, and the two men disappeared into the gray mist that seemed to hover over the island this morning.

Zuriel was still in his robe when Babette knocked on the cottage door, and by the look on his face she surmised that she'd surprised him. He didn't complain, though, but let her in and placed a mug of coffee in her hands before pouring himself another.

"I have a quick question for you—two, actually," she said, wrapping her hands around the warmth of the stoneware mug. "First—do you believe God speaks to us in dreams?"

The line of his mouth curved in his beard. "I do," he said simply, spooning a heaping mound of sugar into his coffee. "Scripture is filled with stories of men who heard the voice of God in their dreams: Joseph, the adoptive father of Jesus; Daniel; Joseph of Egypt; the apostle Peter—"

"What about ordinary people," Babette interrupted. "Like me?"

Zuriel regarded her with an intense but guarded expression as he lowered himself into a wooden kitchen chair. "Yes, I believe God speaks to ordinary people in dreams. Sometimes he must because they will not hear in other ways."

Babette felt her cheeks burn. He had to be obliquely referring to his so-called "message from God." Well, her dream was as convoluted and odd as his message, so perhaps they did spring from the same source. Pure and simple guilt had probably produced that crazy dream . . .

"Imagine, if you will," Zuriel said, his dark eyes twinkling in the morning shadows, "a powerful king who unites many far-flung kingdoms. He yearns to communicate with his new subjects, but they don't speak his language. He could require them to rise to his level, but he loves his subjects enough that he is willing to learn the language of each tribe and clan—even the language of the individual." He sipped from his coffee cup, swallowed, and looked at her over the rim. "God is like that, Babette. He loves each person enough to learn his or her heart language. And however he can best speak to you, that's the way he will speak. If one communication doesn't get through, he'll try something else until his message is understood and received."

Babette struggled to swallow over the lump in her throat. "I thought God spoke through the Bible and preachers."

Zuriel smiled. "Often he does. Often he speaks through circumstances. Sometimes he demonstrates his will in opportunities given and removed. But sometimes he speaks through the intimate language of a dream."

He leaned forward, setting his coffee on the scarred wooden table. "You had another question?"

Babette shook her head as if the motion could clear out the cluttered ideas and thoughts crowded there. "Um—yes." She caught his eye and softened her voice. "How did you know about Edmund? I called Frenchman's Folly after you left, and Annie didn't know."

Zuriel's eyes shone with gentleness and understanding. "I saw Caleb last night."

"Ah." Babette lifted her hand in relief. Of course, Caleb hadn't been in his room when she called. He must have been with Edmund when he died, and he'd met Z when he went to fetch Dr. Marc or something . . .

She managed a soft laugh. "I'm glad that's straightened out. I was beginning to wonder—" She shook her head. "Never mind." She pushed herself out of the chair, then placed her coffee cup in the small sink by the window. "I won't keep you, Z; I only wanted your opinion." She grinned at him. "I don't suppose you do dream interpretations on the side."

A wry half-smile crossed his face. "Sorry. I haven't been given any interpretations for you."

"Too bad." She moved toward the door and placed her hand on the knob, bracing herself for the cold dash back to the house.

"Thinking of Edmund reminded me of something," Zuriel said, stopping her. She glanced back in time to see a slow smile light his face. "Just remember—this life, every moment of it, will one day be the dream. Eternity is what matters, Babette. All of this"—he lifted his hands, gesturing toward the pottery, the cottage, the world in which they stood—"all this is fleeting and temporary. The best is yet to come."

Drawing her collar around her throat, Babette nodded wordlessly, then carried her swirling thoughts out into the falling snow.

Walking backward from the Kid Kare Center, Georgie watched the way his footprints melted the snow that had begun to stick to the sidewalk. Miss Dana's eyes had been red and puffy when he arrived, and after only a few minutes she told Georgie that school would be canceled today.

"Are you sick?" Georgie asked, alarmed at her appearance.

"No, honey." She paused to blow her nose, then wiped her cheek with the back of her hand. "It's not a good day for school. Besides, tomorrow is Thanksgiving. So let's call today a holiday, okay?"

She sent him out the door with a pat on his back. "Tell your mom we'll have school again on Monday . . . after the memorial service and the holiday weekend."

Georgie was about to ask what a memorial service was, but Miss Dana had firmly closed the door.

Now he frowned as he studied his backward footsteps. Something was wrong and all the grownups felt it, but no one would explain what had happened. His mom had been unusually quiet at breakfast. Then Dad forgot to put the chocolate pudding in his snack sack (he knew this because he always ate it on the way to school), and now Miss Dana was sending him home before ten o'clock.

Something was definitely not right. The entire world seemed backward today.

At the corner of Main Street and Ferry Road, Georgie stood next to the wooden street sign and looked up at the sky. The clouds sagged toward the town, nearly touching the top of the church steeple. The heavy air felt like a woolen scarf, only cold, muffling sounds and sights alike.

A man's voice suddenly cut through the silence. Feeling out of place, Georgie ducked behind the huge oak on the lawn of the B&B, then peered toward the source of the sound. Dr. Marc stood on the front porch of Miss Olympia's house, and even from this distance Georgie could see that he was wiping his nose, too. Then the doctor turned and stuffed his hanky into his pocket as two other men, both in dark brown overcoats, carried a small bed out of the house.

Georgie bit his lip and leaned forward, his mittens sticking to the rough bark of the oak. Through the falling snow he could see that the bed was covered in a white sheet, but he couldn't tell who—or what—slept under the covers. He didn't recognize the two men, but as soon as they reached the sidewalk, they pulled out legs on the bed, then rolled it down the concrete toward the street.

Who would want to ride on a rolling bed? Georgie crept out from behind the tree and edged forward, feeling somehow naughty. The two strangers wore stern faces, and something in their manner told Georgie that they were dealing with Serious Business, and that always meant No Kids.

A woman's voice reached him then, and he cringed, half-fearing to hear a rebuke from his mother. But the voice belonged to Miss Annie, who joined Dr. Marc on the porch. She held a handkerchief, too, and her pretty eyes looked like slits in a blotchy face.

Georgie twisted his mouth. He knew what that face meant. Like Miss Dana, Miss Annie had been crying.

He opened his hand and counted people on his fingers. Annie lived in Frenchman's Folly on weekends, and she looked okay. Dr. Marc lived in the garage, and he looked okay, too. That left Miss Olympia and Caleb and Mr. Edmund . . .

He tilted his head as the light of understanding dawned. Mr. Edmund had been sick for a long time. His mother never said his name in anything but a sad whisper, and Georgie could hardly remember the last time Mr. Edmund had been able to attend church. He used to carry red-and-white peppermints in his pockets, but he hadn't given Georgie a candy in a long time. Mr. Edmund must be the one in the bed—and he must be very, very sick.

Caleb came out of the house then, followed by Miss Olympia, and Georgie saw Olympia hug Annie. Then Olympia lifted a big Christmas wreath, except this one was completely black, and Annie helped her hang it on the door. Then Dr. Marc hugged Miss Olympia, then he hugged Annie, then the three of them watched Caleb follow the two men who were rolling the bed on wheels toward the dock.

Unable to see down the hill, Georgie slipped his hands into his pockets and walked toward the ferry landing. He formed his lips into a pucker and tried to whistle the way his dad did when he set out for the newspaper, but his lips were too frozen to whistle . . . and he'd never been very good at it.

His steps slowed as he neared the ferry. The boat rocked gently in the swells, but it shouldn't be at the docks now. In the winter it wasn't supposed to come until noon.

The grownups on the porch of Frenchman's Folly didn't seem to notice him, so Georgie crossed the street and hid behind one of the tall, bare trees across from the Mercantile. From his position he could see the strangers and the bed—and Captain Stroble talking to Caleb as the men carried the bed aboard the ferry. The wind whistled across the dock, flattening the men's coats against their legs, then a corner of the sheet lifted and flew upward, stopped only by a belt over the bed—

Georgie felt his stomach drop. A body lay on the bed, a body that looked like Mr. Edmund, but wasn't. The man's skin was blue gray, and the face seemed hollow and shrunken like a scary cartoon. That couldn't be Mr. Edmund, it was a frightful thing, and suddenly Georgie realized that he was seeing his first honest-to-goodness dead person.

He felt a cold hand pass down his spine. A voice inside his head whispered that he ought to look away, but his eyes wouldn't close, wouldn't even blink. Torn between fascination and fear, he stared until one of the men caught the fluttering sheet and pulled it back down, covering the dead man's head and shoulders again.

Overcome by a bad feeling he couldn't name, Georgie turned and ran for the safety of home.

Babette cleared her throat softly and hugged Annie, then Olympia. Strange, how frail Olympia felt. Babette had always imagined that Olympia de Cuvier had steel in her spine, but the slender woman in her arms felt almost birdlike, a fragile creature of cartilage and feathers.

Babette blinked the preposterous image away and whispered in Olympia's ear. "I'm so sorry, my dear. We've been praying for you all morning."

Olympia pulled out of her embrace, nodded briefly, and dabbed at her nose with a handkerchief. For a moment she stood straight and tall, then the facade crumbled. "My Edmund," Olympia whispered, the tears beginning to flow again as her shoulders slumped, "I wanted to tell him good-bye, but he slipped away before I could!"

"There, now, honey." Edith Wickam came in from the parlor and put her arms around Olympia, managing to give Babette a smile as she did so. Babette willingly stepped back, eager to let the pastor's wife handle the condolences.

While Edith walked the sobbing Olympia toward a quiet corner,

Babette caught a glimpse of Barbara, the Lansdowns, and Winslow in the kitchen. Winslow was on the telephone, jotting down a message, while Barbara hovered near the coffee maker. Floyd was frowning at a flower arrangement that had just been delivered. "What in tarnation am I supposed to do with this?" he asked, his voice drifting out in the hall.

Not wanting to get in the way, Babette wandered into the formal living room, where Annie sat on the couch, an open photograph album on the cushion next to her. Caleb, the old butler, sat stiffly on a chair, a strange smile on his face.

Shock, Babette thought. The reality hasn't hit him yet.

"Miss Babette." Caleb rose to his feet as she entered, then gestured toward the sofa. "Would you like to sit and share a cup of tea?"

"I don't need anything, Caleb, so please don't trouble yourself." Babette exchanged a smile with Annie, then took a seat on the far end of the sofa. Pointing toward the photo album, she said, "Taking a trip down memory lane?"

"Ayuh." Annie's tired eyes glowed with wonder. "I never knew Uncle Edmund was a pilot! But here he is, flying one of those old—what were they called, Caleb?"

"Biplanes," the butler answered. "Oh, yes. Your uncle was quite a daredevil in his younger days."

"Famous, too." Annie pointed toward a black-and-white photo, then turned the album so Babette could see. " 'Edmund Shots and his Amazing Flying Fandango.' Can you believe it? He and his brothers were into wing-walking and all that stuff."

"Edmund Shots?" Babette glanced at the butler. "I thought his name was—"

"Olympia never liked the name," Caleb explained, a blush lighting his cheekbones.

"Oh." Babette clapped her mouth shut, knowing better than to pursue what had to be a touchy subject. She looked down at the photos for a moment, then purposefully looked away, intuiting that Annie wanted to concentrate on the pictures. Why did young people wait until death to appreciate the folks they'd known all their lives?

Babette crossed her legs and cleared her throat, her gaze flitting around the room. Frenchman's Fairest was still a regal house, though there were definite signs of wear on the Oriental carpet. The heavy drapes in this room had to be twenty years old, and the antique sofa sorely needed reupholstering.

What had Edmund done with his money? She hadn't known him in his stunt pilot days, but she'd known him when he was a successful investment banker. Of course, his illness had eaten away at their savings, and a place like Frenchman's Fairest took far more than Social Security to maintain. And there was Annie, whom Olympia and Edmund had taken in after her parents died.

But Annie had gone to college on scholarship, hadn't she? And they hadn't spent too much on housing, for this place needed help, and quickly. She lifted her gaze and spotted the telltale signs of stained wallpaper at the junction of wall and ceiling. So—the roof of Frenchman's Folly leaked, too. Wonder how much the repairs on this monster would cost?

She blushed when her gaze crossed Caleb's. How long had he been watching her?

"Mr. Edmund," the old butler said, a reproving note in his voice, "believed in laying up treasures in heaven, not on earth."

Babette's heart jumped in her chest. Had he read the expression on her face and guessed her thoughts? Or was this the typical kind of comment one made during sympathy calls? She hadn't done this sort of thing enough to know how to respond.

"Treasure in heaven?" She tilted her head and tried to keep her tone light. "What did he do, buy heavenly savings bonds?"

"No, missy." His smile deepened. "Edmund invested his life in things that count for eternity. I was with him at the end, and I can testify to the fact that he looked forward to receiving his eternal rewards."

"Look at this!" Annie said, jabbing her finger at another picture. "I never knew Uncle Edmund worked at a church camp!"

"He not only spent the entire summer as a camp counselor, but he also paid expenses for twenty kids from inner-city Boston that same year." Caleb kept his gaze fastened firmly on Babette. "He gave money whenever he saw a need. He gave quietly, often anonymously, and always freely. He used to say he was just a channel, that God was the real supplier."

Huddled over the album, Annie laughed softly. "I remember this," she said, her fingertip caressing another photo. "Uncle Edmund decided to sponsor a dozen kids from the Angel Tree project. He sent Christmas presents to all of them, and instead of decorations that year, we had the kids' pictures hanging on our tree."

Babette leaned sideways and twisted her head to see. The snapshot had been taken years ago, for Annie looked to be fifteen or so, but there was no mistaking Olympia's slender form and Edmund's wide smile. In the photo, he had one hand on Olympia's narrow shoulder and the other tucked inside his coat pocket—the same pocket that had always held peppermint candies for Georgie.

Edmund de Cuvier had spent his lifetime . . . giving. In the light of his gifts, what did aging drapes and worn upholstery matter?

Babette looked up and caught Caleb's eye as the light of understanding dawned in her heart.

Zuriel half heard the thwacking sound before he actually noticed it. It must have begun while he was throwing the pot, for it blended into the rhythms of the spinning wheel and the rise and fall of his fingers. But when he switched the wheel off and sat observing his work, the thwacking sound continued . . . and came from outside the cottage.

He rose from his stool and crossed to the window, then stared out across the side lawn. Surrounded by the stiff, brown stalks of last summer's flowers, Georgie sat in the garden swing, mindlessly smacking a stick against the angled frame of two-by-fours.

Zuriel didn't wait to be told the boy needed him. Clearly, if an active child like Georgie had been sitting still for more than two minutes, something was wrong.

He pulled his coat from the peg near the door, then stepped out into the overcast day. Thrusting his hands in his pockets, he hurried forward until he reached the swing, then stood for a moment. Georgie didn't speak—another sign of trouble.

Zuriel jerked his chin toward the empty space on the long swing. "Mind if I sit down?"

Georgie shrugged in response.

Taking that as permission granted, Zuriel sat on the swing and pushed off, using his long legs to advantage. Georgie stopped smacking the stick against the support posts and let it fall to the mulch beneath the swing.

Zuriel waited, rocking the swing in a silent rhythm. Finally, the boy spoke: "I saw a dead man."

A tremor of alarm touched Zuriel's spine, then he realized what must have happened. The ferry would have come this morning for Edmund's body.

Zuriel made a soft sound of compassion. "Mr. Edmund is in heaven now. Did no one tell you?"

Georgie shook his head. "I saw the black wreath and everyone crying, but no one would say anything. And then the men came out with the rolling bed, and the sheet flew up." He lifted his head then, and Zuriel saw shadows behind the boy's brown eyes. "The body looked awful. It didn't look like Mr. Edmund at all."

"What you saw wasn't Mr. Edmund." Zuriel paused to let the truth sink in. "What you saw was only the shell that housed Mr. Edmund's spirit while he lived."

Georgie screwed up his face. "People don't have shells."

Zuriel laughed softly, realizing that the boy had to be thinking about shellfish like crabs and lobsters, common fare on the island. "We don't have shells like sea creatures, true. Our shells are flesh and bone. This"—he held up his arm and pinched the skin on the back of his hand—"is temporary. My body is a vessel I can wear on earth, but the moment I go to heaven, I have to leave this shell behind."

Georgie lowered his gaze, long lashes hiding his eyes. "If we don't have a body in heaven . . . are we all indivisible?"

Chuckling, Zuriel turned and rested his arm on the back of the swing. "Spirit things are invisible to humans," he said, crossing his legs, "but that doesn't mean they're not real. After all, you can hear and feel and smell the wind, but you can't see it. And it's very real."

Georgie looked up, his gaze clouded in thought. "So Mr. Edmund is a spirit now? Like a ghost?"

"Not a ghost, George. But yes, he's spirit, and he's in heaven with Jesus. If you were in heaven, you'd see him plain as day. You'd recognize him in a minute. Because you'd be spirit, too."

Georgie hugged himself. "I don't want to die like Mr. Edmund. And I don't want my mom or dad to die or Mr. Caleb or Miss Annie or Miss Birdie or Miss Bea—"

"Georgie." Zuriel dropped his hand on the boy's shoulder. "You don't have to fear death, and you certainly shouldn't worry about it. All things die." He hesitated when Georgie flinched. "It's like this," he said, leaning closer. "Look at your body—your hands, your fingernails, your hair. Every little part of you is alive as long as it's attached to the living part of you, your soul. But if you trim your fingernails or get a haircut, pieces of you fall off and get thrown away. Are you sad about losing those pieces?"

Georgie shook his head. "No, 'cause the barber gives me a candy bar if I sit still for the haircut."

"Well"—Zuriel spread his hands and lifted a brow—"it's the same thing. The things that die aren't important because the part that's alive keeps going on. When Christians die, their spirits go straight to heaven, and their worn-out bodies get . . . put away." He paused, lifting his gaze to the steeple on the church across the street. "I'm always a little amazed when people cry at funerals. There's really no reason for them to be sad. Their loved ones aren't gone; they've only relocated. And the reunion will come soon enough."

"I know why they cry." Georgie spoke softly, and when Zuriel looked down, the boy was staring at his mother's frozen flower bed, still dusted with this morning's snow. "They cry because they miss the person. And heaven is very far away."

Zuriel sat silently, absorbing the human perspective revealed in the boy's words. Truth to tell, he had forgotten how limited human understanding could be. They didn't have the luxury of zipping to heaven in the twinkling of an eye, and they didn't have the ability to see beyond the physical dimensions of earth. Though the Lord had given them clear insights, instructions, and assurances in the written Word, not all of them believed it . . . or even bothered to read it.

"I suppose you're right, George," he whispered, feeling the chill for the first time since stepping outside. "But man was not created for this world. God created humans for heaven, for eternity, and all their longings will be fulfilled when they finally reach their home. Heaven is all you could ever imagine . . . and more."

Georgie didn't speak but leaned forward, his elbows propped on his knees, his chin on his fists. His mouth hung partly open, and Zuriel could see the tip of the boy's tongue worrying the loose tooth in the center of his mouth.

"You ever seen heaven?" Georgie asked, not moving.

Zuriel glanced upward for inspiration. Though the angels would never lie to their human charges, sometimes it was wise not to share everything . . .

But didn't Jesus himself thank the Father for hiding the truth from those who thought themselves wise and clever, while revealing it to the childlike?

"Ayuh," he said, after a moment's reflection, "I've seen it."

"What's it like?" Georgie tilted his head and looked at Zuriel with something very fragile in his eyes. "Is it cold?"

"Cold?" Zuriel smiled. "Why would you think it's cold?"

"Well"—Georgie shrugged—"the other place is hot, right? And if heaven's in outer space, it must be black and cold and dark."

"It's none of those things." Zuriel glanced toward the leaden sky and wished he had the authority to part the clouds with a breath. "To be absent from this body is to be present with the Lord, in his holy Temple. And that is a place of warmth and brightness and music. Your human eyes cannot see all of it, nor can your ears hear, nor can your nostrils"—he leaned forward and gently tweaked Georgie's snub nose—"breathe in all the sweet scents of heaven. But when you enter it in spirit, you will know you have finally come home."

The slamming of the storm door broke into their conversation, and both Zuriel and Georgie waited silently to see who would come out of the house. A moment later Babette's head appeared over the porch railing, and her face brightened when she saw them on the swing. "There you are," she said, crossing her arms across her chest. "Stay there, Georgie. I need to speak with you."

Zuriel rocked silently, wondering if he should go, as Babette disappeared, then reappeared a moment later, rounding the hedge that bordered the porch. A moment later she stood before the swing, her face splotched and her eyes swollen. But she wore a smile and she gave it to Georgie.

"Honey," she said, running her hands over her sweatered arms, "I'm glad I found you. I have to tell you something."

Zuriel stopped the swing, ready to rise. "I should go."

"No, Z. Please stay." Babette returned her gaze to her son. "You can hear what I need to tell Georgie."

"I know about Mr. Edmund," the boy said, lowering his gaze. "I know he's in heaven."

"Ayuh—but that's not what I came to tell you." Babette threw Zuriel a quick glance, then reached out and caught her son's hands.

"Sweetheart," Babette said, kneeling on the dark mulch beneath their feet, "I want to apologize to you. I've been doing a lot of thinking, and I realize now that I've been asking you to fulfill my dreams. You painted me a puffin, a beautiful gift, but I was wrong to ask you to paint more. I was wrong to promise puffins without asking you first, and I'm going to call Mr. Bedell and tell him the deal's off. I won't make you paint puffins. And if you do paint other puffins, I'm keeping them here, to display in our gallery. I don't want to make money so we can be comfortable—I want to be a good wife and mom and take care of my family. That's the most important thing in the world to me."

Zuriel felt his heart warm at her words, but Georgie said nothing. He kept his gaze lowered, his feet hanging motionless over the swing.

Babette rubbed the boy's hands, warming them with her own. "You are my precious son," she said, her eyes damp. "You are God's gift to me, and I've been wrong to depend upon your talent instead of God, who gives us all good things. I've told the Lord I'm sorry, Georgie, and now I'm telling you. Will you forgive me?"

Georgie looked up then, and beneath the soft fullness of his face Zuriel saw a suggestion of motion and flowing, as though a hidden spring were trying to break through. For a moment the boy said nothing, though his lower lip trembled, then he threw his arms around Babette's neck.

Holding her son, Babette made soft soothing sounds and rubbed his back. Tears gathered in the corners of her eyes and slowly spilled from the ends of her dark lashes.

Watching the tender scene, Zuriel felt a trembling from the depths of his own soul. He had never quite understood forgiveness, having never needed it, but the power in that profound act never failed to move him.

Swallowing the lump that had risen in his throat, he reached up for the chain of the swing and tactfully shifted his gaze to the wide sky above. And then, in a breathless moment of epiphany, he understood. Today, for the first time in his short life, Georgie had learned how to forgive. And how could he understand God's forgiveness unless he had experienced giving it himself? Very soon, today or tomorrow or the next day, the boy would realize his own need for forgiveness, not from his mom or dad, but from God himself. And in that moment, Georgie would experience the same sweet release that now rained tears over Babette's lovely cheeks.

As a stream of sunlight broke through the cloud cover above, Zuriel breathed a deep sigh of contentment.

Leaving her son with Zuriel, Babette climbed the front porch steps and ran her hands over her arms. While sitting in the faded parlor of Frenchman's Folly, she'd realized how big a mess she'd made, but she could set things right again. Life was too short to spend even an hour in anger or regret.

She entered the house and paused at the bottom of the stairs, suddenly missing the noisy click-clack of Charles's old typewriter. The new computer made nothing but soft tapping sounds, ghostly in the nearly-silent house. She didn't even have the plink-plink of the leaky roof to keep her company any more.

She placed her weight on the first tread and smiled as it creaked. Maybe their house wasn't meant to be quiet and sedate. Maybe it was meant to be filled with clacks and creaks and plinks, overspread with the giggles of an active little boy.

One thing was certain—the silence that had fallen between her and Charles was not a companionable quiet. Though he had not said a cross word to her of late, he hadn't said much in the way of regular conversation, either. She had another overdue apology on her "to do" list.

Charles was sitting in his new computer chair when she entered the office, but his hands were not on the keyboard. They were holding a heavy stack of white pages surrounded by torn brown paper. Someone had stuck a yellow Sticky Note to the first page, scrawled with a short message.

Charles's manuscript had returned . . . again.

She sank into the spare dining room chair against the wall, then pressed her hands together. "Charles?"

Staring mournfully at the manuscript, he shook his head. "Dull, trite, and plodding," he said, his voice heavy with defeat. "Utterly unpublishable."

Purpose and determination kept her from arguing. "Charles, I was wrong to say those things. If you believe in your dream, you should pursue it. I don't know what will happen, but if you really believe this is something God wants you to do—"

"You didn't say those things." His heavy finger thumped the Sticky Note. "Stellar Cross did."

She hesitated, blinking with bafflement. "*The* Stellar Cross?"

"He returned my manuscript." Charles heaved the mountain of paper onto his cluttered desk. "He obviously thinks I should stick to my day job."

Babette lowered her gaze. She had come up to encourage her husband, to apologize for her bluntness, and to give her blessing so he could continue to exercise his creativity however he saw fit. But Stellar Cross had smashed Charles's dream more effectively than she ever could.

"I'm surprised," she began, proceeding carefully, "that a busy man like Stellar Cross would even take the time to read a manuscript from . . . well, from an unknown. The fact that he did says something, Charles."

"Ayuh, it does." He lifted a folded sheet of paper that had fallen to the floor and handed it to Babette. "Read that and you'll understand everything."

Babette unfolded the letter, a handwritten note, and saw that it had been signed by Florence Cross, the famous novelist's wife.

"My husband does not read unsolicited manuscripts," she had written, "but he recognized your name and decided to make an exception. He loves your art, Mr. Graham, and one of your seascapes is hanging over the fireplace in our library. My husband is a harsh critic of writing, I'm afraid, because he has spent years studying the craft and has little patience for beginners. So forgive his brusqueness . . . and know how much we appreciate your beautiful artistry."

Babette folded the note and held it for a long moment before speaking. "Honey, I came up here to apologize."

"No need. You were right. I stink."

"You don't stink." She sighed. "You have a great gift, but maybe you're neglecting it. Maybe you're like a kid holding a whole bag of peppermints, but you keep reaching for somebody else's lollipop."

Charles's mouth took on an unpleasant twist. "I guess I'm not the Renaissance man I thought I was."

"Maybe not." Babette stood and walked to him, then bent and draped her arm around his shoulder. "But you're the Renaissance man I love. And you're the father Georgie adores. You're a wonderful artist, and the people in this town respect you."

"But my painting—" A muscle flexed at his jaw. "It's not good enough to support this family. We couldn't afford to fix the roof, and we had to rely on Georgie to buy a computer—"

"Your art is good enough. It's great." She bent until they were eye-to-eye. "But you've only been painting six months out of the year. Maybe our profits would increase if you painted a few months more . . . and you would satisfy your need for variety if you painted something besides seascapes. You're a talented artist, Charles, and you know the great Creator. Don't sell yourself short."

"Art won't pay all the bills."

Babette drew a deep breath, feeling a dozen different emotions collide. Part of his glum reaction was her fault, for she had whined about the bills and the budget, wanting Charles to feel guilty for allowing her to carry the burden of bookkeeping.

But God had given her a head for figures, so the burden was a byproduct of her own stubbornness. For years she had scrupulously trusted God to handle the tidy ten percent she gave him each month but refused to trust him with the ninety percent she retained. Clinging to their dollars, she had fussed and fumed over expenses while Edmund de Cuvier personified the key to accumulating eternal treasure while living in peace on earth.

Be a channel of blessing.

"Honey," she softened her tone, "God will supply our needs. He always has . . . I see that now. We can trust him for the future, too."

"You think so?"

The computer chair creaked as Charles's hands closed around her waist and pulled her onto his lap. Babette giggled as she and her husband tilted backward at a dangerous angle.

"I know so," she whispered, running her hands through the wisps of her husband's hair.

Creeping up the stairs, Georgie turned the corner of the landing, then slapped his hands over his eyes. His parents were both sitting in one chair, kissing!

"Mom and Dad," he yelled, trying not to look, "there are men downstairs to see you."

"What?"

When he lowered his hands, his mom stood by the desk, smoothing the wrinkles from her jeans. Dad stood, too, and he was grinning.

"Who's downstairs?" Mom asked, moving past Georgie toward the landing.

"The puffin man," Georgie said, following her, "and some guy I never seed before."

"You've never seen," his dad corrected, dropping his hand to Georgie's shoulder. "Did you leave them alone in the gallery?"

"Z's with them." A tingle of excitement, a feeling almost like Christmas, moved through Georgie. He didn't know what was happening, but this was not like any other day-before-Thanksgiving he could remember. First of all, there was all that stuff with Mr. Edmund going to heaven, then his parents were kissing, and now the puffin man was downstairs with a stranger who carried a video camera and a big black bag of stuff.

Eager to discover what it all meant, Georgie skipped down the stairs behind his mom and dad.

Grateful that she wouldn't have to postpone her explanation to Pierce Bedell, Babette smiled in relief when she crossed the foyer and saw him in the gallery with Zuriel. The two men, accompanied by a stranger, were standing before one of Charles's seascapes. She caught herself hoping that Bedell would be as taken with Charles's work as he had been with Georgie's, but when she entered they turned to face her without a backward glance.

"Madame Graham," Bedell said, coming forward to greet her with a warm handshake, "I am so glad to find you at home today. I'm sorry we didn't call ahead of time, but John thought it might be nice to catch you unprepared—so we could have sort of an impromptu visit." He laced his fingertips beneath his chin, then forced his hands outward in an explosive gesture. "Ta da! Surprise!"

Speechless with astonishment, Babette looked at the third man. He wore a denim jacket and jeans, but he carried a video camera on his shoulder, while an impressive array of gadgets littered the floor by his feet. "You must be John," she said.

"John Wilkerson, from WCSH," the man said, awkwardly shifting the video camera in order to extend his hand. "News at Five, Channel Six."

Babette turned to Bedell. "I think we'd like a full explanation."

"Ayuh." Charles's voice echoed from behind her. "We would."

"Of course." Bedell blazed his smile around the room. "Marcia Goldman, program director for WCSH, has hired me to do a segment on our genius Georgie. I'll interview him, John will record the interview, and we'll be live at five on the local news. Marcia's hoping the network affiliate in Boston will pick up the clip, then we should get some major national coverage before the week is out—"

"I've seen the puffin paintings," Wilkerson interrupted, shifting his gaze from Babette to Charles. "They're magnificent."

"Mr. Bedell," Babette began.

"I know this is irregular," Bedell said, spreading his hands again, "but this is a bit of an unusual situation. Ordinarily the station would send a reporter and a news truck, but with the holiday, there's no way we could arrange a full news spot. So I'm going to act as interviewer, and John will tape the piece—"

"Babs," Charles's voice dripped with weariness, "will you handle this, please? Georgie and I are going to go upstairs and play a computer game."

In dazed exasperation, Babette watched her husband and grinning son move toward the stairs. What was she supposed to do? She had promised Georgie there would be no more puffin paintings, but she hadn't counted on Bedell showing up with the local news and plans for national exposure. If she sent these two away without a full explanation, she might look as though she were trying to hide the truth about Georgie. But if she painted him as a child prodigy, she'd be right back in the quicksand she desperately wanted to escape.

She lifted her gaze to the ceiling, murmured a quick, "Lord, help!" and then caught Zuriel's eye. Some secret twinkled there, and she felt a wave of relief when he stepped forward.

"Babette," he said, his smile deepening the dimple at the border of his beard, "maybe these men would like to see Georgie's work at the Kid Kare Center."

Then, in a barely comprehensible flash, she knew the answer.

After nodding her thanks to Zuriel, she gave her visitors the brightest smile she could muster. "Gentlemen," she said, leading the way toward the front door, "follow me if you want to see some real works of art."

The scents of cinnamon, roasting turkey, and spice candles greeted them when Dana Klackenbush opened the door of her home. "Why, Babette," she said, taking in her visitors with one wide-eyed glance, "I didn't expect company today. We're baking for Thanksgiving dinner."

"I know, and I hate to bother you," Babette said, gesturing toward the two men behind her. "But these gentlemen would like to see your classroom. I know you have some of Georgie's pictures on the wall."

Dana's face brightened as she stepped back to let them in. "Indeed, we do. We have an excellent program for day-care drop-ins and full-time students, even though Georgie is our only resident student right now—"

"Just a quick look, Dana," Babette interrupted, stepping into the foyer, "that's all we need."

Dana pointed to the doorway at the right of her foyer, and Babette led the way into the sunny space that served as the Kennebunk Kid Kare Center classroom. Four low tables occupied the center space, but the visitors' eyes were drawn to an array of colorful pictures on the wall. Smiling, Babette crossed her arms as Bedell and Wilkerson exclaimed over the vibrant portraits of puffins, sea gulls, and whales.

"What colors! What style!" Bedell gushed, applauding one particularly exuberant painting of a lobster. "I didn't know our boy liked to paint anything but puffins."

"He likes to paint all sorts of animals," Dana said, shooting Babette a curious glance, "most children do."

"Such an air of whimsy," Wilkerson said, lifting his camera to his shoulder. He put his eye to the viewfinder, then pulled his head back and motioned for Babette to step aside. "If you'll move to the right, Mrs. Graham, I'll get a shot of Pierce and these paintings. We'll do a voice-over about this evidence of Georgie's budding talent and expanding interests—"

"Georgie's talent?" Dana shot the cameraman a twisted smile. "What about the others?"

Wilkerson froze.

Bedell's mouth tightened. "What others? I thought Georgie was the only student."

"He is the only resident student," Dana said, looking to Babette. "But other kids drop in quite often. These pictures"—she gestured around the room—"were painted by many children, from several different places and walks of life."

Bedell's face rippled with chagrin.

Crossing her arms, Babette gave him a confident smile. "Ayuh," she said, "these are great works of art. They are simple, whimsical, and beautiful. But they're not particularly unique. Almost all children paint with this kind of freedom and perspective."

Bedell frowned, his gaze level under drawn brows. "Impossible. I know art, and I know genius when I see it."

"Perhaps," Dana said, reaching out to touch the textured surface of a child's seascape, "all children are geniuses when it comes to art. I know they see a much simpler world than we do. Or maybe they see with innocent eyes."

Babette pointed to a wide painting of a spouting whale, marked in the lower corner with Georgie's trademark initial. "Georgie may have talent, but it's too soon to force him into professional painting. I want him to be free to explore all the gifts God has given him. As for his art—it is lovely, but any mother in America probably has had something just as priceless on her refrigerator door."

She motioned for Wilkerson to lower the camera. "My Georgie isn't going to sell any more puffins. I was wrong to take the joy of painting away from him. I'm not going to do that anymore."

"But," Bedell stuttered, a cold, congested expression settling on his face, "what about the paintings? What about my reputation? I told people those paintings were art—"

"They are art," Babette answered, moving toward the door. "And the people who bought them from you got a bargain. To me, they're priceless." When she reached the doorway, she turned and lifted one shoulder in what she hoped was an elegant, casual shrug. "If you want a refund, Mr. Bedell, I'll give you one. But I'd want the paintings back, of course."

"I can't retrieve the paintings." Bedell raked his hands through his hair. "And we have a contract!"

"Consider it canceled," Babette said. "Payment was upon delivery of each painting, and there will be no more deliveries. So that settles everything."

She nodded farewell to Wilkerson, blew a kiss to Dana, and gave

Bedell a final smile as she lingered in the doorway. "I wish you both a blessed Thanksgiving, gentlemen."

After a dinner of chowder and tuna fish sandwiches, Charles went into the gallery to check on his paint supply. Babette stepped into the foyer to watch him a moment, then smiled and returned to the kitchen.

He would learn to celebrate his gift. In some ways, he was a little boy at heart, a lot like Georgie.

And for all her budgeting and planning, she had to learn to live by faith. Through her beloved son, God had given her a precious gift and used that first painting to supply some urgent needs.

She glanced up at the ceiling, where nothing but a brown stain remained of her near-constant leak. Next weekend, after the holiday, she would pick up some white ceiling paint from the Mercantile and freshen this room.

She ran water in the sink, then squirted a capful of dishwashing liquid beneath the streaming hot water. As the bubbles foamed around the dirty dishes, she realized how close she'd come to breaking her son's heart.

"Lord, forgive me," she whispered, trailing her hand through the bubbles. "When I think of the wall I was building between me and Georgie—"

"Mom?"

She turned. Georgie stood beside her now, holding one of his Sunday school papers.

"Mom"—Georgie wore a serious look as he contemplated a picture of Jesus on the cross—"Zuriel says we have to ask forgiveness when we do wrong, but Jesus never did wrong things. I don't understand why he had to die."

In that moment, just before turning to answer her son, Babette silently lifted another prayer of praise and thanksgiving.

Fortified by coffee and free doughnuts, Buddy Franklin delivered nine more bags of mail throughout the morning. Shortly after the noon ferry arrived, he returned to the bakery with bad news.

Twenty-one additional sacks had just landed on the dock. And Captain Stroble sent word that future deliveries would be deposited at the ferry office. The citizens of Heavenly Daze would have to transport and deliver the mail from that point. In other words, Birdie deduced, the captain's bad back was acting up.

Vernie came in around one o'clock to deliver Birdie's and Bea's turkey. The mostly-thawed bird had to be stored in the refrigerator, she warned, as if Birdie had never cooked a turkey in her life.

As Abner took charge of the poultry, Vernie moved to the window and shook her head. "Terrible thing about Edmund," she said, her voice dropping to a desolate tone. "I suppose you've heard by now."

Birdie hurried to the window. "I hadn't heard. Did he pass?"

"Last night, apparently. I haven't heard the whole story, but I know Pastor Wickam's been over there this morning. And I saw them carry the body out a while ago."

Turning, Birdie caught Abner's eye. After wiping his hands on a towel, Abner removed his apron. "If it's okay with you, Birdie, I'll go see if Caleb needs anything."

He returned later, his eyes gleaming with compassion as he told Birdie, Bea, and Vernie that Edmund had passed away in his sleep.

"Oh, my," Birdie murmured, wiping at sudden tears. "He was a good man."

"Ayuh," Abner seconded, "he's always trusted in the Lord for his strength."

Without another word, Birdie and Bea slipped into their apartment, and emerged a few moments later in visiting clothes. Abner had guessed their intentions, for he handed three wrapped loaves of focaccia for Birdie to take to the family.

The sisters walked across the island in silence, then knocked at Frenchman's Fairest. When a red-eyed Annie opened the door, Birdie extended her arms. The young girl fell into her embrace, openly weeping.

"Thank you for coming." she whispered, her voice breaking. "Aunt Olympia needs friends right now."

Smoothing Annie's back, Birdie nodded. "We'll do all we can to help her through this."

They stayed only briefly, for many people were coming and going. In the midst of hushed conversations about the funeral, Birdie heard someone say that Olympia had asked that the services be held Saturday in Heavenly Daze. The island was Edmund's home, so Pastor Wickam would perform the eulogy and Edmund would be buried in the cemetery behind the church. It seemed only right, somehow, for Edmund to take his place beside Jacques de Cuvier and the other sea captains who had spent their last days on the island.

Before they left, Olympia embraced Birdie and Bea on the porch, holding onto the women for support. For the first time in years, Birdie sensed genuine appreciation from the island's female curmudgeon.

"Thank you for coming," Olympia whispered. For the briefest moment she broke down, her frail body shaking as she openly wept into a handkerchief. Birdie patted her back, understanding that Olympia needed to allow the months of pent-up emotion to escape. When the wave of despair passed, she leaned weakly against Birdie for strength.

Birdie held Olympia tight. "If you need anything—"

"Yes, anything," Bea echoed. "Anything a-tall, Olympia. We want to help you through the next few months."

Olympia straightened and pulled out of the embrace. "I'll be fine. Annie's here, and I have Tallulah and Caleb."

Wiping her eyes, Olympia turned to greet the Klackenbushes, who were coming up the walk with a covered pie plate.

"Bea, we saw all that mail piled on the dock," Dana said as she came up the path. "Where in the world is it coming from?"

Birdie stiffened, knowing this was not the time or place to discuss such things.

"Bea and I will take care of the mail, Dana." After a final wave to Olympia, she descended the steps, pulling Bea with her. Across the street she spotted Zuriel walking to the dock with Georgie Graham.

As the two sisters rode back to the bakery, Birdie prayed that Olympia would have strength for the dark days ahead. She'd never been a wife, so she couldn't really imagine all a widow might feel, but she'd stood by her sister when Frank Coughlin died.

Life was so brief, so temporary. Like a fragile vapor, a soul passed from earth to eternity in the blink of an eye. Edmund de Cuvier was a Christian, so now he was enjoying heaven, but that comfort didn't lessen the fact that others would mourn.

And tomorrow was Thanksgiving.

The holiday would be celebrated in Heavenly Daze as it was in homes across America. Grateful hearts would gather around bountiful tables and give thanks for blessings large and small.

But for Olympia and Annie, it would be a day of mourning. There would be no roasting turkey at Frenchman's Fairest, no fragrant aroma of pumpkin pies, no air of celebration.

Only an empty house filled with memories of happier days.

CHAPTER THIRTEEN

"Buddy!" Birdie gaped in surprise. "Why, you look so distinguished!"

Buddy Franklin stood before her in black tails, a white shirt, and a red satin cape. His long face gleamed in a bright spotlight, and beyond the edge of the stage, she could hear a spattering of anticipatory applause.

"They're waiting," he said, winking at her. "And you look pretty foxy yourself."

Birdie blushed. "Aw, go on."

"No, Birdie, you are a vision of loveliness, a comet of cuteness, a shooting star from Saturn." He paused as the orchestra music swelled. "You look just like . . . whatever."

While she watched, Buddy swept past her, his red cape flashing as he began a routine with moves like Fred Astaire.

Birdie blinked. She didn't know Buddy could dance. When did he learn to waltz like that?

As the audience went wild, she turned, a little surprised to find herself in the wings of a stage. She glanced down as a feather rose in the heat of the lights and tickled her nose.

Why was she wearing a red feather boa?

Just then, Bea walked up in black fishnets, a sequined bodysuit, and a three-foot tall collar of ostrich feathers. "Out of the way, Sister," Bea said, pushing her aside. "It's showtime!"

While Birdie watched in horror, Sister sashayed into the spotlight, joined at center stage by Vernie Bidderman, who wore a similar outfit of sequins, feathers, fishnets, and combat boots. As the crowd surged to their feet, Vernie and Bea linked arms and began a high kick that would have put the New York Rockettes to shame.

As Birdie clung to the curtains for support, a man in the audience tossed a long-stemmed rose onto the stage. Bea dove forward, gave him a wink, then placed it in her mouth, never missing a beat.

From the side of the stage, Buddy tapped his cane and called, "Step right up, ladies and gents, to see the brightest lights and the prettiest girls east of Las Vegas!"

Birdie bolted upright, abruptly coming awake as sweat dripped from her forehead. She opened her eyes, blinking the nightmare from her field of vision. The aromas of mincemeat and pumpkin pies drifted from the kitchen and reminded her who and where she was.

Feeling lightheaded, she exhaled in relief. Bea was up early, stuffing the turkey, setting hot rolls out to rise, and baking the traditional pies.

The familiar sounds and smells of a holiday morning should have brought her a sense of joy and well-being, but Birdie couldn't forget that these were dark days indeed. Her friends and neighbors were peeved at her, and Olympia's loss lay heavy on her mind. Edmund was gone, and Birdie supposed she'd never bake another apple strudel without thinking of the banker with the kind heart.

Edmund loved apple strudel. His eyes would brighten and he'd give her a jaunty wink whenever she offered him one of the flaky delicacies. "Birdie," he'd say in that gentle voice, "you make the best strudel in the State of Maine."

"Edmund Shots, you're a smooth talker if ever I saw one," Birdie would tease back. They'd share a good laugh and then Edmund would make a pretense of searching his pockets for change to pay her. Birdie never charged Edmund for strudel. The look of sheer ecstasy that transformed his face as he devoured the warm pastry was compensation enough.

In later years, after Edmund developed diabetes, Birdie and Abner concocted a slightly-revised version of strudel using artificial sweetener and a less fatty crust. Though Edmund loved the original strudel best, he ate the new version with relish and appreciation, tempering his praise only slightly: "Birdie, you make the best cardboard-crust apple strudel in the State of Maine!"

Chuckling at the memory, she swiped at tears dropping from her eyes. "I hope you're eating all the strudel you want right now, Edmund. Save a piece for me."

Curling tighter under her blankets, she entertained the thought of staying in her pajamas all day. Could a body do that on Thanksgiving? Bea could attend the church service, and when she got home they could eat a quiet dinner with Abner. Later they could play a few games of dominoes: chicken foot or mexican train. She wouldn't have to face anyone today or see irritation in her neighbors' eyes.

Oh, they would get over it, as Grandma Bitts used to say, but every time they looked toward the ferry office and saw a new mountain of mail sacks, they'd grumble her name.

Never mind that she didn't start that silly e-mail. She'd encouraged Bea to answer the first letter, and she'd been foolhardy enough to send money to a little girl who asked for it. Now only heaven knew what trouble tomorrow would bring.

Swallowing, she realized her throat was sore. Stress, cold wind, and bad weather had taken their toll.

She threw the covers back, then padded into the bathroom. Switching the light on, she opened her mouth and peered at her throat in the medicine cabinet mirror.

Red as a turkey's wattle.

Drats.

When she walked into the kitchen a moment later, Bea, still in her terry-cloth bathrobe and hair curlers, glanced up. Dropping the baster, she eyed Birdie with a calculating look. "You look a little streak-ed this morning, Sister." Birdie opened her mouth to speak and nothing came out. Swallowing, she tried again, but nothing but a rusty squeak escaped her lips.

"Oh, my," Bea said, clucking. After shoving the roaster back into the oven, she shut the door and beckoned to Birdie. "Come with me."

Birdie shook her head, realizing too late the torture Bea had in mind.

Throat swabbing—the purest form of inhumanity.

For a moment they slapped at each other like little girls, then Bea latched onto Birdie's hand and dragged her through the hallway and into her bathroom. Amidst retching and many emphatic stamps of her foot, Birdie endured the archaic treatment of having her throat swabbed with Mercurochrome. When it was over, she went back to her bedroom and dropped to the quilts for a moment, wondering why she couldn't just suck on a throat lozenge like anybody else.

Islanders were already pouring into Heavenly Daze Community Church by the time Bea and Birdie finally arrived.

Few scowls were evident this morning; only friendly faces met the Wester sisters as they climbed the steps. Birdie greeted her neighbors with a closed-lip smile, praying her teeth hadn't been permanently stained from the Mercurochrome.

"Sister's sick this morning," Bea announced to no one in particular as she planted herself on the piano bench.

Standing at the pulpit, Micah lifted an inquisitive brow in Birdie's direction. Shrugging, she pointed to her throat.

"She's lost her voice," Bea announced, rapidly flipping through the hymnal on the piano. She looked up, fixing the song leader in a direct gaze. "I'm not in the mood for traditional hymns today. Since this is a holiday, I thought something special might be in order, so let's start with 289 instead of 217, then sing 276 before 137, followed by 310 before we move right on to 452."

Frantically trying to keep up, Micah flipped through the pages and scribbled changes on the bulletin. Leaving Bea, Birdie hurried to find a seat in the rapidly-filling church.

Somehow, Micah adapted to the change of program. The song service was uplifting, and Birdie felt her heart rejoice as an assortment of voices rattled the rafters on a cold, sunshiny Thanksgiving morning on the island of Heavenly Daze. Thundering praises vibrated against the windows as they sang praises to the great I Am, the Exalted Jesus Christ, King of all kings and Lord of all lords.

Unable to sing over her aching throat, Birdie enjoyed listening. The powerful hymns washed over her, assuring her of God's love and filling her with a heady elation she sorely needed.

Beside her, Vernie Bidderman belted out the old hymns in her husky alto, occasionally clapping her coarse, work-worn hands in disjointed rhythm.

Across the aisle, Mike and Dana Klackenbush sat beside Babette and Charles Graham, two young couples with their whole lives ahead of them. Young Georgie scribbled on a notepad, occasionally reaching over to filch a breath mint out of his mother's purse. Babette and Charles smiled adoringly at their son's antics, then looked at each other as if they shared a secret.

Birdie lifted a brow, wondering what it was.

She was a little surprised to see Olympia and Annie in church, but there they were, in the center of the de Cuvier pew just ahead of her. As the music swelled, Olympia reached out to hold Annie's hand, and something in the gesture twisted at Birdie's heart. And something seemed odd—as a rule, Caleb sat with the island's other single men at the back of the church, but this morning Zuriel, Yakov, Abner, and Elezar sat on the de Cuvier pew, almost as if forming a protective shield around the mourning women. "Thank you," Birdie whispered, knowing they couldn't hear, but feeling grateful all the same.

She felt Edmund's presence as surely as if he sat in the pew next to Olympia. How wonderful to know that for those in Christ, partings like these were but brief absences.

Buddy Maxwell, wearing his usual muddy boots, sat toward the front, and that was a miracle in itself. Dana must have bribed him into attending. The Lansdowns and the Higgs sat next to Edith Wickam, while Dr. Marc sat at the end of the pew. Captain Stroble had even come to church this morning.

Oh dear! Birdie slid lower in her seat as the significance of his presence hit her. Surely he hadn't come to deliver more mail—not on Thanksgiving!

She lowered her gaze, then felt herself flushing even more deeply, rattled by a sudden self-awareness. She'd been scanning the audience and taking a mental roll call because . . . she was looking for Salt!

Thank the Lord, he hadn't come. She'd die if he caught her looking for him.

When the last amen died away, Pastor Wickam rose from his chair and walked to the pulpit. The middle-aged minister wore fall colors—a handsome brown tweed coat with a buttercup yellow shirt set off with a cinnamon and yellow striped tie. Birdie made a mental note to congratulate Edith on her splendid job of dressing him for the occasion.

After reaching up to smooth his mostly nonexistent hair, he opened his sermon notes, glancing up only briefly when Micah quietly moved to sit on the de Cuvier pew.

Birdie had to smile when she saw the pastor's automatic head patting gesture. Winslow had come a long way since his fascination with hair. These days he wore his bald spot like a badge of honor, openly declaring that vanity and preoccupation with shedding follicles was a waste of good time. A couple of weeks ago when Birdie caught him in the Mercantile, he flashed a grin and told her he'd discovered certain advantages to going bald: one, he could comb his hair with a washrag, and two, with just a little more hair loss, he would look like he had a continual halo 'round his head.

And that, Winslow had humbly confessed, was exactly the effect he wanted.

Pastor Wickam stood silently for a moment, gazing out at his flock.

Then slowly he closed his Bible and opened his eyes. "For a moment, we're going to talk about the life of Edmund Shots de Cuvier. Saturday we'll gather once again and ask the question, 'Death, where is thy sting?' Olympia has lost a mate of forty years; Annie, a beloved uncle. All of us have lost a friend; the world, a great benefactor. Edmund will be missed."

Olympia sniffed audibly, and from the other side of the room Birdie saw the flutter of tissues being pulled from pockets and purses. She lifted her own handkerchief and dabbed at her eyes.

"Which brings me to my topic for this special Thanksgiving service. We all suffer from emotions, whether from irritation or grouchiness or depression. The events of the past few days have shown me how quick we are to show emotion, but how reluctant we are to show true compassion and love.

"Some of us here this morning," Winslow continued, "have been blessed beyond our wildest expectations. And some of us are hurting."

The congregation shifted and shuffled. Birdie felt a collective movement of heads turning to look toward Olympia and Annie.

Winslow paused, apparently sorting his thoughts. Birdie tightened her grip on her handkerchief. Long pauses weren't Pastor Wickam's style; he usually plunged headlong into his message, well aware that pies were cooling and potatoes waiting to be mashed for the holiday dinner.

After a long moment, he lifted his gaze and looked directly at Birdie. "Some people here today are hurting, and, may God forgive us, we are the source of that pain."

Voices whispered, eyes lowered. Birdie could have heard a pin drop as the meaning of Pastor's words penetrated hearts and souls.

Next to Birdie, Vernie shifted, then a rough hand reached out to cover hers. Without a word, she gave Birdie's hand a gentle squeeze.

The pastor's gaze remained on Birdie. "Birdie, we are your family, too, and I fear we have lost sight of that fact. What you did last week by helping that little girl was a Christlike thing to do. I've thought about it often, and I've been ashamed of my own response." A blush ran like a shadow over his cheeks. "In our selfishness, we tend to cling to what we think is ours—the island, the budget, the wonderful peace and privacy we enjoy here in Heavenly Daze. Often we don't want to share. We want to be God's people, but we want to be left alone—"

"Preacher?"

Every eye swung to the front pew, where Floyd Lansdown had just stood.

Birdie stirred uneasily in her seat. No one ever interrupted the message, not even if the sermon stepped on a few toes.

Pastor Wickam's face went blank with shock. "Is there something you wanted to add, Floyd?"

"Not add," Floyd said. "Maybe correct."

Winslow smiled. "Why not? This is the day for sharing."

Floyd turned slightly to face the congregation. "It's not that we didn't want to help that family," he said, casting a quick look at Cleta. "All of us saw the need, but what about the furnace? That old thing's about to go. If we took money from the furnace fund to help the Akermans, then when the furnace died we wouldn't have one red cent to fix it."

From the piano bench, Bea piped up. "The money for that family came from me and Birdie. For heaven's sake, why is everyone making such a big deal out of one letter? This is Thanksgiving. Let's forgive and forget and get on with the service." She turned to her hymnal, flipping heatedly through the pages. "The way some of you have been treating Birdie is a crime. She did what she felt was right, and that's the end of it." She paused, snapping the hymnal closed, then dropped it to her lap and crossed her arms.

Vernie waved her hand. "What about the grant money we received from Rex Hartwell? Have we spent all of that?"

Floyd shrugged. "Not all of it—we put that new roof on and made some foundation repairs. There's a little left, but we haven't bought a dishwasher for the parsonage yet."

Edith Wickam timidly lifted her hand. "I don't need a dishwasher," she said, looking at her husband. Emboldened by his smile, she shifted and looked out at the congregation. "I've been doing dishes by hand for years and it hasn't hurt me a bit."

Floyd shoved at his glasses. "The point is, we've stretched what we have until it's screaming for mercy. Most of us don't like saying no any more than Birdie, but we don't have the means to help others. Apart from the Gettys and Gates of the world, who does?"

Words bubbled in Birdie's throat, but pain stopped them short. She grinned, suddenly grateful for the laryngitis. God was allowing her to listen for a change.

"Money is always a concern with a small congregation," Winslow admitted. "But how we treat each other shouldn't be."

"Money may not be a pleasant subject, but it is a necessity," Vernie pointed out.

"That's the truth!" Cleta stood. "We don't mean to be callous, Pastor, but the Lord expects us to plan ahead and save for a rainy day. Too many folks spend without thinking, then suddenly they're down and out looking for help."

Several in the congregation amen'd the sentiment.

Cleta lifted a warning finger. "What if another emergency comes up—maybe someone gets sick and can't take care of himself, or they raise the church insurance premium? What'll we do then? We'll have no emergency funds whatsoever if we start trying to answer all those angel letters. Don't we need to think of our welfare first? We can't take care of everyone. We're not God."

"That's right, preacher!" Floyd nodded with such force his glasses slipped from his nose.

"May I speak?" Dr. Marc stood up and folded his hands. "Speaking for myself, I know that in a case of unforeseen illness I would care for the patient without any regard for compensation."

Cleta wagged her finger at him. "You do that anyway, Dr. Marc, and we're beholden, but what about medicine and special treatment? You can't cover it all. Medical expenses these days can run into the millions."

"Then we couldn't help, regardless," Dr. Marc gently pointed out.

"My point is that I'd do what I could. We should all do what we can."

As Abner rose to his feet, heads rotated to watch him. Pastor Wickam inclined his head toward the baker. "You have something to add, Abner?"

"Thank you, Pastor." Abner's gaze moved over the congregation. "Brothers and sisters, I urge you to think. When has God ever failed to meet even one of our urgent needs?"

Silence fell over the room. Pointed looks were exchanged, then eyes lowered.

"Really," Abner pressed. "Who among us has been deserted by God when we most needed him?"

Silence reigned in the sanctuary. No one offered a rebuke.

Closing his eyes, Abner softly recited: "Doesn't life consist of more than food and clothing? Look at the birds. They don't need to plant or harvest or put food in barns because your heavenly Father feeds them. And you are more valuable to him than they are. Can all your worries add a single moment to your life? Of course not. . . . Look at the lilies and how they grow. They don't work or make their clothing, yet Solomon in all his glory was not dressed as beautifully as they are." He opened his eyes, focusing on Floyd. "And if God cares so wonderfully for flowers that are here today and gone tomorrow, won't he more surely care for you?"

Clearing his throat, Floyd dug in his pocket for a handkerchief. "It's not the same," he mumbled.

"Ah, but it is. We must trust God to care for our needs. Anything less is a lack of faith, and those who come to God must believe, for without faith it is impossible to please him."

As Abner sat down, Birdie saw Yakov lean close. "Thank you, brother," he said, his whisper reaching her ear. "That was a most appropriate response."

Grinning shyly, Abner dropped his head. "Wish I had thought of it first."

Pastor Wickam cleared his throat in the microphone, redirecting the congregation's attention to the front. "Many of you know that I like to take long walks along the shore," he said, a smile ruffling his mouth. "Yesterday morning, while I gazed out at the sea, God spoke to me. Oh, he didn't adopt a booming voice and literally say, 'Winslow, I want you to take this message to my people.' But I felt his presence. I heard his voice in the soft wind, and I heard him speak to my heart. He said, 'Everything I permit has a purpose.'"

Winslow looked out at his people, the light of conviction in his eyes. "And then it came to me—perhaps our loving, personal God has singled out Heavenly Daze to give help and hope to a dark world."

He paused, letting the silence stretch. "I know about the e-mail chain letter going around," he said. "At first I was like most of you, annoyed to think that such a silly thing would inconvenience us, then I applied the Lord's word to my heart and remembered what he told me: Everything he permits has a purpose. And then I asked myself, 'What if God has decided to allow us to serve him in a way most Christians only dream about?' How often do we say, 'Oh Lord, here I am, use me,' but we never expect him to actually take us up on our offer? Oh, we might volunteer to usher, serve communion, or teach Sunday school, and those are all valuable services to God. But what if he wants more from us who live in Heavenly Daze?"

Annie Cuvier raised her hand. "What do you mean, more? Are you suggesting God has singled out Heavenly Daze to deal with all the world's problems? With all due respect, Pastor, that's impossible."

Winslow gave her a patient nod. "I was thinking that perhaps God has singled us out to care."

"Care?" Vernie echoed.

"To be a voice of encouragement where there is none, to offer hope to those who have reached the end of their rope."

That sobering thought lingered with Birdie long after Winslow finished his sermon and the worshipers filed past Olympia and Annie to offer hugs and heartfelt condolences.

And as she walked home with Bea, she asked herself if it could be true: Had God actually anointed Heavenly Daze to be a beacon of hope? The idea seemed ludicrous; that sort of thing didn't happen in today's world.

Or did it?

As Birdie took the golden brown turkey out of the oven, she considered the challenge the pastor had given them. God worked in mysterious ways, so could the angel letters be part of his plan for the town?

One thing was certain—Pastor Wickam's challenge to care had been immediately answered.

Bea raised her voice above the whirl of the mixer. "I caught everyone, I think. They'll all be at Olympia's house by one o'clock.

"Good," Birdie said absently. "Good for all of us to pitch in and care."

Today, at least, Heavenly Daze would live up to its reputation.

The house was quiet, so deathly quiet.

Sitting in the warm kitchen nook, Olympia was staring out at the sea when the chime of the doorbell shattered the stillness.

As the doorbell pealed again, Caleb shuffled from the stove to answer it. Glancing toward her, he softly mused, "Wonder who that could be?"

Olympia shook her head. Everyone from church had gone home to gather with family.

Cruel death was no respecter of holidays.

The smell of baking ham drifted from the oven, but Olympia had no appetite. Caleb was trying to maintain the de Cuvier holiday tradition, but today seemed surreal. She thought of Edmund lying in the funeral home—no, Edmund was with God, but his body lay in the cold funeral home. And his mother, Edie—though the old woman had been informed of her son's death, Olympia knew she needed to go personally to the nursing home. She'd go tomorrow. She couldn't possibly summon the strength for such a somber trip today.

She heard the creak of the front door, then the sound of voices. Floyd Lansdown's bass growl rose above Mike Klackenbush's husky baritone. And was that Vernie Bidderman's gravelly alto?

Rising from her seat, Olympia ventured into the hallway. A virtual mob filled her foyer and front porch, and everyone carried a dish. Her eyes skipped from bowl to platter, spying cranberries, pumpkin pies, mashed potatoes, and gravy.

Birdie was struggling under the weight of the biggest turkey Olympia had ever seen!

Babette Graham smiled, holding up a bowl of pistachio salad, Olympia's personal favorite. That little scamp Georgie carried a plastic-wrapped blueberry gingerbread loaf in one hand and a rolled-up parchment in the other.

Speechless, the matriarch of Frenchmen's Fairest stared at her neighbors. They should have been home celebrating around their own hearths, but here they were. Edith stepped up to embrace her. Holding her close, she whispered, "Your family has come to share Thanksgiving with you, Olympia."

Overwhelmed, she could only point toward the dining room, where an empty table waited to receive a feast. She stared in stupefaction as Barbara and Russell, Birdie and Bea, Edith and Winslow, Cleta and Floyd, Babette, Georgie, and Charles, Dr. Marc, Vernie, and all the Smiths—Yakov, Micah, Abner, Zuriel, Elezar—trooped into the room. Buddy Franklin brought up the rear, red-faced and bearing a large basket of yeast rolls. For once, Olympia noted, he was wearing shoes instead of boots.

Water welled in her eyes and rolled unchecked down her cheeks. Annie came up beside her, her young eyes bright with unshed tears.

Turning to Olympia, Annie smiled. "Isn't it wonderful, Aunt Olympia? I never expected this." She reached out to catch Babette Graham's hand. "Thank you so much."

Standing quite still, Olympia heard her pride break. It was a small, clean sound, like the snapping of a toothpick. But the brokenness healed immediately as love washed over her like a tide of rich, warm honey.

"See?" Caleb whispered at her ear. "Miracles do happen."

Swiping self-consciously at her wet cheeks, Olympia eased Caleb aside to throw open the door of Frenchmen's Fairest to the late arrivals: Captain Stroble, Butch, and Tallulah, all three of whom stood panting on the porch.

"Come on in," she whispered, smiling. "Anyone and everyone is welcome in our home."

As Babette moved down the groaning dining room table, Charles stepped into the space at her side and slipped an arm about her waist. "Congratulations, Madame Graham," he said, nuzzling her neck. "I don't know how you convinced him to paint again, but I just saw Georgie give Olympia a puffin painting."

Babette gaped at him. "Really? But I thought he would never—"

"Apparently he changed his mind." Charles picked up a plate and fork, then scooped up a slice of Babette's blueberry gingerbread. "I think it's his way of comforting the lady."

Babette thought for a moment, then moved down the line. Amazing that Georgie had begun to paint again. And more amazing that what her son wouldn't do for money, he would do for a friend.

A huge meal usually calls for a huge nap. As Birdie and Bea gathered the coats and empty dishes, she heard the men talking about football games and afternoon hibernation.

She wouldn't mind a little snooze herself.

It was late afternoon before she, Bea, and Abner met in the bakery with several of the latest sacks of mail. Each of them sat at a separate table, deciding to read and sort the letters before answering them. Some petitions required prayer, others action. If nothing else, the trio decided, they could pray over the requests, even those without return addresses. At least they'd be able to know they'd done something to ease the problem represented in each letter.

Shortly after six, Captain Stroble popped into the bakery to see how their work was progressing. Because of the holiday, he'd received no more mail, but he made a point of shuddering when he mentioned what he feared the next day would bring.

By seven, there were papers piled on the counter, behind the register, and on every table. The industrial-sized mixing bowl held the urgent requests, most involving money or a miracle, neither of which Birdie, Bea, or Abner could provide. Cures for cancer and pleas for mortgage money were automatically dropped in the mixer.

The bread pans in the empty display case held the more trivial requests—for new bicycles and video games, new dresses for mommy, new golf clubs for daddy.

Birdie thought some of the letters would be funny if not for the obvious sincerity of the author:

Dear Angel,

My daddy got all his hair burned off lighting the bar-b-q. Can you make my daddy's hair grow back 'cause Mommy says he looks like a crazed cue ball.

Others were heartrending:

Dear Angel,

Can you please tell God we need money? Grandma is very sick and Momma says she needs to go somewhere where somebody can take good care of her. Momma wants to take care of her, but she has to work since Daddy died and we don't have anyone to take care of us anymore. Grandma needs to be at a nurse's home, but we don't have enough money to put her there so she stays alone here in the house all day while I go to school and Momma works at a macaroni and cheese factory. Grandma cries a lot and says she's nothing but a bird den, then Momma starts crying and says no, no, that's not true.

I don't understand because Grandma don't attract birds, not that I can see, but she thinks she's a lot of trouble for Momma. Grandma Yance smells funny sometimes, but I love her and she isn't too much trouble. So please, Angel, talk to God about Grandma. She doesn't want to be a bird den, she just don't want to bother anybody.

Birdie's back ached and her shoulders burned with strain as the minute hand slowly swept the clock. More than once she had to stop reading to wipe away unexpected tears.

The clock had just struck the half-hour when Birdie heard a rap on the front door. She looked up to see a mob at the front door.

"My lands, they've come to string us up," she warned, glancing at Bea. "They've forgotten every word Pastor said this morning."

"Hush, Birdie." Bea went to unlock the door. "Give 'em a chance."

In a moment, the Lansdowns, the Higgs, the Wickams, the Klackenbushes, the Grahams and Georgie, Buddy Franklin, Vernie Bidderman, and even Annie and Olympia de Cuvier had filled the room, their faces whipped red by the wind and holiday atmosphere.

Lowering the letter in her hand, Birdie stared at them in astonishment. "The bakery's closed," she called above the excited chatter. "If you're looking for dessert, well, we don't have any tonight."

"We're not here to buy anything." Cleta straddled a pile of mail bags, crossing her beefy arms.

Stiffening, Birdie braced for criticism. This had to be a lynch mob.

They had all come to tell her, "I told you so." They'd looked in the window and seen this blizzard of mail, and now they wanted to assure her that she'd ruined the island's reputation forever.

Well, maybe they were right.

She opened her mouth, about to speak, but just then Abner and the Smith fellas came in through the bakery kitchen.

Caleb, Micah, Yakov, Zuriel, Elezar, and Abner stood behind the counter, their arms crossed, their presence almost overpowering.

Birdie's heart sank. Had they come to fuss at her, too?

As the front door opened again, Dr. Marc squeezed in, accompanied by a gust of chilly air.

The room quieted as Birdie's gaze moved from family to family. What could she say? Heavenly Daze might never again be the peaceful island they'd grown to love, and all because Bea and Birdie had taken it upon themselves to answer a few little letters.

Cleta jabbed Floyd.

Clearing his throat, he met Birdie's questioning eyes. "We've come to help."

Birdie's jaw dropped. Had she heard right?

Nodding, Cleta spoke up. "Tell us what we need to do, and we'll do it."

"But"—Birdie glanced at the piles of mail—"there's so much, and it's likely to keep coming no matter what we do."

"Ayuh." Floyd nodded. "We know."

Pastor Wickam threaded his way to the counter. "We're here to help, Birdie. We were wrong to question an unselfish act. We ask your forgiveness and hope you'll grant it." He gave her a heartfelt smile. "Now, where would you like us to start?"

A rise of sudden emotion blocked Birdie's sore throat. They weren't here to fuss; they were here to help. Amazing.

Annie shouldered her way through the crowd. Stooping to give Birdie a hug, in a loud voice she said, "I think what you did was wonderful."

"No use wasting time." Dr. Marc hefted a sack of mail to his shoulder. "Dana, you and Mike, Buddy, Babette, Charles, and Georgie can help me. Caleb, Micah, Yakov, Elezar, and Zuriel can work with Abner. The rest of you pair off and keep those sacks moving!"

The bakery erupted in a beehive of activity as everyone assumed battle stations. Bea explained the way Birdie had organized the requests, and Abner passed out empty bread trays to hold more letters. With lightning efficiency, envelopes were opened, read, and passed down the line.

Birdie and Bea ferried the requests to the proper staging area where Cleta and Vernie marked *urgent* on the most pressing and set them aside for Pastor Wickam to consider. With pen and paper in hand, Edith and Olympia sat at a table and wrote three heartfelt sentences across the bottom of the more simple requests: "Your letter was received. We prayed for you. God loves you." On a few others, they added: "Give all your worries and cares to God, for he cares about what happens to you."

Dana Klackenbush pulled out of the assembly line long enough to tell Birdie: "We can use the Kid Kare Center for overflow. The bakery can't hold all this mail, and Georgie will be my only student until spring. I can use the classroom for an operations center."

"God bless you." Overcome with gratitude, Birdie hugged Dana, nearly forcing her to drop an armload of envelopes.

The young woman grinned. "Oh, he has, Birdie. He has."

The town worked late into the night, sorting letters, answering each missive with the simple message. Neither Birdie nor the residents of Heavenly Daze knew how long they could keep up the pace, but for as long as God had a purpose, she reckoned they could come up with a plan.

With a little luck and an e-mail blitz to point out that Heavenly Daze was only a simple town inhabited by simple people, perhaps the angel mail would slow and the island would gradually settle back into a normal routine.

As Birdie served coffee and day-old doughnuts to her friends and neighbors, her heart overflowed with gratitude and love. This Thanksgiving in Heavenly Daze had been one to remember. Only one thing could have made it more perfect: Salt Gribbon's attendance at church, the dinner, and this impromptu gathering.

Outside the bakery, snow had begun to drift down, white bits of light shining in the golden glow from the windows. Pressing her nose against the frosted glass, Birdie thought of Salt and wondered if he were watching the snowfall. Poor, lonely man . . .

She swallowed the despair that rose in her throat. The old skipper had come a long way in the past month, and who could say what the future held for him? After all, wasn't December the month for miracles?

Smiling at the thought of taking him a chocolate Christmas yule log, she turned and lifted the coffeepot. "Who's ready for a fresh cup?"

EPILOGUE

As the clock strikes midnight and concludes another Thanksgiving holiday, my own spirit is warmed by the grateful hearts in Heavenly Daze. Though there is one less human on the island tonight, every heart is blessed to know that Edmund de Cuvier is at home in heaven.

And every man, woman, and child who wrote to Heavenly Daze, for whatever reason, will realize God has provided a place of help and hope, of prayer and genuine caring. Such a message cannot be valued in terms of money, for honest compassion, in this age, is priceless.

The angels, however, both on earth and in heaven, are giving thanks tonight for a far different reason. Far more significant than Edmund's homecoming is Georgie's adoption into the family of God. Having been prepared by loving parents, faithful teaching, and the Spirit, this November Georgie placed his faith in the Son of God.

And we rejoice.

Birdie, by the way, would love to share her pattern for hand-knitted dishcloths. You'll find it on the next page.

Until we meet in December, we wish you warm nights and heavenly days.

—Gavriel

Birdie's Deceptively Simple Dishcloths

Materials needed:

Size ten knitting needles

Peaches and cream or sugar and spice yarn, any color

(Birdie favors buttercream yellow; Vernie likes red)

To begin: Cast four stitches onto a size ten needle.

Row 1: Knit four stitches.

Row 2: Knit two stitches; increase one stitch in third stitch; knit one.

Row 3: Knit three stitches; increase one stitch in fourth stitch; knit one.

Row 4: Knit three stitches; yarn over; knit to end of row.

Continue knitting as in row four until there are forty-six stitches on your needle. Return; knit two; knit two together; yarn over; knit two together; knit to end of row.

Continue this until eight stitches are left on needle. Then on the next row, knit one; knit two together; knit two; knit two together; knit one (you should have six stitches remaining on your needle).

Knit one; knit two together twice; knit one.

Bind off the four remaining stitches.

Take a crochet hook and tuck in the loose thread. You have now finished one of Birdie's Deceptively Simple Dishcloths. Launder as you would a towel; no special handling required.

IF YOU WANT TO KNOW MORE ABOUT . . .

- Angels as servants and messengers: Genesis 24:7; Exodus 23:20; Hebrews 1:14
- Angels are as "swift as the wind" and "servants made of flaming fire": Hebrews 1:7
- The angel who was detained on his mission to Daniel: Daniel 10:13
- Angels' special care for children: Matthew 18:10
- Angels as protectors: Psalm 91:11–12
- The heavenly throne room: 2 Chronicles 18:18; Psalm 89:14; Psalm 11:4; Revelation 4:1–6
- The prayers of the saints: Revelation 8:4
- Angels' limited knowledge: Matthew 24:36
- Angels eagerly watching humans: 1 Peter 1:12
- The third, or highest, heaven: 2 Corinthians 12:2; Deuteronomy 10:14; 1 Kings 8:27; Psalm 115:16
- Seraphim: Isaiah 6:2
- Cherubim: Genesis 3:24
- Satan as the prince of the power of the air: Ephesians 2:2
- What happens when we die: 2 Corinthians 5:8; Philippians 1:23
- The resurrection of believers: 1 Thessalonians 4:15–17.
- How to invest in eternal treasures: Matthew 6:20; Matthew 19:21; Luke 12:33; Philippians 3:8; 1 Timothy 6:19

For a copy of Babette's Maine Blueberry Gingerbread recipe and the latest news from Heavenly Daze, visit

www.heavenlydazeME.com

Also Available from Angela Hunt

Angela Hunt, with prophecy expert and apologist Grant Jeffrey, spin a chilling tale surrounding computer genius Daniel Prentice and a secret "millennium code." The code is used to solve a national bank chain's Year 2000 computer crisis which ultimately leads to a dangerous entanglement with a one-world government.

In this thrilling sequel to *Flee the Darkness*, the Y2K crisis has passed, but Daniel Prentice is faced with an even greater crisis as the ancient prophecies foretold in the book Ezekiel begin to unfold. The forces of evil have never been stronger nor the world's destruction nearer than in *By Dawn's Early Light*.

In the sequel to the popular end-time thriller *By Dawn's Early Light*, evil ruler Adrian Romulus seems to have the world's political matters firmly in control. But underneath his powerful facade is an evil madman bent on destruction. Can he be stopped in time?

A man claiming to be 2000 years old says he is on a holy mission to prevent a global catacylsm. To uncover the truth, heroine Claudia must re-examine her beliefs as she delves into ancient legends of the "Wandering Jew," biblical warnings about the Antichrist, and eyewitness accounts of the Crucifixion, the Inquisition, and the Holocaust.

WORD PUBLISHING